PRAISE FOR
PIVOT

"Beyond good and evil, *Pivot* juggles archetypes until you're not sure which ball is airborne and which is still in the author's hand. A story about cracking free of your intended role in life, as plot and depth travel at the same exceptional speed."

—**Josh Malerman,** author of *Bird Box*

"Impressive and arresting prose drives this vivid debut. (...) Barlow's gorgeous writing will easily propel readers through the rest of the series."

—**Publishers Weekly**

"Horrifying yet so compelling. I enjoyed every page!"

—**Brienne Dubh**, Escapology Reviews

"I'm not entirely sure how I would describe this book except to say go read it! (...) I enjoyed it immensely and fully recommend."

—**Diary of a Reading Addict**

"*Pivot* is an exciting, dark, intriguing, and ultimately enjoyable book. The pacing is exciting, and the development of Jack from innocent child to indoctrinated assassin to an aware, empowered young woman is masterfully done."

—**TehBen.com Book Reviews**

"A brilliant blend of mystery and horror. (...) *Pivot* is well plotted and the author introduces twists that readers won't see coming. L.C. Barlow takes readers on a perilous journey, crafting scenes that are emotionally charged and focused and creating characters that are both complex and real."

—**Readers' Favorite Book reviews (five stars)**

"An engrossing read full of twisted relationships and otherworldly powers. Barlow managed the feat of giving both the characters and the world a sense of depth. The supernatural powers—Cyrus, his enemy the man with stars in his body, and the mysterious red box that gives and takes his abilities—all have a weight and history to them, a sense of rules, that intertwine with the characters relationships in a satisfying way."

—**Antonio Urias**, author of *The Chronicles of Talis*

"An intelligent, beautifully written thriller."

—**Charles Baker**, IndieReader

PIVOT

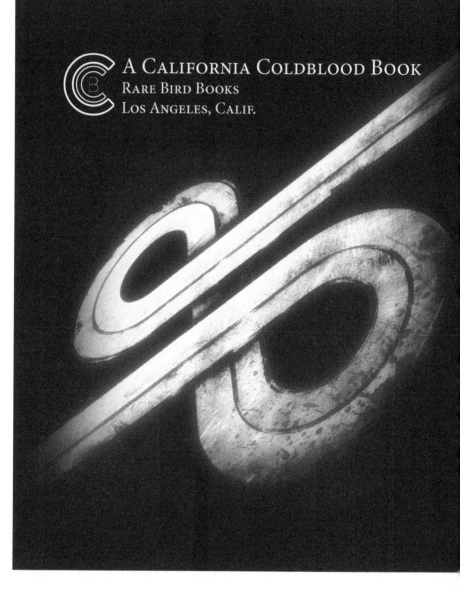

A California Coldblood Book
Rare Bird Books
Los Angeles, Calif.

PIVOT

L.C. BARLOW

BOOK ONE
OF THE JACK HARPER TRILOGY

THIS IS A GENUINE CALIFORNIA COLDBLOOD BOOK

A California Coldblood Book | Rare Bird Books
californiacoldblood.com
rarebirdbooks.com
Copyright © 2019 by L.C. Barlow

ISBN 978-1644280539

Set in Minion
Cover design by James T. Egan of Bookfly Design LLC
Printed in the United States
Distributed by Publishers Group West

Publisher's Cataloging-in-Publication data

Names: Barlow, L. C., author.
Title: Pivot / L.C. Barlow.
Series: The Jack Harper Trilogy.
Description: Los Angeles, CA: California Coldblood Books, An Imprint of Rare Bird Books, 2019.
Identifiers: ISBN 978-1644280539
Subjects: LCSH Cults—Fiction. | Magic—Fiction. | Brainwashing—Fiction. | Paranormal fiction. | Horror fiction. | BISAC FICTION / Occult & Supernatural | FICTION / Horror
Classification: LCC PS3602.A77561 P58 2019| DDC 813.6—dc23

For Mom, Dad, Sebron, and Adam.
Words cannot express how meaningful you are.

CHAPTER 1—WAKE UP
AGE: 7 YEARS OLD

THE FIRST TIME I KILLED a man, Cyrus made me do it. We stood in a small room in the basement of his mansion. One bare bulb hung from the ceiling. There were no windows. The only objects within the room were a chair for me to stand on and a table with flat blue ropes that strapped the man down.

The man was not awake. He was alive, though, and breathing loudly. His skin shone a beautiful dark shade, character built into his face by way of lines and furrows. He was older and gray but still had all his hair, including what sprouted on his chest and stomach. Climbing to stand on the chair, I bumped into him by accident. His body barely shook, simply rested like a stone, and his skin was rough, like sand. The look of him made me queasy.

The truth was that I did not want to kill him, and so I said to Cyrus, "Why do I have to do it?"

"Because you need to learn how," he said. "You need to get used to it. Now look," and he set before me what appeared to be a metallic fishing fly. "We are going to do this simple."

Something in me curled up and died at the sight of the needle. But so I would not disturb my own dead self, I watched and listened and obeyed Cyrus rather than argue.

"This is a butterfly needle," he said, "and it slides into veins to let out blood. You are going to insert this needle into the vein, here." Cyrus pointed to an indigo line in the man's neck. "It'll take you a few tries, but trust me. You can't be worse than many nurses."

I did exactly as he said. I pressed my feverish fingers upon the thin man's cool neck, and I took the needle just so in my right hand. On my first try, I punched a hole straight through the vein, and Cyrus said he knew that was so by the black bruise that instantly covered the area.

After a while of prodding, though, I finally found the tunnel through which the fluid of life flows, and I inserted the needle deep inside. Warm blood poured out.

I cried as my hands were washed with crimson, and Cyrus grabbed them. "It's all right," he said. He took a handkerchief from his pocket and delicately wiped my palms. "The job is done."

I barely heard him.

The fount poured along the man's neck and spread beneath him, splattering before me a cherry mirror in which I could see the glare from the overhanging bulb and in that glare my face.

Cyrus held my right hand in both of his, and he squeezed it gently. He moved my arm above the man and slid my hand so that it rested upon his chest. His beating heart pulsed beneath my palm.

"His heart will eventually stop," Cyrus said. "Feel for it." Suddenly, I could not breathe. As I pressed my hand upon the man's chest, and as the black bruise in his neck began to expand, I sensed an inextricable link between myself and the blackening of his face. It was as though he was transforming into a demon and within solely me lay the perversion capable of it. I tried to lift my hand, but Cyrus settled his own on top, locking mine against the man's waxy skin. No matter how I resisted, Cyrus would not release me.

"Stop!" I cried.

Blood flooded off the table. The dribbling sounds upon the floor were a heavy bass in my ears. The man's face continued to blacken, and

I became hysterical, trying to tear myself away from the beating heart buried beneath the bone. If I could break contact, the horror might stop.

Cyrus held fast to me, though, pinning me down to the dying body, clamping me to the death itself. The heartbeat quickened. I imagined that heart struggle left and right beneath my hand, pulled as if by a million different wires until it stretched and shrieked in the only way it could, with a hot, flashing pace.

When I did open my eyes, I saw only the blood sliding, spreading its tentacles like a voracious vine across the floor, beneath the man who was both blackening and whitening simultaneously. His hands unconsciously searched for his face, searched for me, but the blue ropes held him fast, and eventually all movement ceased.

In every whiff of the pervasive blood were millions of pennies in sugar.

The heart slowed under my hand, like a flower closing its petals to the night. It slowed like rain turned to snow. Then, as though electrocuted by my very touch, the man's body began to twitch and contract like a spider that had just been swatted. I had to close my eyes again to stand it.

When I could no longer feel the heart, I cried, a cold stone lodged low in my stomach. I wanted to press my hands to my belly to rip it out, but Cyrus's own hand was still like a manacle upon mine. When he finally let go, I jerked back, breaking the link between me and the dead. I vomited.

For the longest time Cyrus tried to comfort me, but every word he said meant nothing. That is, until he shocked me with the following.

"I have every intention of bringing him back, Jack. There is really nothing to worry about."

Through eyes flooding with tears, I looked up from the floor at him, gazing at this demon, who suddenly began to sprout wings. I hungered to hear those words again.

"That would make things easier for you, right? If I were to bring him back?"

"Yes," I said, not believing or disbelieving him, just following my choking desire. "Yes, please. Please bring him back." I clutched the soft cloth of Cyrus's pants. I whispered the same words over and over. "Please, Cyrus. Please."

Cyrus grasped my arms in his hands and gently lifted me to my feet. He wiped the tears from my eyes, just like he had wiped the blood from my hands, and he ran his fingers through my hair. He held me close and calmed me.

"His name is Roland James, and tonight he'll be back, alive. I swear it to you, Jack. No worries." Cyrus kissed the top of my head, and I relaxed against him. After just a few minutes, I passed out.

CHAPTER 2—ROLAND
AGE: 7 YEARS OLD

I woke in the bedroom that had been provided for me in the west wing of Cyrus's home. The ceiling of ornate wood was sectioned into squares with swirls in their centers. As my eyes traveled over their twists, I thought of the dead man, Roland James.

He would be alive again, Cyrus had said. He was to be resurrected that very night. Outside the windows that opened to the back of Cyrus's property shined the moon and freckles of stars. I had slept the whole day.

Though my eyes were puffy after shedding their tears, my cheeks still flush, I calmed. The man I'd killed was supposed to return. Magic was in the air, like a funeral slowly being replaced by Christmas.

The doorknob creaked as I sat at the window, and I turned, expecting Cyrus to greet me. Alex, his son, appeared instead.

Alex was shorter than me, his hair blond, eyes blue. His face was round and his cheeks plump. He wore a black, long-sleeved shirt, dark blue jeans, and white socks. He did not appear a child but rather a small adult. He stared at me without emotion.

Neither of us spoke. His breathing was loud, and, though he did not look angry, there existed a fount of emotion behind each breath.

"Hi," I said, at last.

"Hi," he mirrored. "What did you and my father do this morning?"

I cocked my head to the side, trying to register what he was asking. "What?"

"This morning, when you went to the basement—what did you and my father do?"

A red flag waved in my head. "I can't tell you."

"Why?"

"Cyrus wouldn't want me to."

Alex stood motionless. His blue eyes, which were locked on me, distanced, and he bit his lip. "You might be older, but I can do whatever you can. When Dad teaches me, I'll be better than you, and then he won't want you anymore. You'll be lumped in with the others."

"What others?"

He did not answer.

With little more than a smirk, he left. His footsteps softly thudded as he exited the room, and he disappeared. A few seconds later, a distant door slammed.

All I could think of was finding Cyrus, and also that I was hungry. Alex quickly disappeared from my mind, as if he had never been in my doorway.

I headed to Cyrus's kitchen, which was located at the northern center. It was very close to the den and also near what I had labeled "the White Room"—a room decorated with modern white carpet and walls, platinum drapes, and a glittering white marble pool table with velvety white felt.

The chairs, tables, molding, baseboards, and windowpanes were all white. The tremendous chandelier was like a ghost pinned midair. The room frightened me. Without color, it seemed a starved thing, hungry for something human.

When I entered the kitchen, Cyrus's laughter rang, arriving from the direction of the White Room. I walked slowly toward the double swinging doors to the west and pushed through them. I arrived at the great white whale of a room just a short way down the hall. Through the open doors were a white desk and a man sitting behind it. Cyrus held a cigar in his hand. Big white puffs of smoke colored the air about him with pallor. In one of the plush, thick velvet chairs in front of the desk sat the man I had murdered that morning, Mr. Roland James.

Roland was not only alive but smiling, laughing—exuberant. He was the human thing that the room hungered for. Wearing a bright blue suit and khaki shirt, he looked to me to be the very paradigm of health.

Except for his neck and his face. The areas that had blackened that morning after I plunged the needle through his vein were still a bit darker than he was.

While I stood, staring at his neck, Roland James turned to me. He smiled.

"Jack," Cyrus said. He beckoned me with a wave. "Come in."

"Yes," said Roland.

Under the spell of the dead man, I drew closer to him, hypnotized and curious, until I arrived at the edge of Cyrus's long desk. I placed my hand upon its cool, white surface and swallowed hard.

Roland smiled, his eyes eerie. Cyrus stripped some of the ash from his cigar onto the white ashtray before him, as though not a thing in the world had happened. Only after he finished did he look at me. His demeanor was cheery. "Well, what do you think?"

"I..." I looked back and forth between Roland and Cyrus and wished I could speak to Cyrus alone. "Does...does he know?"

Cyrus lifted his eyebrows and leaned forward. "Does Roland know that you murdered him today?" he confirmed. I grimaced at the blatant question.

I expected them to laugh, but they didn't. Cyrus drew again on his cigar, blowing a smoke ring into the air.

"I know," Roland said. He looked at me again with a cunning that I had also seen in Cyrus. "And it's okay, Jack. It's all right. Cyrus told me you were worried, but there isn't anything to worry about anymore. Here," he said, "have a seat." He patted the pillowy chair, identical to his, beside him.

I pulled myself into the chair, positioning myself on the edge. I felt as though I were in the presence of God.

"I intended," said Cyrus, "that we would begin this way. I would assist you in killing a person for the first time and then have that person returned for you. Obviously, we have done just that. This morning, we took Roland's life, and now I have fully returned him. Do you agree?"

I regarded Roland once more. He smiled at me and held out his hand. I took it in my own and recognized for certain that he was the man on the slab that morning. He was not a twin; this was not a charade. The man who sat beside me and requested my company was the person I had let liters of blood pour out of only hours before.

How is this possible? How can he be living and breathing again?

Roland leaned forward in his chair, his bright blue suit crinkling as he moved. "I want you to know that what you did earlier is all right. Cyrus was training you, and he wanted to train you well, so he asked me to help. As you can see, I accepted. I was here for you before and am here for you now. I am going to help you learn how to kill and to understand killing." He smiled widely, wider than I had ever seen anyone smile. "You know, don't you, that someone who would sacrifice himself for you has your best interest at heart?"

I nodded, mesmerized.

"Roland has done a magnificent job," said Cyrus. "And perhaps we will do what was done this morning a few more times. You will kill Roland, and I will bring him back. And what you will learn from this is that you are not really killing him, not really. He is like a boomerang. He simply comes right back to life, no matter how many times you take life from him. But eventually, Jack, eventually, we'll move on to another person."

My heart fluttered, and my attention shifted from Roland's kindly face to the man responsible for life and death.

"And you will kill as we have taught you. When it comes to that other person, he won't return like Roland has. But hopefully you will keep in mind that you aren't really murdering that person, or any other, not really, just like you're not really murdering Roland. Rather, we're just not bringing that person back to life. Do you understand, Jack?"

I looked to my right at Roland's eyes. They twinkled like a starry night. "Yes," I said.

"Then say it with me," said Cyrus. "Say, 'I'm not really killing anybody, I'm just not bringing them back.'"

I swallowed a bit of sticky saliva so the words flowed freely from my mouth. "I'm not really killing anybody, I'm just not bringing them back."

"'Just like Roland James,'" said Cyrus.

"Just like Roland James."

"Thatta Jack." Roland patted me on the back.

CHAPTER 3—PERFECTION
AGE: 7 YEARS OLD

WITH THE MAN I'D MURDERED leading the way to my future murders, my path was paved with ease. How was I to say no to him? I had taken his life, and so I owed him mine. Thus, I obeyed whatever he said, which was a lot. He took over in teaching me how to kill.

Roland never showed me any malice; rather, he brought me occasional gifts. He never revealed even the slightest pain, anger, or disapproval of what I was doing to him in the deep, dark mornings. The weight of his blood shrank from a bucket to a teaspoon.

How did Cyrus do it? How did Roland return? These questions wracked my brain. Early on, I ruled out the theory that Roland was simply the twin of the man I'd originally killed—he would have had to be an identical quadruplet or quintuplet, as many times as I killed him.

I shot Roland and stuck my finger in the burning hole in his chest, as commanded by Cyrus. I strangled him to death with piano wire, placing my foot against the back of his neck and pushing as hard as I could, until I thought my foot would tear my arms from their sockets. I stabbed him to death, practicing in the most real of terms the twelve angles of attack: left femoral, right femoral, left ribs, right ribs, abdomen, heart, left clavicle, right clavicle, left eye, right eye, beneath the neck, vertical through to the top of the head. Repeat. Finally, I killed him with a ball-point pen. Each and every time, Roland returned.

In the hours when Roland was alive, there might be some sign of what happened to his body in the hours before, a scratch here or a little nick there, but the man was always cheerful and content. Murder was only a shadow upon him.

There was also no question that Roland actually died. Each time, I checked his pulse, as I was told. Each time, there was the almost purple blood, the lack of body heat, the complete and utter stillness after a series of spasms. And that sigh, like pressure in the room being suddenly released. There was that, too.

I believed wholeheartedly that I had murdered Roland James a multitude of times. Cyrus was right, though. Like a boomerang, Roland kept returning.

It made me wonder if there was something special about Roland himself—if it were not that Cyrus was returning him but rather that something within Roland made him a revenant. Perhaps it was a joint effort. I did not know.

Cyrus made sure I spent plenty of time with Roland. I experienced my first cigarette with him—clove, black, cinnamon, sweet. It was with him that I first fired a gun. With him, I watched movies and heard about his life.

He was a musician—piano, sax, clarinet, and trumpet—and he'd played in many clubs, he told me. He said he dabbled a little in "hollerin' and moanin' at the mic." He taught me to play the piano a bit, as well as the alto sax. When I first started to play the saxophone, I bit the reed so often my mouth burned and my lip bled. When I complained he said, "The skin learns not to bleed and hurt after a while. You just gotta give it time. And then you can play the blues, if you want, or something classical. Just make sure you don't get out of practice, because the callus won't stay if it isn't encouraged a little now and again. Still, no matter how long between playing, it's always easier to build up that callus after it sprouts the first time."

Often through the crack around the door, Alex watched me with Roland. His perfectly trimmed blond hair gleamed in the darkened hallway; his eyes shone in the light. Eventually, Cyrus or Roland would discover him, and they'd send him on his way.

Aside from playing beautiful music, Roland cooked exquisite meals, and we often worked together on them. Brandied carrots and parsnips, sage-crusted pork loin, pecan-crusted chicken, Brussels sprouts au gratin, chess pie—these were the silver linings of our days. A little blood in the morning and by evening a little salty and sweet to wash away all those pennies in sugar. Poor and often hungry before I met Cyrus, I frequently dreamed of food. Roland fulfilled my dreams. I'd kill the cook and then later dine with him. Sometimes I imagined he cooked better each and every time he was brought back.

When food was there, when I could smell the cooking meat and carrots and potatoes and warm myself beside the hot oven, when my best friend in the world—the person I kept sending away but who always came back for me—was playing the piano and singing "In the Pines," an ineffable magic filled the air. It's something I wished I could bottle, so I could spray it, and taste it, and keep its little drops forever. It was that important to me.

"Jack," Roland said to me one evening, "come sit beside me for a moment. There's something I want to talk to you about."

He sat on the cobalt velvet couch near a small, cozy fire in a fireplace surrounded by gray-green slate squares. He patted the seat beside him, and I hopped up, leaned against him, and absorbed his delicious calm.

The stereo on a wall twenty feet from the couch played a classical piece. It was soft, melodic, easygoing, pianissimo. Interspersed with Roland's words were the *plum...plink...plink* and *ploom...plink...plink* of music.

"Jack," he said, "I've always been a man who sang for others, but there was an evening not long ago when a man sang for me. One night I was drunk, stumbling through the woods close to the Meddlesome Myth—a bar where I'd just played. I heard it! The sweet wooden vibrations of a violin and, when I closed my eyes, the deep tones of a voice that sang an odd tune. My ears led me exactly in the direction I needed to go.

"With only a cigarette in my hand to light my way, I stumbled and crawled in those woods, through those trees, until I came to a small pond—and then I could hear both the violin and water sloshing.

"Who did I see but a man standing out in the middle of it, his back to me, the tips of his toes pressed in the moonlit water, dangling there by some unseen force, swinging his hand back and forth like he was sawing into the instrument. And the cross that hung round my neck—a silver one given to me by my momma—became so hot I had to take it off. When I held it out in front of me, it glowed white, and then it shriveled up into a little ball—all its corners turning in and meeting one another. If the thing had been alive, it wasn't anymore. It went cool again, and the light disappeared.

"The man on the pond turned around, like he was now free to face me, and he quit playing that violin, quit singing. He walked toward me a few yards, to where I could barely make out the lines of a face, and he stopped. 'Hello, Roland,' he said, and then straight under the water he dropped, without a splash. It's like the water sewed him up. The surface was as still as if he had never been there.

"That was the first time that anything I would have deemed 'impossible' ever happened to me. It was purely supernatural, Jack, and it was good for me—not just the experience itself, but the knowledge of it...It took me out of this world a bit.

"It made me less concerned with what was going on here. What was going on here didn't bother me anymore. Him showing up on that lake, just playing that violin and singing, and dipping back through the water like a damn fish in a three-piece suit was enough medicine to keep me from ever being a victim of this world again. That's the nice side of the dark things—they are victimless. With what I've given you, you too should be victimless now."

He smiled at me, and he patted my hand. He looked around for a second. "I kept the cross to remind me. I keep it in my pocket always. The metal isn't as smooth as it used to be." Roland reached into his pocket. "It shrivels a bit more every year." He pulled out a decrepit-looking spherical cage and dropped the little ball into my palm. I ran my hands over it, registering its little grooves, looking at what appeared to be a tiny withered windowpane. It smelled like ash. I returned it to Roland, and he eyed it appreciatively before he dropped it back into my hand.

"Keep it," he said. "Keep it safe."

I rolled the cross in my palms, in awe, and thanked him.

Roland smiled. "It's hard not being a victim in this world, but that's what we're working on for you and for others in Cyrus's little group. The supernatural...That's where getting beyond what's here lies. The darkness— well, evil can't be a victim. It's easier to accept the hell of this world when you're comfortable with the fact you deserve it. It's calming."

He looked me up and down and smiled slowly. "Yes, you are innocent and guilty as hell. It's a strange mix, and not one for everyone. The world can't affect you as well as you can affect it. That's good. We'll get you there."

With that, he patted my leg and rose from the couch. He slipped his hands into his pockets and stared at the small fire in the hearth before he walked over to the piano and pushed the cover back from the keys. He played the all-so-familiar E, A, G, B, E chord variation, and as he played, he sang slowly,

"Little   girl,   little   girl,   don't   you   lie   to   me,
Tell   me   where   did   you   sleep   last   night
In   the   pines,   in   the   pines   where   the   sun   don't   ever   shine,
I   shivered   the   whole   night   through."

I sat there, and I listened to Roland. I was so at home in that moment that it could have been a dream. I never would have known the difference.

As for Roland, no matter what he told me, I could stomach it, for he always came back, always sang to me, always taught me and cared for me, and I wholly loved him, this man I murdered. People I let live have rarely meant so much to me.

CHAPTER 4—THE BOX AND THE CHURCH
AGE: 7 YEARS OLD

SLOWLY, THE KILLING LESSONS RECEDED into the background of my days. They did not hurt me like before, and eventually, once I got into the rhythm of things, the rhythm took over. It was a lot like listening to Roland play music or sing and then joining him. He led the way, and I let the tune be what it was. My voice melded, low, with his.

The only thing that remained difficult for me was not knowing *why* Cyrus was teaching me how to kill. Though I had been in his home for many months, I still did not understand how I had come to live with him, why he kept me so close, or why numerous people visited his home. So many strangers arrived and left that I lost count, and it seemed I never saw the same face twice, which couldn't possibly be true.

I never asked Cyrus what was going on. The very idea terrified me. Instead, I slouched toward that steady rhythm and allowed it to pull me along. I obeyed what I was told and never looked up from my task. I did not want to be punished.

A few months after starting with Roland, Christmas approached, and a gigantic Christmas tree sat at the foot of the stairs. I often went and sat beside it, tapping all the beautiful red, gold, and blue ornaments, in awe of all the sparkling trinkets. The tree stretched upward forever.

While at the foot of this tree, a loud commotion erupted down the hall. I stared across the empty marble stairs to a hallway that led from the front of the house to the very back.

Sparkling dust caught the light. Cyrus's voice shot to me.

"You think you know better than me?"

Cyrus wasn't talking. He was *yelling*.

My finger trailed along the edge of a bright crimson ornament, sensing its cold, smooth surface, as I stared, wide-eyed, and listened. Goosebumps prickled the back of my neck, tickling me.

Though an open door on the left hand side of the hall, men exchanged muffled words.

Several individuals had been in that room for nearly an hour, as they were on most days, having a meeting. There had been a lot of talking, and they drank and smoked. Everything had been fine.

Now something sharp was in the air. Multiple people spoke loudly, and I cocked my ear. My heart thudded hard.

"Let me remind you, once again, that I was the one who founded this church. And I decide who stays and who leaves!"

Roland appeared beside me, his eyebrows drawn into a deep V, his lips parted.

"Stay here," he said. His energy was grim, but he nevertheless smiled at me briefly and winked. He walked toward the tumult.

Compelled against my own will, I walked after him.

My footsteps were so quiet that Roland didn't notice. We both made our way toward the incessant shouts, the arguing voices. My body trembled.

A sudden blur of motion made me jump back.

Cyrus lunged out of the room. He gripped a man by his sandy brown hair, dragging him backwards, while the man screamed and kicked at the floor, his black rubber soles squeaking and streaking the marble. He clawed Cyrus's arm. His teeth were bared, and spit sprayed from between his lips.

Cyrus hauled the man forward one step at a time. More people entered the hallway, wide-eyed and open-mouthed.

In his other hand, Cyrus held something dark red and rectangular. He swung it back and forth with each heave. It was a box.

Cyrus pulled the man into a room at the end of the hall. He slammed the red box down on a table inside and released the man, who instantly scrambled to his feet and bolted from Cyrus, toward us.

The door to the room slammed shut.

My eyes widened. My whole body felt electrified, struck by lightning. My mouth went dry. Had the door just moved on its own?

From inside, the man's incessant screams stopped. The silence in the hallway thickened, something that could be sliced into. It enveloped me.

The door creaked, dividing the smooth silence. It did not open enough, though, to reveal anything inside. My breath nearly nonexistent, I found one of my feet had moved forward and then the other.

"Don't," Roland said. He tugged at my arm, but I continued.

Nobody else said or did anything to stop me. They had frozen with fear. The door swung wide.

The room was not the same. It had whitened. The floor, the walls, the cushions, the couch, the drapes, the other side of the door—everything was impossibly white, like it were made of stone. It was a perfect image of the White Room upstairs, the one where Roland appeared the first time he was brought back from death.

Cyrus walked into view. He stared at us, catching his breath, and seemingly floated midair. His black shoes and the top of his head were equidistant within the doorframe. He stood on nothing. Everything around him was one color, lines here and there defining a couch, a pillow, a desk, but they were unreal. Nothing appeared three dimensional.

Cyrus stepped out of the room onto the ivory-colored marble, re-entering our world. He ran his hand through his silver hair and heaved several breaths.

"Problem solved. Thornton is dead," he said.

He gripped the red box's handle tightly. From the corner of his fist, a trail of blood dripped onto the box. The blood disappeared into the top. The velvet drank it.

Cyrus strode forward. The others made way for him. One man dropped to the floor and crawled backward.

Cyrus paused, looked down at him, and laughed. He lifted the red box, shook it with both hands. "It's shut," he said. "The only time you have to worry is when it's not."

He continued on his way, leaving us.

I walked down the hall, closer to the freshly whitened room. Thornton's face slowly entered into view on the white floor. His head tilted up and toward me, his dark eyes wide and staring from beneath a patch of thick brown hair. He was not moving, and not a sound came from him. Just like Cyrus, he floated in that room, suspended amid all the white.

I exhaled a breath I didn't know I had been holding.

I told myself, then and there, to do whatever Cyrus wanted, always and forever, so I would not end up like Thornton, floating in the hungry white. I would do everything to ensure that the box, the thing that killed men and drank blood, would not hurt me.

-

Later in the evening, Cyrus called me to his office. The red box sat on his desk, between us, as he took a seat in his big brown leather chair. I tried not to stare at it, its dark red velvet and damaged corners, its squeaky handle and almost purple sheen, as he spoke.

Cyrus's voice was soft, much softer than it had ever been. He told me he had not wanted me to see what had happened earlier that day with Thornton, that I was not yet old or prepared enough to know what the box could do. He became quiet. At last, he cleared his throat, and he said that I would learn everything when the time was right.

His eye gleamed as he talked about how well I had taken to my training. He told me I had impressed him.

"Do you know," Cyrus said, "that you are a very lucky person, Jack? You are a very lucky person indeed. There are mounds of things in the world to seize—knowledge, power, love. The world is ripe, absolutely overflowing with the potential for things for you to have. I could never name all that is open to you, for it multiplies every day into infinity. There are worlds beyond your world, pieces of you beyond yourself, and you cannot know how important it is to know all these things until you know them. You're just a child, after all." He smiled, and he tapped his finger on his chin contemplatively. "You are a blank slate, like them all—the *tabula rasa*. But you are a very lucky blank slate, because *I* am willing to do something with that. I am willing to help raise you as as my own. I am going to let you know of all the things that are in this world. I am going to strengthen you so that you may venture through it unharmed. I am going to let you tell the lies from the truth. I am going to show you something that nobody else in the world can show you except me." At this, Cyrus leaned back against his desk, his hand reaching out to rest upon it, and his fingers slid ever-so-delicately over the velvet lid of the red box before they touched down on the wooden desktop with a loud *clack!* from his ring. "And when I ascend, you will be there."

He stiffened in his chair and fixed his gaze on me. "As you know," he said calmly, "what I run here is my church…*our* church. What we do—well, it would probably be best explained by telling you what we do not do. You see, there are people called 'Christians' in the world. And, as you will soon find out, there are those who believe more in Satan than they do in God. Satan makes more sense to them. And the others out there—the others in our little group—most of them believe in Satan, and they say that God does not exist. This is obviously false. The things that I have seen that eventually you will see as well should convince you that God can do nothing but exist. Nevertheless, we are not ones who follow Him. For that will not sustain us." He looked at the box. "The only thing that sustains this church, this assemblage of ours, is devolution, chaos, and the downfall of innocence. It is through them that I will ascend. And how you will, eventually, will take my place, how you eventually will ascend. That is, after all, why you are here. Do you understand?"

Slowly, I nodded, even though I did not entirely comprehend.

"But have no doubt," he continued. "It will tempt you—the God-ish side. And I want you to remember, no matter what those who live in Heaven say, Hell is what saved you before you knew what saving was. The pacifists and Christians, the people with their perfect families and dogs and colleges, those who have all the chances you never would have had without me, they will condemn me. But I, one sort of hell, saved you from the other. You will not be raped—not because of their charity but because of my gun. You will not be murdered—not because of where their faith resides but because of where mine does. You will not be a victim—not because a shelter or a missionary found you but because a little red box sits in this house, and it waits for another bite of the flesh of fools who dare blaspheme.

"So if you ever start thinking that they're right and I'm wrong because their arguments seem logical and what I require of you seems so horrible—if you ever start to hate what you once loved—remember this moment and all moments with me, with whom you are perfectly safe, and realize what a tragedy it would be for you to leave all that I have provided.

"What I bestow upon you is *unconditional* protection—the kind of protection that people eat their hearts out for. You have it. As long as you listen to me, as long as you keep your faith in me, as long as you follow me and learn from me you are safe—and the journey will be hard, undoubtedly, but if you keep at it nothing can harm you. No one can touch you. I am sealing you off from the rest of the world, Jack. The world can fuck itself like it always does, but it won't be fucking you. And I'm going to help you get revenge for all the things it could have done, were I not here. Revenge for all the horrible futures that will not be.

"I love you. I love the best and worst parts of you. And you will love them too. There is nothing more important than that. What is here and now, and what lies before us, together, is more important than any other thing in the world. Do you understand?"

"I understand," I told him.

"But if you do stray..." He tapped the case. "All of my protection ends."

I didn't even know how to stray, and I told him so.

"It will come," he said. "It always does. The choice."

Sitting in the chair, across from Cyrus, I thought of Thornton suspended, as if caught up in a white picture that had swallowed him. A shiver ran itself through my body on an endless loop. I told myself one thing and one thing only.

I would not lose the way.

I would not lose the way.

CHAPTER 5—ECONOMICS
AGE: 10 YEARS OLD

Not nearly as numbly before, I did my best to keep pace with the rhythm of Cyrus's home and all that it brought me. By the time I was ten years old, I had been training with Roland for three years. In the prior two, I had begun the earliest of my lessons with Cyrus. These did not revolve around killing or murder but something much more ordinary—money.

I was given a set allowance each week. Cyrus did his best to con me out of it in every way possible. Following these cons, twice each week, we would discuss rational and irrational choices and what made them such.

One day, he might short my allowance by folding bills over so that when he counted them, there appeared to be far more bills than there actually were. His lesson was "Take all the money into your own hands, and count it yourself. Don't trust anyone else." Another day, he might write me a check and, later, offer to cash it. When he cashed the check, he would do so incorrectly. Either he would short me by an entire decimal point or he would "misread" the amount. His lesson was for me to scrutinize the numbers and remember that they can always be fiddled with, especially if there were multiple checks, especially if I myself had not added up the totals. Another day, he might do something as simple as offer me extra dessert after dinner in exchange for one of my ten-dollar bills.

"If you were at a public school with other children," he told me during one of our recaps, "you could employ these tricks on them. If you packed your lunch, you could exchange your favorite dessert for a few dollars. You increase the price at the right moment—when someone is hungry. That way, they're least likely to say no.

"Don't worry," he added with a smile. "I'm going to repeat these things again and again. You won't forget them."

Perhaps the most important thing that he hounded into me was not to deal in any way in cash over ten thousand dollars with a bank because of the way the federal government tracked the money with Currency Transaction Reports. Not only that, but Cyrus reiterated that we must avoid banks so that an equally dangerous Suspicious Activity Report wasn't created. Cyrus never exchanged more than nine thousand dollars in cash with a bank, and never often. More importantly, Cyrus never exchanged more than nine thousand dollars with "followers," as he called them.

"Generally, if there is cash, it stays in the vault here," he said. "And I—we—never ask others to donate more than nine thousand dollars each once a week. A lot of them can't donate that much, of course, but the ones who can… We have to milk them slowly, otherwise they will withdraw the cash from their bank, and their bank will create a CTR for that money. It's possible we will be discovered."

"By who?" I asked him.

His eyes shined. "By those on alert for drug traffickers, terrorists, and others of nefarious means. But we are not like those. Our following is not like those. Are we?"

I shook my head. Of course not. Not if Cyrus said we weren't. What "the following" was, was exactly what Cyrus said it was, just like everything else.

"But you can often get more out of a bank than they intend to give. It happens all the time." Cyrus smirked. He leaned toward me, and his short, thick silver hair glowed in the light. "For instance, if I go into a bank, I walk up to the teller with a smile on my face and say that I need to withdraw five thousand dollars, and I would appreciate it in a strap. 'You know, a brick,' I tell them. Sometimes I will actually get a brick, even if they know that is incorrect." He winked at me.

"The fact is, a brick isn't five thousand dollars—it is ten thousand dollars. I know perfectly well it isn't, and they know perfectly well it isn't. Still, that's what I *request*, and sometimes, even if the bank teller explains my incorrect assumption to me, the *idea* of the brick is lodged in his or her head, and I get just that.

"Several times I have successfully exited a bank with double the amount of money in my pocket than what I had written down on the withdrawal slip. Ten thousand dollars strapped in a five-thousand-dollar label, all because of the power of suggestion.

"And what's wonderful is that the bank system will never know. Not until the end of the day, when the teller tries to balance. By then, it's very difficult to figure out where the money went, because that amount was never entered into the system. Yet I never threatened anyone, did I?"

I shook my head as I stared into his cold, gray eyes.

"I merely suggested." He leaned forward. "Suggestion is so *powerful*."

The way he said that dazzled me.

He leaned back in his chair. "I'm teaching you complicated things right now, but I want you to realize what an effect there is in the slightest alteration of words. Under the right circumstances, sometimes a few sentences can yield five thousand dollars."

He smirked and tilted his head toward me. "Wouldn't you prefer to double your money?"

I nodded.

"Everybody would," he said. "All right. We're done for the day."

Of course, I learned other types of economics from Cyrus, ones that dealt with death and blood and were indeed just as frightening as my lessons with Roland. One of them occurred on the first day that Cyrus taught Alex to kill.

Cyrus had an old dog that needed to be put down. It had been moaning for days. We—me, Roland, and Alex—were led to the back of the property, to a wooded area with a small stream, to complete the work.

Cyrus never told me or the others point blank why we were going into those woods on that particular day, but we knew—I knew. Alex knew.

Roland knew. Even the dog knew. His head hung low, his ears drooped, and he shook all over. Alex didn't shake. He never did like that dog.

Frankly, the dog didn't like Alex either.

Cyrus was using his resources wisely. He had a dog that needed to be put down, and he had a son who needed to learn how to put "dogs" down. It was economical. A death that might otherwise come naturally was permuted into a lesson.

When Cyrus put the .357 in Alex's hand, though, something wasn't right. Something about the way Alex twisted the gun, took off the safety, turned his head—my heart leaped. Roland leaned against a tree, stock still, and folded his arms. So I went still too.

Cyrus told Shakespeare, the German Shepherd, to lie down. He motioned for Alex to stand a few feet behind him, and Alex did. Then we all put bright orange earplugs in our ears.

Cyrus put his finger on one of the skull bones that protruded over Shakespeare's neck. "Right here," he said to Alex and handed him the gun. "One bullet here, and we start digging."

Alex cocked the gun, and before I could blink he fired. One. Two. Three. Four. Five shots. They were so loud, I smacked my ears with my hands and shut my eyes tight for a split second.

A high-pitched ringing filled my head. Then I could make out more sounds. They were coming from Shakespeare. He was still alive, whimpering, quivering, crawling along the dirt. Alex had not pierced his skull.

The dog was bloody, and a milky white foam seethed from a hole in his back. His left paw was almost completely blown off.

My throat stiffened. Shakespeare's tongue lamely licked at the dirt and rivers of blood trailing down the coarse fur on his back onto the sparse grass.

"Goddammit, Alex!" Cyrus roared. Alex stared blankly at his father. Cyrus grabbed the gun from his hand and knocked him in the face with it. Roland, meanwhile, calmly strolled from his tree and retrieved a pistol from his inner pocket.

"Move out of the way, so I can do your job for you," Roland said. Alex scooted toward me. Roland shot the dog in the back of the head twice, and Shakespeare stopped turning. He lay in the dirty, surreally still.

"Need I remind you that I am in charge?" Cyrus said. He stamped across the dirt and leaves and pushed Alex to the ground. "What the hell were you thinking?"

Alex stared at Cyrus. That was the bravest moment he had ever had. He did not look away. His courage quickly broke, though, as do all great things supported by bad deeds. Alex began whimpering. "I just..." Alex said.

"You just what?"

"I just wanted to do well. To be better than the others."

Cyrus shoved Alex to the ground with his foot. "What is it exactly that you think we do here? Hm?"

"I...I...don't know." A tear trickled down Alex's cheek.

"Exactly. You don't know." He pointed at Shakespeare. "You don't fucking know. Well, here is your first lesson. We never do *that* to one of our *own*. Never! You want to torture something and you choose the family dog?" Cyrus shook his head and ran a hand through his hair.

"I'm sorry," Alex whispered.

"Fuck you are. Get up!" Cyrus yelled. He removed his foot from Alex's chest. "You're going to dig that damned grave on your own. I want it perfect."

Alex pulled himself up, wiped his nose, and slunk past Shakespeare to where one of the shovels lay against a tree. "You'll need the spade first," Cyrus said. Alex winced, walked two feet to where a spade lay on the ground. He reached down, his shiny blond hair falling, obscuring his face.

"Now start digging. And you'll keep going until your body hurts. And then you'll still keep digging. And then your arms will give out. Then you'll claw through that dirt a spoonful at a time. You won't stop until I say." Cyrus's eyes shot sparks. It was not the dog that had angered Cyrus but the failure of his lesson. He had desired to accomplish two things at once: Shakespeare's death and teaching his son. He had fulfilled neither. That meant he had lost control.

Alex sniffed, looking less like a king and more a pawn. He squinted at the ground below his feet. Halfheartedly, he broke the surface with the spade, splitting the first slice of soil in two, wedging the pieces apart until he could gain further leverage.

He pierced a new section of soil and repeated the same thing. And again. And again. He did this for a good hour. Tiny beads of perspiration formed on his forehead and rolled down the sides of his face. Grit collected in the tiny crevices between his nose and cheeks. Light seeped from a part in his mouth until there was only an exhausted, drained husk of a boy. This contented me.

Roland leaned against his tree, a thin line across his neck—evidence of my killing him just two days prior. Cyrus clenched his fists now and again. I stood, too wary to move among the enormous strands of tension strung through the air.

As time passed, my attention shifted to the leaves in the trees surrounding us. They blew in the wind, dropping sometimes, red and yellow blotting out the darkening ground, sometimes landing on Shakespeare, sometimes hitting me. They reminded me of butterflies with broken wings.

After the first hour, the three of us found seats in the dirt. After the second hour, rigor mortis had set in for Shakespeare, but Alex was moving fervently, toiling to show that he could not be beat. After the third, the sun had gone down, and Roland went to the house and returned with food for himself and me and Cyrus. He brought flashlights—giant, million-candlelight ones—and set them up in a circle around Alex.

Dirt flew through the air surrounding the flashlights like a cleansing mist.

After the fourth hour, Alex finished digging. Cyrus gently placed Shakespeare into the hole, kissed his head, and apologized for his son's behavior. We all filled that hole in together, packed the layers neatly, like files in a filing cabinet.

We retrieved the flashlights and trekked back to the house, heading to one of the east wing's dens. Cyrus escorted Alex to a corner of the room. Roland and I watched from a distance as my mentor lectured his son.

Roland, who stood beside me, said quietly, "What would you call that?"

"What Alex did?" I said.

"Mm hmm." He peered at me through the dim light.

"I don't know. I don't understand. He went insane."

Roland looked at his cuticles without seeing them. "And that's just the beginning." He gazed up at the ceiling and cocked his head.

"I'm not going to work with him, teaching him to kill...It won't be me. Not how I was with you." His right hand went to his hip, and he leaned against the wall.

Alex's head turned to us briefly, as though he had heard Roland's words.

"That means Cyrus will teach him. One thing you should remember, Jack. Just one thing. Nothing comes between a man and his son. No matter how bad the boy gets, his father will stick by him. And that means he will help Alex with whatever he wants.

"What that means is that you need to steer clear of Alex. Don't seek vengeance. Don't seek equality. Let him be. You don't want to give Cyrus any excuse to think ill of you. Believe it or not, staying in this house is the best of your two choices. Don't let Cyrus contemplate the alternative."

Roland always understood so well what was going through my head.

Neither of us spoke. At last, Roland nodded and broke the silence. "Just don't mistake what I'm saying. I'm glad I taught you well. I'm glad you were the first to learn."

I smiled proudly and, sensing that we'd shared a moment of deep, secret honesty, for the first time I asked a question I had been wondering for a while. "Roland," I began.

"Hm?"

"Are you the only one Cyrus can bring back? I mean...could he bring me back? Like he does with you?"

Roland smiled at me. "Yes, he can."

His words were so quiet, they sounded like the beating of a heart.

"And...if Alex dies, can Cyrus bring *him* back?"

Roland pulled out his pack of cigarettes and tapped the box against his palm. He stared at it. "Yes," Roland said. "He can bring you, Alex, me, and everyone else he wants to back...as many times as he wants."

"How?" I asked.

He paused.

"There's another man," he said. He brought a cigarette to his mouth, and it bobbed up and down as he sought his lighter. His words were sharp and stilted, and he did not look at me as he spoke. "He helps Cyrus resurrect them."

"Oh!" I said. My heart filled with fiery curiosity.

For the past few years, in absolute childlike wonder, I had believed Roland was perhaps magic. Then that Cyrus was. It had never occurred to me that there might be a third person lurking in the house—that the sparkling enchantment that made everything possible was not located in either of the men who taught me but in a mysterious stranger.

Yet there it was. The enigmatic web of my youthful ignorance began disentangling.

I started to ask Roland more, but Alex's steely-eyed stare stopped me. Rather than give in to my desire, I shut my mouth, wary of being spied on.

Roland smiled. "Now is the time for you to get to bed." He spun me around and ushered me in the direction of the stairs. "I wouldn't have answered your question anyway."

"How did you...?" I started, but Roland had a knowing look on his face. I was an all-too-easy-to-read book.

"Have a good night, Jack." With that, our conversation was over.

I made my way toward the doorway. "Goodnight, Roland."

-

I paused while ascending the staircase to the second floor. I was thinking about him—it: the someone or something lurking in our basement. I tried to imagine what he might look like. If he was a shadow. If he had red teeth and green eyes; if he had thick black fur—or if he looked like a normal man, in a tailored suit and hat.

More than that, though, I wondered where I could find him. Was he, perhaps, in one of Cyrus's bedrooms? Did he live in the library? Or did he move around the house, shifting in the shadows?

It hit me. A particular synapse of my brain fired, as if I had been working on the mystery for years. Roland had always left the basement *alive* after I had killed him. Cyrus never carried his body out of the basement. He never had to. If Roland always exited the basement alive, that must mean...

The man was in the basement. Of course. Cyrus kept the scene of the kill and the scene of resurrection in the same place.

Cyrus appeared at the top of the stairs, cutting short my thoughts. He descended.

"Goodnight, Jack," he said as we met on the same stair, and he placed a kiss on my forehead.

I smiled.

His silver eyes peered down at me, as though studying a curious text. "You know...you are doing well here. Better than I expected. I never would have dreamed that you and Roland would befriend one another, that you would take to your role in killing him so well. But that has...worked out for the best. I expect you'll end up staying."

"Where else would I go?"

He cupped my face with his hand, his expression keen. "With the other children. They live in a place not too far from here."

This was the first time Cyrus had mentioned any "other children." A sting of intuition told me to run from the topic as fast as I could, in case I somehow became entwined with it. Another part of me, though, desperately wanted to know what he was talking about.

"What other children?" I finally said. "What kind of place?"

"It's not worth getting into, now." He gave me a look that stopped everything in its tracks.

I blinked and, to sweep the topic away, smiled, pretending he had not just terrified me. It was a smile that said, "I love you, and I'm sorry for asking," as my mind said, "I fear you." We bid each other goodnight, and then his hand slipped away. He continued down to the first floor.

Pausing only for a moment, long enough for my smile, which had no more purpose, to fall away, I climbed the steps to my room, opened the door, and flicked on the light. Alex stood at the foot of my bed appearing dreadful—covered in dirt, eyes red, hair disheveled, his body almost lifeless.

"What are you doing here?"

"I just need to tell you something." He slouched toward me until his face almost touched mine. His salty breath tickled the hairs on my face. His eyelids drooped just below the tops of his blue irises.

"What?" I asked.

"I told you I'd do it better than you when Dad started teaching me."

"I don't know what you're talking about," I said. "I could have killed five dogs. You didn't even kill one."

"But I made him *feel* it," he said. "I made *all* of you feel it."

"Why does that matter?"

"It's the only thing that matters," he said before he shoved me.

I didn't even think. I pulled out the knife I always kept in my back right pocket, the silver-handled one given to me by Roland, and sliced Alex's face with it, a two-inch cut across his rosy-red cheek, the same cheek that Cyrus had struck with the butt of the .357.

Alex slapped his hand to his face, his eyes stretching wide, his mouth dropping open. "I'm telling Dad!" he yelled. He dashed out of the room.

He did tell Cyrus, but Cyrus did not bring it up with me. Instead, Alex was locked in his room for the night.

Alex being shut away didn't calm me though. All through the night, he fiddled with the lock on his door, trying to pick it. He muttered to himself, over and over, "Must do better. Must be better. So I don't end up where the others go."

I began to sense for the first time that Alex and I were on the edge of some abyss, some dark place that might swallow us whole. He was compelled to find his own path away from it, and that made me begin to wonder...

If I needed to fear it too.

CHAPTER 6—WOOL BETWEEN THE SLATS
AGE: 10 YEARS OLD

KNOWING A MAN WAS RESPONSIBLE for Roland's resurrection and that he was living in Cyrus's home, most likely in his basement, inspired me to charge through the floorboards and meet him, whether or not he was a terrifying monster.

I did not ask my mentor about the mysterious stranger because it might tip my hand. Cyrus might punish me for my curiosity or, at the very least, keep a stricter eye on me. After seeing what Cyrus could do to people and rooms with his red box, more than anything I feared his punishment.

I decided against exploring the basement alone. For one, it was too large, stretching beneath the entire base of Cyrus's mansion like a concrete maze, with too many hallways, cubbies, and rooms in which I might get lost, never to be found again. There were also strange noises and smells in that basement that warned me against unaccompanied exploration.

Instead, I spied on Cyrus as often as I could, waiting patiently for him to descend the cellar stairs to meet with whoever or whatever it was and usher in the next miracle. I hoped he would take a body with him when he did, so I might see the corpse reignite, witness what had been hidden behind a large brick wall for so long.

Approximately five days later my dedication was rewarded.

One particular evening, when I was supposed to be asleep in bed, I was watching Cyrus in the White Room through a crack in the door. On his desk, he had placed the dreadful red box, which he had retrieved from his office.

I kept my attention half on the box and half on Cyrus as he searched through the desk drawers. In the large right bottom drawer, he found what he was looking for; he retrieved it and slipped it into his pocket. Red box in hand, he walked to the door.

Quietly, I bolted. From around the corner, I watched him leave the room. I trailed him.

Cyrus wandered to the east side of his mansion and descended a set of stone stairs that led to the basement.

I waited several seconds before following him. When I finally reached the basement floor, I was unsure which of the alcoves he had entered. I might have been too cautious and lost the trail completely.

I listened and waited. There was only silence.

So small I nearly missed it was the barest hint of a shadow slipping across the brick wall to my left. I smiled.

I tiptoed in that direction, down a long corridor that led me to the wine room. I walked between wooden crates and racks of red and white wine to another threshold, one I had never seen before. Usually, the thick, large metal door that barred the way was shut. This time, it was wide open.

Tentatively, I stepped just past the threshold to study the vault-like door. To my right, the hallway dead-ended. It led to just two rooms. That wasn't much, I thought to myself, to require such a large metal door to keep people out.

The antechamber was well lit; three bare, clear bulbs hung overhead. To my right, the closest of the doors was ten feet away. The other was twenty.

A man spoke quietly, like a radio turned down low or buried beneath a pile of sheets. I took two steps in and held my breath to hear better.

The hairs along the back of my neck prickled. A strange noise flowed through the wall, harsh and eerie, as though it were coming from something dark and spindly, with sharp tentacles that could attach themselves to the brick and lunge some massive, quivering body toward me. I froze, midstep.

The growl continued, expanded.

Alarmed, I retraced my steps. As slowly as I could manage, attempting to calm myself, to prove to myself that nothing all that horrific was occurring, I backed through the doorway one step at a time and entered the wine room.

A deafening scream exploded just as I reached the island in the room. Fear struck me. I slapped my hands to my ears and dropped low, close to the bottom tiers of wine, shoving my forehead against my knees. The scream thrust itself inside my head, until I was the one screaming, like I might never stop.

I was sure the whole house could hear it, certain the nearby forest was waking to the sounds of hell in Cyrus's basement, that birds were flying from their nests and crickets burying themselves deep underground, just to get away from that scream, so loud it was science fiction.

It reminded me of a lamb, a beautiful, cream lamb, in the midst of slaughter.

When the shriek finally stopped, I remained frozen for a long while, too fearful of moving in case it returned. Eventually, though, when my legs were cramped from squatting, I stood and pressed myself against one of the metal storage racks.

I tried to swallow and noticed there was nothing *to* swallow. I opened my hands wide, realized that they were shaking despite my fierce attempts to control them. I breathed deep.

Placing one of my trembling hands upon the wall firmly, I clasped the red brick and rounded the corner.

I walked across the threshold just as carefully as I had before, hoping to observe a clue as to what the hell had just happened.

It was unfathomable.

The hall's red brick had blanched to white, as if I were standing in the remnants of an explosion that had destroyed every particle of color. Other than a few spots of red here and there, the majority of the blast zone was as white as sugar, as salt, as snow. Even the light from the three overhead bulbs was white, not yellow like before. It was exactly like the White Room or the small sitting room where Cyrus had killed Thornton three years before.

As I observed the quartz-looking bricks, however, suddenly they... weren't.

In the cold, dank hallway, as my heart pulsed faster than the wings of a hummingbird, the brick slowly turned pink, and then orange, before reddening again, as if the bricks were bleeding back to their original color. If the antechamber were a limb, the circulation was returning.

The door closest to me rattled. The knob turned.

I launched through the large metal door, out of the wine room. I silently ran to the next hallway, and then I bolted up the stairs. After quietly closing the basement door, I rushed all the way to my room and climbed into bed.

There, I quieted my heart, slowed my breath, closed my eyes, and waited for Cyrus to arrive.

Eventually he did. I pretended to be nearly sleep. He sat down on the bed and kissed me goodnight. I whispered "Goodnight" in return. I sensed him breathe a few breaths, the smell of it sweet, like he had just eaten chocolate. He got up from the bed, walked away, and closed the door. He continued to Alex's room. They spoke for just a moment before the sound of Alex's door clicked shut. Cyrus's footsteps retreated down the hall.

The slowest hour in the world came and left. I lay beneath the sheets and stared at the clock, deciding what I should do and when.

Eventually, unable to rein in my curiosity, I got up and slipped on my shoes. I crept out of my room.

I tiptoed to the end of the hall and then to the left, past the balcony that overlooked the den, down the stairs. Carefully, I made my way to the basement, but a realization came to me. The large metal door would most likely be locked again. How was I going to get past it?

As though a part of my brain had been working on the problem before I even thought to ask the question, I remembered Cyrus slipping something from his desk into his pocket. Might it be necessary to open the door? I altered my path and went to Cyrus's office.

I inspected the contents of the upper right desk drawer. Nothing looked like a key, but I lifted a white card and thought it might have been what Cyrus took with him—it was the only thing there that was small enough to fit into his pocket and was simultaneously worth taking. The rest—a stapler, a folder with papers, a box of pens, a book, several notepads, paper clips, dark blue ink in a clear bottle, a gun wrapped in a cloth, and a small cologne sampler—were unremarkable. The white card, the only thing that looked remotely important, was somewhat thick and had a stripe on the back of it, kind of like a credit card. I slid my hands across the sturdy plastic. Satisfied with my choice, I placed the item into my pocket, shut the drawer, and, relieved that I did not see the red box anywhere in the room, continued on my way.

In several minutes, I was facing the same wooden door that led down to the basement.

Slipping my small hand through the circular handle, I gripped the metal lightly and pulled. In the quiet, its groan was thunderous. I shushed the door, wincing.

Very distant, but distinct, moans rose from downstairs. I pressed myself against the closed door, using it to shield me from the anguished sounds.

Whatever was in that room, it was louder than any human. For its voice to penetrate two doors, one of them metal, meant that this creature, whatever it was, owned a voice that passed through brick as if it were little more than Sheetrock and cardboard. Nevertheless, my hands and heart were steady. I didn't fear him.

I slipped down the stairs slowly and soundlessly.

I passed through the walls of wine and stood in front of the gray metal door. There was a handle and above that handle a black slot, but not like for a key. It appeared, rather, as a vending machine would, with a slot for money. I retrieved the card from my pocket and gazed at the dark brown strip on one side. It appeared well-worn and scratched.

Holding the card strip-side up, I slid it into the slot above the shining metal handle and waited. Nothing. I tried the handle, and it would not budge. Frowning, I removed the card and then slid it inside again, with no result. Sighing, I flipped the card so the strip faced down and tried again. Something inside the door, an internal switch of some sort, clicked. I smiled.

The handle moved effortlessly, and I slung all my weight back. The door opened with a squeak. Fearing it would close on me, I set a bottle of wine that had been sitting on the island in the doorjamb. At last, I crossed the threshold.

I walked into the deeply red hallway and listened to whatever person or thing was whimpering. I pressed my hand against the rough brick and mortar and listened so intently and for so long that my feet began to ache. I had been standing on tiptoe without realizing.

After another brief whimper, the moans dissipated to almost nothing, and in the reassuring quiet, I walked the ten feet and arrived at the wooden door.

Flickering light danced beneath the door's lower edge. It didn't quite reach five inches beyond the frame, but it touched the tips of my shoes. It was like a reflection of moving water at the edge of a pool or fire reflecting off glass. Mesmerizing.

I bent low, dipped my hand into the light, and then placed it firmly on the brick floor. I lowered my head and attempted to peer inside. The gap between the door and the floor was too narrow, and I rose again, disappointed. I accidentally banged the door with my right foot.

The crying stopped.

Silence.

I held my breath, waiting, listening. Finally, knowing the jig was up, I asked, "Are you okay?"

There was only that shimmering light, the basement's familiar moist, cold smell with the rotten undertone, and the quiet.

I repeated, "Are...are you okay?"

The thing or man or whatever was inside did not answer. Tentatively, I touched the doorknob. The old, complexly cut glass knob seemed like a stone for a giant's ring. I gripped it in my small hand and tried to turn it.

It budged perhaps a centimeter, but no more. It was locked, and I did not have a key for this second door.

My mouth slipped open, a question poised at the tip of my tongue. "Are you the one who has been helping bring Roland back to life?"

Again, only silence.

"If so..." I searched for the right thing to say, "thanks."

No response.

Sensing that this was as far as I would get, I decided to leave. "All right, well...goodnight," I told the mysterious being. My own words made my heart swell. The emotion surprised me. It had been so long since I had experienced much beyond fear. I wasn't sure where the sensation came from or why it happened, but the fact that it occurred at all satisfied me. Slowly, content I had made contact and willing to wait for anything more, I left the place, glancing back at the wooden doorway only once before returning to the metal door. Ensuring that the white card was still in my pocket, I lifted the wine bottle, pushed the door firmly shut, and then returned the bottle of wine to the island, facing it the same way it had been facing before.

I went upstairs, returned the card to the desk, and slipped back into my room. It was a long time before I slept.

-

For the next two days, I thought upon the fact that I had been able to get past the more challenging of the two doors, and I tried to decipher a way to unlock the wooden door and see whatever was inside.

I considered asking Roland if he might be willing to train me—or find someone who could train me—in picking locks. Almost immediately, I realized this would hinder more than help, as Roland would invariably ask *why* I wanted to learn how to pick locks. It was hardly the best option.

I marched through the mansion, thinking, pondering.

I pictured the wooden door again, the wavering light hitting my shoes like the waves on a pool in the calm early evening. A brilliant idea hit me.

I might not need to open the door. It wasn't that I necessarily needed to enter the room, or that the being inside needed to come out. It was only important that *something* would be able to go into the room and return.

The gap between the bottom of the door and the brick floor was two inches. I could slip something small, like a letter, or even something a little bit larger, maybe a hundred-page book, or even, say, *a mirror*, beneath the door frame with no problem. There could be another form of communication, a creative way around the roadblock.

Then, an even better idea plied its way into my brain. If he was indeed the one who could resurrect the dead, I might be able to bring something small to him and have him resurrect it. My heart leaped at the possibility. I could very well witness, via the small crack between the door and the floor, a miniature miracle.

A grasshopper or a snake would be small enough to fit beneath the doorframe.

As I was walking along a corridor, though, I came across something better than any grasshopper or snake or cricket or cicada or toad.

Three dozen red roses glowed in a white and silver vase. Their edges were just beginning to blacken, the drooping petals showing the barest signs of their inevitable death.

I plucked a limp red flower from the vase and gazed upon it. It could work.

Swiftly, I carried it upstairs and hid it beneath my bed. I did not want the flower simply limp when I brought it to him; I wanted it dead, dried, and crackling. I demanded the miracle as miraculous as it could be.

Several days passed, and the flower shriveled and dried. The smell of the fragrant rot intensified, and I wrinkled my nose every time I smelled it. By the end of the week, it was exactly what I needed: thin, fragile, and as light as a feather.

The night of the seventh day, I was lying in bed with plans of carrying the flower down to the basement as soon as Cyrus tucked me in. When he entered my room, he was dressed in a coat and shoes, ready to go out. I asked him, "Are you going somewhere?"

He nodded.

It was late, and that confused me. "Where?"

"To check on the other children. See how they are doing."

"Oh. Are they sick?"

"No, no." Cyrus smiled. "Every Monday evening, a few more children arrive, and I have to go and meet them."

I thought of the many rooms in Cyrus's house and did not understand why Cyrus would need to leave at all. "Why don't they live here?"

"Only the lucky ones live here. Alex is a lucky one. You are a lucky one."

"And what are they?"

Cyrus's eyes shifted. "They are...*almost* lucky." He shifted his head forward. "You would rather be lucky, yes?"

I nodded.

"That's all that matters... Time to go to sleep."

He patted my arm once and rose from the bed. He walked to the door and turned back once to wink. He left.

I waited, watching the clock. Twenty minutes passed. That should have given him enough time to leave. It was a good time for sneaking.

I slipped my shoes on, retrieved the dead rose from beneath my bed, and moved to my door. I opened it, peered out, and made sure no one else was in the hallway. After several minutes of silence and stillness, I quietly exited and shut my door behind me. I tiptoed to the end of the hall, to the left past the balcony, and down the stairs.

Soon, I again faced the wooden door that led to the basement, card in hand. I took several deep breaths before placing my hand on the door handle. Trepidation sped my heart, but I was used to trepidation and used to a speeding heart. These sensations did not stop me.

I reached the lower level in no time, skipping past the wine. I grabbed a bottle from the island and slipped the white card into the slot above the door's handle. I pulled the door open, set the bottle of wine against it again, and entered the familiar red hallway. I crept to the wooden door, my pulse thumping in my ears, and bent toward the flickering light beneath it.

When I dropped the rose to the brick, its petals fractured and made a delicious crunching sound. I shoved the crumbling petals through the gap under the door, so that only half of the long green stem remained visible. The sound of petals scraping against the floor could not be ignored, not in that quiet hallway. Believing that whoever was inside had to have heard it, I searched for a shadow. I waited, giddy with anticipation.

Something shifted on the other side of the door. There was the sound of footsteps.

"It's me," I said when someone, something, approached. Realizing I had never introduced myself, I said, "My name is Jack. I was here a few days ago. I thanked you for resurrecting Roland."

Slowly, a shadow blocked the light from beneath the door, and the rose stem edged its way under and disappeared without a sound. The shadow quietly vanished, and all that was left was the flickering, shimmering light on the red brick.

I gulped, a tad embarrassed. I stammered and asked if he could bring the rose back to life. "You don't have to if you don't want to," I said, "but I just would like to see it happen. You know...because it's amazing."

Near one of my bare feet, the tip of the rose's stem came into view.

I slowly withdrew the stalk. The plumpest, healthiest rose slipped between the door and the floor. The enormous bloom flared open as I righted the flower.

The blossom pulsated with life, larger and fleshier than it had been four days before. It was more real, more alive, than any rose could be. It was not simply resurrected. It was improved—pure crimson beauty.

I had found him, the being who helped Cyrus bring Roland back to life, who could bring me back, if needed. What had Roland said? Anyone at any time?

The rose's phenomenal scent was strong and sweet. "It's so beautiful," I sighed as I brushed the ruby petals against my nose. "Thank you."

Trying the knob once more, I found the door was still locked and solidly so. Knowing I should not linger too long, I said, "Goodnight, whoever you are," and made my way back down the hall, glancing once more at the miraculous monster's doorway. "I'll be back later."

I clasped the rose to my chest as I crept back to my room, and I slept with it on my pillow beside me. That night, as I rested, I dreamed I was eating a piece of pie made with bits of apple wrapped in petals; there had never existed any food so delicious.

-

I brought that rose back to the man on several Mondays after, excitedly awaiting each evening that Cyrus would be away checking on the other children. Each time the man beyond the door quietly transformed the flower and returned it to me, my skin flushed and my heart bloomed as large as the rose. The miraculous process became a weekly habit.

Then, another strange, delightful idea hit me.

After breakfast one morning, I placed my empty bowl of cereal in the sink and left for the sitting room in the back of Cyrus's mansion, the one where Thornton had been killed. I slipped into the den.

I had not been inside the room before. The need to investigate the place where Cyrus had used the box had never called to me; the truth was that I had tried to avoid it. Now, I ignored any fear, glided into the room quietly, and shut the door.

No window shades were drawn, and it enhanced the blankness of the room. The den floors were hardwood, and the wood was terribly white. It was solidly furnished with sofas, a chaise lounge, a piano, several bureaus and buffets. An empty birdcage near one of the tall windows was bordered by lush satin curtains.

At one time, those curtains had likely been light blue with gold stripes, just like in some of the other rooms. The couches had perhaps been a soft cream, the molding gold, the birdcage a bright, electric silver. The entire room, like the rest of Cyrus's mansion, must have been arrestingly elegant.

It wasn't brilliant, now. Rather, it was like the White Room. The image of Cyrus dragging Thornton into that very room by his hair and Thornton's eerie upturned face came to my mind. I shook the memories off.

There was a similarity between the events in the basement and the events in that den. The color had been sucked from both rooms.

There was, of course, one notable difference. Unlike the room where Thornton had been killed, which was still white, in the basement the red had returned, and the man in the room was still alive, whereas Thornton was not.

This begged an experiment.

I withdrew my knife and approached one of the white curtains. I cut along the base of the fabric until I'd freed a square about twice the size of my hand. I folded it and slipped it into my pocket. I situated the curtain so the cut could not be seen.

This piece of curtain I kept beneath my bed beside the plump rose.

On a Monday evening, I waited once again until fifteen minutes after Cyrus had left my room.

Just a little after eleven, I slinked down to the basement and stood outside the familiar door, the white fabric clutched in my hands. Like a messenger delivering an envelope, I carefully dropped the fabric to the ground and slid it under the door.

Breathlessly, I watched. Within a few moments, the man arrived. The fabric disappeared. I bit my lip and pressed my ear against the door. Shuffling, perhaps, but that was all I could detect. Light flickered at my feet, like a quiet fire was burning inside the room.

A corner of fabric appeared in the light.

I tugged it. The fabric was not glistening white platinum cloth, but rather two very light blue stripes and two brilliant gold ones. The brilliant hues shimmered at me beneath the yellow overhead bulb.

"How do you do that?" I asked. "Who are you?"

Silence.

I pressed my ear against the door, listening hard for any detectable sound. Someone might be quietly breathing, but it also could have been my imagination.

I folded the cloth and slipped it into my pocket. I turned around.

Cyrus stood there, a red box in his hands. "What are you doing, Jack?"

I gasped.

He wasn't supposed to be in the house. He was supposed to be gone. Wasn't he? I racked my brain, trying to remember if I had actually seen him leave. I didn't know. There had been too many Mondays for me to remember. Under his gaze, I could barely contain these thoughts; in the weight of his presence, they evaporated.

"I..." I shook my head, stammering. Cyrus stood inordinately still, his gaze as hard and unrelenting as a statue's. He squatted to my level, and though there were times when he had hugged me, tucked me into bed, kissed my forehead, was kind, there was no hint of those moments. It was like gazing into the eyes of a snake.

"Where is my key card?"

I reached into my back pocket and retrieved the white card. I held it up, and he took it. His attention shifted from it to the door.

"Who told you about this place?"

"No one."

"Then how did you find it?"

Every muscle in my body tensed. My heart hurdled over my ribs. "I followed you one night."

"Did you see what's beyond that door?"

This question carried an immense weight.

"No."

"But you wanted to?"

Slowly, I nodded.

He stood again. "Are you not happy here?"

"I am," I said.

"Because I'd hate for you to have to leave after all we have accomplished."

I shook my head, gripping my hands into fists tight enough that my fingernails cut into my skin. "No, no, no. I don't want to leave."

"And I would hate to have to begin again. It is very difficult for children so advanced in the process to begin again."

"No!" I said, terrified.

"Then," he said with gritted teeth, "do not follow me or sneak through this house looking for treasures that do not belong to you. Do not steal from me." He lifted the key card. "I won't have anyone who lives here stealing from me."

Warm tears slid down my cheek. "I won't steal from you."

"Believe me. You would not like it outside of this house."

"I know. I'm sorry."

I wiped my eyes with my palms and could no longer look into his frightening, unblinking gaze.

"You will be punished for this, but right now I want you to go. To. Bed."

"Yes, Cyrus."

I quickly stepped past his hunched form toward the exit, my footsteps sounding outrageously loud.

I reached the exit to the wine room.

Cyrus said, "Jack."

I turned.

He stood in front of the creature's door. "If I catch you down here again, that will be it."

I gasped. "I won't."

As I ascended the stairs out of the basement, an anguished scream reverberated through the air.

I clapped my hands to my ears and hunkered on the steps, unable to move, waiting out the horrific noise. The sounds went on and on. It seemed the screaming would never end, that it was knocking me over, freezing me, hurting me.

Suddenly, there were warm, comforting hands on my own. I opened my eyes and saw Roland. He lifted me up, telling me, "You don't need to be down here, not when Cyrus goes to harvesting." He set me on my feet and held my hand. Side by side, we escaped the shrieks that sapped all my energy.

Outside the basement, Roland shut the door. The yelling continued, resonating beneath my feet—faint vibrations in the floorboards. It was almost like a wounded sheep was in the wood—wool between the slats.

Roland scooted a chair from a nearby table across the floor, and I sat in it. He leaned on the table edge.

"I can't stand that screaming," I told him, wiping tears from my face.

"You want to know a secret?" he asked, his voice exceedingly kind. "Neither can I."

This confused me. Roland was always solid, impermeable to weakness and moral throes. The look on his face said otherwise. All the muscles had collected inward. "If things weren't the way they were..." he said. "Well, I guess my point is, I shouldn't have to hear those screams, and neither should you. Because he...shouldn't have to scream."

"Why is he?"

Roland winced. "Cyrus doesn't want you down there, and he doesn't want you to know about that man. I won't be the one to endanger you by telling you. You have to understand..." he held in a breath and paused. "What Cyrus is attempting here with you and Alex, he has never attempted before. There is no need to give him reason to think it was a mistake to keep you two in his home. He's just as willing to live without you as he is to live with you."

He stood and held out his hand. "Come on."

We left the small room, and the farther we walked, the less those vibrations stung my feet.

When we reached the upper floor, Roland said, "Don't go down there anymore. Don't go seeking things in the basement. Don't test Cyrus again."

I nodded slowly and thought about Cyrus's threat to send me where the other children were. It made me shiver. "I won't."

Sensing we were about to part for the evening, I hugged Roland. He paused before returning the hug and squeezed me tight. When I pulled away, he smiled.

"How is it that, no matter how dark, or old, or weary a man gets, a child can change him?" Roland asked. "Hmm? How is it that I am changing now, when for fifty-some years I have been what I am? How am I regretting?"

"What are you regretting?" I asked.

He shook his head.

"I love you, Roland," I said. "I love you more than I love Cyrus."

"Jack," he replied, "I love you too, but don't ever say that again. Not in this house. Not ever."

-

Cyrus woke me in the middle of the night. He sat quietly on my bed.

He appeared gray in the dark. There was a bit of blood on his neck. I touched a speck of it and wiped it away. He caught my hand, retrieved his handkerchief, and wiped my finger clean. He dabbed the cloth against his neck.

"You can't go down to the basement again."

"I know. I know. I won't."

He gazed out the window beside my bed. A shadow of the trees in the wind danced across his face. His eyes glittered.

He held up his hand. "Two days," he said. "No food. You stay in your room. Two days. That will be your punishment."

"Starting when?"

"Now."

Rising from the bed, he replaced his handkerchief in his pocket and then walked to the door.

"Cyrus."

He turned.

"I'm sorry."

"Don't be sorry. Just be better," he replied. He opened the door and left.

The next few days passed slowly. I was tired, restive, and hungry. By the middle of the second day hunger overwhelmed me. My head fogged, and all my thoughts and recollections came to me covered with a sickly film.

I found a watermelon ChapStick in my nightstand and ate it. The wax coated my stomach, but only for a short time. Eventually, I was hungry again, and there was no ChapStick or anything else.

By the night of the second day, the pangs of hunger had stopped toying around. I lay on my bed, simply waiting, my hand curled around a limp rose wrapped in a piece of blue and gold fabric.

I expected Cyrus to come to me that night, but he did not appear. It was the next morning that he arrived, unlocked my door, and let me out of my room. He walked with me down to the kitchen. When we arrived, a plate of eggs, toast, and bacon awaited me. I dove to the chair, took my seat, and immediately began eating.

My mentor watched me for a long time. When I was finished, he said, "You must think I am cruel."

I shook my head.

"You should." He spoke wistfully. Then he straightened and added, "But as much as I am cruel to you, I am kind."

He rose from the kitchen chair and walked past the cupboards, past the island, and out of the room. When he returned, he carried a cardboard box that he set on my lap.

Inside was a black and brown puppy.

I gasped. The high from eating doubled.

I reached inside and withdrew the tiny sleeping German shepherd, and I cradled him. The box slid to the floor.

"Seemed right," Cyrus said, "since Shakespeare is gone. What will you name her?"

"Her?"

Cyrus nodded.

I smiled and peered down at the tiny head covered with the softest, shiniest black hair. I thought hard. "Rose," I said, looking up at Cyrus.

"*Ciao*, Rose," Cyrus said. "Welcome to this world." Cyrus patted Rose's head, and then my own. "You are still part of this house, Jack. As long as we get along well."

I looked down at the puppy in my lap. "We do."

CHAPTER 7—BEHEADED
AGE: 10 YEARS OLD

KNOWING THAT CYRUS HAD MULTIPLE uses for the man in the basement intrigued me all the more. Not only was he responsible for bringing Roland back to life, but he was also responsible—according to Roland—for protecting all of us from death. It barely registered that Cyrus and this man were not friends, that this man was locked in a room, and that Cyrus was apparently hurting him, somehow, with the red box. My focus instead revolved around discovering the new location of the key card, despite my promise to Cyrus.

It was no longer in his desk drawer, and it only took me six days to discover the new place he was stashing it—on a bookshelf behind his desk in his office, between the top two books on the left.

As I stood in front of the towering bookshelf, I wanted to hold the card, to slip it from between the books and look at it again. Even if I didn't ultimately return to the basement, I wanted to have it in my hands. I stared at the little piece of white plastic sticking out from between the top two books on the twelfth shelf and could not rein in my desire. I prepared to climb.

As I reached for the edge of the sixth shelf, my foot slipped, and my hand shot forward, landing on top of a book. My fingers latched onto it, my fingernails bending back as I clasped it in desperation. As I fell, the book jerked toward me, and I lost my grip on it entirely. I landed with a hard thump.

After the initial shock and pain disappeared, I stood.

The book jutted forward at an angle in the middle of the row, baring its golden edge. I pulled Cyrus's brown leather swivel chair close to the bookshelf and stepped onto the seat to reach the book—the more intelligent approach I should have taken in the first place.

I could not push the book back in place. The spine was cold, hard, and unyielding. It wasn't a book at all. The gold gilt on the outer layer of the pages overlaid metal. I tapped my finger on its edge. *Tink tink tink.* I tested the rest of the books. They, too, were metal. Every single one was fake.

Pushing the jutting book with all my might, I tried to force it back into place, but it would not return. I strained against it until my hands were bruised.

My heart pounded, pierced with fear. If I couldn't return the nonbook to the way it had been, Cyrus would notice, and he would realize I had been in his office. There was only one thing left he could do to me—send me off to the mysterious, dark abyss with the other children.

My mouth going dry, the world around me swaying out, I stepped off the chair and rolled it back to Cyrus's desk. With a sticky swallow, I retreated to the hallway outside his door and leaned against the wall. There was no way to saw through the metallic book; there was no way to cover it up; there certainly was no way for me to move it back into place.

Roland, I thought. *I can tell Roland.* Roland, though, was with Cyrus, and it would be impossible to get him alone without arousing suspicion.

For a good two hours, I paced the house, my heart whirling, my mind foggy with fear. I had been stupid to try and get that card. I had been stupid to even think about holding it again, especially so soon after I had been discovered in the basement.

I caught sight of Cyrus walking to his office. I froze, watching him approach the door. My fear level shot to its apex. My mind went wild, searching for some tale to explain.

Cyrus entered his room and proceeded to his desk chair. Without so much as a glance at the shelves behind him, he took his seat and proceeded to rifle through a set of white and yellow papers.

My eyes still wide, my heart still hurdling over each rib, I approached the room quietly.

I glanced at the bookshelf, and my mouth opened. I nearly collapsed with relief. The purple book, miraculously, no longer protruded from the shelf. It was back in line with the others. It must have moved back into place on its own. I could have cried with joy.

Cyrus looked up, noticing me. "Hello, Jack. Are you all right? You look...pale."

I broke into a smile that was not entirely disingenuous. "I'm fine," I said.

He gazed at me inquiringly.

Under the pressure of his look, I blurted out the first thing that came to mind. "I was wondering if I could...borrow a book." As soon as the words left my mouth, I wished I hadn't said anything. I was tempting fate.

Cyrus smiled, his gaze never veering from me. "The library on the *third floor* is full of books."

I nodded, glancing at the shelves behind him only once. "Yes."

"Pick a good one."

"I will."

He returned to the papers on his desk, and I left.

The horrible two-hour ordeal over, I was shaken, but my curiosity was not destroyed. If anything, my failure stoked the coals hotter and brighter. I was determined to figure out just who this mysterious being was and what else he could do.

-

A week after the incident with the bookshelf, I was riding in Cyrus's car with him, returning from a restaurant where we had picked up food to go. A woman toddled along the side of the road near one of the little cafes. Her wild gray hair was squashed beneath a tight hat, and she swung back and forth, left and right, as she walked. She wore a thick dark jacket, a dirty brown bag in tow.

Cyrus pulled the car over, close to the woman, and stopped. He rolled down his window and called to her. "Miss! Would you like some help for the night?"

Cyrus did not sound like his normal self. His voice was pitched higher, his eyebrows raised, his face the opposite of analytical. He was completely transformed. He was charming.

She turned and looked at him, straight on. She stared at him like she knew the sort he was. Her thin lips pursed into a frown. As she was about to continue on her way, she spotted me. She looked at me for a long time.

"That's my daughter, Jack. I just bought dinner for her, her brother, and myself. There's plenty. You're welcome to share some. Spend a night inside with us, free from this cold weather."

It might have had something to do with Cyrus's inflection, or that she could probably smell the food from where she stood, or because a ten-year-old child sat beside him, but the woman tentatively approached the car.

"And why would *you* help *me*?" she asked. The words were accusatory, but her tone was inquiring. Her eyes sparkled.

"Because I know what it's like to be hungry," he said in the kindest way I have ever heard a person speak. "When I was a child, I had very little to eat. One night, I had only an onion for dinner. It was so hot when I bit into it, it made me angry, and I threw it against the wall of the kitchen. Once my tongue cooled off, I picked it up again and took another bite. It was that type of hunger. When I was older, I promised myself I wouldn't be hungry like that again, and I wouldn't see anyone hungry like that again."

"I could simply give you the food," he said, reaching to his right and lifting the bag beside me. He showed it to her, and she stared. "Or you could come with us, have a warm bed for the night and some company."

The woman nervously squeezed the front of her coat, the handles of her brown bag wrapped around one of her wrists. She looked at me again, as though a child in the ritzy vehicle was enough to validate this stranger's innocence. As her eyes swept over me a third time, she stepped to the back of the car. Cyrus unlocked the doors, and she opened the one behind his.

"What's your name?" he asked as she slid into the seat.

"Lynn," she said quietly.

"Hi, Lynn. My name is Cyrus. This is Jack."

I said hello. Her stained and raggedy clothing made me sorry for her. She appeared as old as Cyrus, but the disparity between them was startling. He looked like he was meant to survive. She did not. I was witnessing the other side of the line, the line that Cyrus could make me forget existed.

The ride was quiet. At home, he brought her to the living room and set his own food down for her. He gave me Alex's food and my own and sent me on my way to the dining room. We ate separately from him and the new, interesting woman.

As I left them, he said to her, "You don't need to worry, anymore. Not tonight. Not ever again, if you don't want to. I'll protect you from the cold, all the kinds of cold."

Lynn stayed at the house that evening and the night after. She never left. She was there all the time, wearing clothes Cyrus gave her. Though Alex and I never spoke with her, I was aware of her presence, for she had eventually asked Cyrus what she could do to repay him. He said he didn't need money, and, frankly, he knew she didn't have any. If she would help around the house here and there, that would be enough. She cleaned the dishes, washed the laundry, and swept the sidewalk.

Slowly but surely, others appeared—David, Carl, Jim, Sarah, Amy. He'd find these people, these homeless residents, easily; they seemed compelled by some sort of magical, magnetic pull. He helped them, providing the nourishment their bodies needed, the community their spirits craved. As with Lynn, he came to know them deeply and personally.

Cyrus was always an entirely different individual around each new person. He dropped *everything* he was to become like them for a little while. They inevitably became close to him. Eventually, each individual moved with him, together, synchronous, toward whatever he wanted him or her to be or do.

These people never had to pay him back for his kindness, except with yard work or cleaning, running errands, or finding others like themselves who needed help. Eventually, fifteen individuals were living in one side of the house, rooming with one another, building their strength up, relaxing a little.

After he had collected a fairly large group, he set up little parties. The first ones were small, but soon they became larger and more impressive. The individuals who attended them could not have afforded such extravagance and would usually have been out of place. When Cyrus entered the room, though, he made them feel *in* place, like they belonged. He was what made the amalgam possible, the one who gave them permission to share in the celebration. His exuberance spread among them like ink in water. They forgot that not-belonging had ever existed.

He joked with them. He made light of poverty, not in a way that made fun of them but

in a way, rather, that made the horrible powerless.

These people had been told their whole lives that life was always that which did not include them. They believed that harmony came only to those who could afford cars and clothes and expensive televisions.

Cyrus turned everything they had been told on its head.

"Celebration is important," he preached to them. "Always celebrate who you are. Always. These material items that others hold in such high esteem are a lie."

They bloomed with him. They were now where life was.

Clothes no longer mattered to them, nor did expensive toys. Everything could be celebrated. Their age, the holes in their socks, the pills on their cotton jackets, their thinning hair line—everything was beautiful and worthy. Cyrus gave them what the world should have given them. Thus, they loved him. I could see their love. They'd never understood the beauty of small things until they met Cyrus.

That's who he was for them.

I learned this synchronicity, this performance as normality—to erase oneself in the presence of another, until I am like that other, and then, slowly but surely, I create the slightest tug. The tug is oh-so-slight, so that they lean in toward me, intimately, like we're about to kiss. I make that normality. Instead of walking side by side, they begin to enter alongside my own path. It's all in the tilt.

Though he always knew himself and always returned to himself instantly when he was finshed speaking with them, looking down at me with a renewed coldness, Cyrus knew how to be human, just like them, exactly like them, so that they'd sway with him toward inhumanity. That might have been enough, on its own, to keep them there and with him, following his requests, but that wasn't all he did for them.

Several months after Lynn arrived, she was cleaning the kitchen. I walked in, sleepy, hungry for breakfast. When I saw her, I stopped and gaped. Her hand on a mop, other hand on a hip, she stood before me changed and improved, appearing so much younger and healthier that she was nearly unrecognizable. Slowly, I entered the kitchen and caught a complete view of her in front of the freshly cleaned windows that opened to the distant woods.

Her transformed figure was thinner. Her hair was thick and brown, her cheeks flush. The changes were more than food, more than exercise, more than money could accomplish. Her alteration was impossible.

"Wow," I said. I couldn't stop myself.

She jumped and twirled. "I know!" she whispered, and the largest smile spread across her face.

"What happened to you?"

Lynn pursed her lips; she winked at me, but she would not say. She resumed mopping.

Later, the others improved just as utterly as Lynn. The lines and furrows all but disappeared from their faces. Their eyes were brighter, as though they had spent the day in the sun, and they did not totter back and forth. Jim's limp disappeared.

Cyrus had given them something. That was obvious. What he'd provided, though, I had no idea. I simply knew that he could, and had, made good on his promise. He had given his fellow travelers the experience of transformation. Whatever the spell or elixir, he'd healed them and solidified the magic of his charm. He dazzled them.

My curiosity pained me. I mentally urged Cyrus each and every day to explain this mystery, and I hoped that my thinking about it might somehow make him do so. I waited and waited for any explanation, seeking any sign of enlightenment.

A few weeks later, just after dinner on a Tuesday evening, Cyrus brought me and Alex into the foyer, something he rarely did, and regarded us seriously. My heart sped.

"It's time the two of you see what else I do. What *we* do," Cyrus corrected himself, "for the others."

Cyrus pulled on his jacket, and he handed us ours. He told us we were going to the Havingers'—the house where a family of his followers lived. It was a relatively short drive away.

"Why?" Alex asked.

"Evelyn's mother is dying of cancer. We are going to cure her because that's what we do for people that support us. We heal them."

My mouth dropped, and Lynn's image immediately flashed in my mind, how healthy she had become overnight, how refreshed and glowing. Was it possible Cyrus was about to make another metamorphosis take place?

I stepped closer to him. "How do we heal them?"

He winked. "Magic."

"The same kind of magic," I asked, "that brings Roland back to life?"

Alex also searched for a response from his father. Cyrus placed one finger to his lips as he stared at me and said, "Yes, but that's our little secret."

I nodded. Inside, something flared. I burst alive at the revelation. One more piece of the puzzle had fallen into my hands, one more gap closed, and the picture was on the verge of becoming intelligible, if not nearly complete, of both the man downstairs and Cyrus's operations.

"We will go there now," he said.

We exited the house and went to the car idling in the circle. I was not about to ask unnecessary questions and delay the revelation I had long been waiting for, but it was difficult because the mystery gripped me tight and would not let loose.

I slipped my hands into my pockets, shivering briefly in the sudden cold, and touched the cool metal of my .38. The gun was always in that jacket, but for the first time I was glad it was there; the idea of going to someone else's home was uncomfortable. It was not how we usually did things, and I did not like to break from our normal rhythm. Doing so made me feel lost.

The car ride was silent, and the dark night on the empty roads leading out to land, pebbles, horses, and forests pervaded everything. The scenery slipped by, reminding me of a silent movie.

Driving with Cyrus was always pleasant. The experiences and smells of wealth were calming. Its sounds—clinks and V12 engines and squeaky materials and deep bass—were cathartic. It was like everything could be washed away and everything could be material, even us.

When we got to the Havingers' house, Cyrus parked in front of the long blue wrap-around porch with four small posts and a tiny gate. Two lamps flickered on either side of the door, casting a dim orange light upon two figures standing beside an unpainted swing that rocked back and forth in the wind. We left the vehicle and walked toward them, slipping in the gravel beneath our feet. Mr. Havinger and his wife, Evelyn, took the few steps down the front walkway to greet us.

"Thank you, Mr. Harper, for coming out to help us tonight," Havinger said in a deep voice.

"It's my pleasure," Cyrus said.

Havinger was taller than Cyrus, which meant that he was taller than six foot two, but he was not as thin, and his stomach protruded over his silver belt buckle, shining in the dim light like a star. He wore a long-sleeved plaid shirt and a baseball cap, but it was so dark that, apart from a few reds and yellows, I could not read the colors. The lines on his face were invisible in the dark.

Evelyn stood beside him, the bun on top of her head barely distinguishable from the rest of the night. She wore what appeared to be a cream or white dress. The moonlight resonated with it, and she glowed.

"What can we do to help?" asked Havinger.

"Nothing," said Cyrus. "I will take care of all of it."

Havinger looked to his wife. "All right," he said. "Come on inside. I'll bring you to her."

We entered the house, Cyrus and Havinger leading the way, Alex behind them, and then me and Evelyn.

The interior of the house was bright, almost blinding compared to the dark night. The way the ceiling's track lighting shone upon the golden wood made the home seem on display, like we were about to have our photo taken. We stepped onto a wood floor that creaked with each step.

To my right was a sparse-looking living room with a simple denim couch and two rocking chairs facing one another. There was no television.

A scratched and worn coffee table sat in the middle of the three pieces of furniture, and two cups of coffee, still steaming, deploying a dark bean scent, almost tobacco, waited on the coffee table, without coasters. I imagined the wood bubbling beneath the heat.

To the left was a small and cozy kitchen, clean and filled with many things that Cyrus usually loathed: magnets on the fridge, including a three-dimensional lobster with claws attached via springs; a tiny porcelain mask with purple and green feathers; an alligator with a jester's hat that protruded in three directions, each ending in a tiny golden bell. Hand towels featuring kittens playing with balls of string were folded over the stove handle. What caught my attention the most, though, was a cookie jar at the outer edge of the counter in the shape of a rocket ship. The front of it read Cookies That Are Out of This World. My mouth watered.

Havinger and Cyrus walked between the living room and kitchen and veered left as soon as the kitchen's countertop ended. Alex, Evelyn, and I followed. As we turned past the kitchen, we entered a large hallway that led to several doors and, on our right, a set of stairs to the second floor. We passed the staircase, and I looked up into the dark second floor for a split second. We moved beyond it and immediately arrived at our destination.

On the other side of the stairs was one of several hallway doors. Havinger opened it. He and Cyrus stepped inside, and the rest of us followed. The room was quaintly decorated with a bed, two nightstands, and two dressers in different shades of weathered and worn wood. Near the bed was a set of hospital equipment. An IV stand beside the bed was hooked to the veiny arm of a woman asleep beneath a cream quilt.

Cyrus was already removing his black leather gloves when we took our places in the room, and he laid them gently on the quilt. The bedding stretched into the armpits of the sleeping woman with cotton-white hair that twirled up onto her pillow to a point. Her cheeks were thin, her cheekbones high and slender. Her pained grimace made her appear malevolent.

The smell of the room got to me, a nutty smell, something like peanuts or food gone bad.

I tried to swallow the odor away, observing the shelves and dressers. Blue Willow plates rested on two dressers, the shelves, and the television stand. Those on a shelf behind me depicted Chinese houses, birds, vessels, and crooked fences in brilliant cobalt. The plates reminded me of the magnets on the fridge and the kitten hand towels—they were gaudy but pretty.

The only light in the room came from a lamp on a wooden nightstand, and Cyrus partially blocked it as he removed his jacket. His shadow moved across me. I abandoned the Blue Willow plates and watched him as he worked. We all did.

From an inside pocket, he retrieved a small black glass vial with a corked top. He withdrew the cork with a pop.

"Do you have a syringe?" he asked.

Evelyn procured one from a nearby nightstand drawer and placed it in his hand.

He dipped the tip of the needle into the vial. As the black rubber plunger slowly edged through the barrel, a thick, rusty liquid entered the cavity. When the syringe was full, he re-corked the vial and placed it back inside his jacket. Cyrus held the IV near the woman's bed and injected the liquid into the drip chamber. The plastic hose line shifted crimson.

"Is that blood?" Evelyn asked.

I stared at Cyrus's face, eager, waiting for an answer. Was it blood? Was it, perhaps, blood from the man downstairs? My mentor looked up at her and said yes in such a way that neither Evelyn nor Havinger questioned why he might have a vial of blood on him.

"Agatha," Evelyn said as she approached the elderly woman until their faces were only inches apart. There was no mistaking it; they were mother and daughter, each with large round eyes and pointed chins with a little dimple in the center. Agatha had more lines on her face, and the color had retreated from her hair, but if they had been the same age, they could have been mistaken for twins. Evelyn placed her hand on her mother's arm and whispered her name again.

The blood trailed down the IV, slowly flowing into Agatha's arm. I refused to blink. I was finally allowed to witness the incredible process, and I planned to record the moment. When the red fluid reached her vein, the effect was instantaneous.

The old woman blinked a few times and muttered in a harsh and deep voice, "What is *that*?" She sounded fascinated.

Her lips reddened and her cheeks flushed. Her calm eyes deepened into royal blue. Her breathing softened, and anything resembling a scowl disappeared from her face. The malevolence in her expression vanished.

"Whoa!" she said, and she smiled. "I need some more of that!" She grinned with an impossible vigor. Her voice no longer sounded gravelly but smooth and refined.

She stretched out a hand. The skin of her palm shifted from yellow to pink. Her body filled out, freshened, rejuvenated, and the unpleasant smell diminished. At the sight of her renewal, something deep within me that had been wound up released.

I was reminded of Lynn and Jim and all the others in Cyrus's home he had picked up from the streets, invited in, and transformed. What Cyrus gave Agatha was the same as what he had given them. Blood.

Evelyn bent over the no-longer-sickly woman. Her eyes misted. "Mom," she said. "You look so beautiful."

We were all in a reverie. I was deeply entrenched in it, in awe of the power of the blood.

A noise behind me, a strange one, sounded. I turned.

Havinger stood with his hands in fists at his side. His chest heaved slowly with each breath. Unlike the rest of us, he was not entranced by what had just happened. His large eyes were wide, and his blocky, stubbly face appeared strained.

Cyrus cocked his head, and Evelyn turned slightly away from Agatha. Whatever the sound was, they had heard it, too.

"What is it?" Cyrus asked, his face as still as stone.

"Nothing," Havinger said. "I'm just so happy to have her healthy again. Thank you."

They were the right words, but something was still wrong. My mentor's face lacked any sign of resolution. He did, however, slowly turn back to the two women. Whatever had happened, he ignored it. After observing Evelyn and Agatha for a few moments, he donned his coat.

"I am hungry!" Agatha announced, and she laughed. She placed her hands on her daughter's cheeks. "I can't believe it! I am so hungry!"

Evelyn swore she would cook anything her mother wanted. She thanked Cyrus repeatedly. He, like many times before, transformed himself, playing the part of the kindly stranger who needed nothing in return for a good deed. He said very softly, in an almost cooing tone, "It's all right. Nothing to worry about. I'm glad you are healthy again."

When Cyrus put on the first glove, though, another odd sound erupted behind me. I turned back to Havinger, whose fists were turning white.

"Michael?" Cyrus asked.

Havinger's whole body relaxed, and he lifted his square chin. "Nothing," he said, and he smiled, though a drop of sweat broke out at his temple.

Evelyn and her mother were speaking, but my mind was on Havinger. I was trying to figure out the sound, the one I had heard *twice* behind me. Had he spoken? Had he said something, or had he moved something?

Havinger looked straight through me. The drop of sweat slid from his temple to his jaw, and I waited, watching, until it dripped on his plaid shirt, darkening a red square of fabric. Neither of us moved, nothing happened, and I looked away, against my instincts.

Cyrus pulled his second glove on, and he kissed Agatha's forehead. She swept her palm across his left cheek like a mother to her son. He soaked in this adoration, and he told her to take it easy for several days. He assured her the cancer was gone and would be gone for a good while. He could not promise, however, it would not return. Agatha said that she understood.

The sound repeated itself. It was strange, still unintelligible, though it reminded me of wood dragging across wood or a boot scraping wood.

Something hit me.

I landed hard on my chest. Pain exploded through my core. There was a high-pitched yell—Alex. I couldn't move. My lungs had collapsed. When I tried to breathe, nothing came. After several moments of trying to force air in, I succeeded, and when my lungs finally expanded, a windy moan escaped. I took several big gulps and placed my palms on the floor. When I managed to push myself up, the scene had drastically changed.

Havinger was showering Cyrus, prostrate on the floor, with blow after blow—so many, so quickly, and so hard that I didn't know how Cyrus wasn't dead. Blood pooled on the floorboards, and Cyrus's shiny silver hair was streaked with crimson. Evelyn shrieked.

Havinger punched Cyrus in the mouth, and blood exploded from Cyrus's lips, dripping down his chin and neck into his shirt. It mixed with the blood from his head. Havinger pinned his giant knee against Cyrus's chest to keep him still, and an animal-like wail poured from Cyrus's throat. It seemed to coil in my own.

Evelyn's gaze fastened onto Havinger and Cyrus, and she waved her arms at them. She was in shock. Alex backed toward the door, eyes wide, his face contorted.

I searched my jacket pocket for the .38, the one Roland gave me. I brought it out calmly and quickly and I stood, just as we had practiced.

The next few seconds were the easiest in the world. It was like riding a bike downhill. Havinger was pinning Cyrus with his knee, his back to me, slamming Cyrus with alternating punches.

His fists flew as if in slow motion, and I took one step forward with each punch. In no time, I held the gun to Havinger's head, almost touching the base, where the skull protrudes. I squatted and aimed to the right, so the bullet would not pass through Havinger and into Cyrus, and I pulled the trigger.

Boom! It was like there was a cannon in my hand, not a gun. My ears whined. Havinger's body fell over Cyrus like a door unhinged. I never touched the man.

All was quiet. Cyrus's dazed gray eyes wandered, half-conscious, over the ceiling. He struggled to breathe under the weight of Havinger's body.

"No!" Evelyn's scream stabbed its way through the high-pitched noise in my ears. She lunged at me.

I shifted to the left. On my knees and one hand, I raised the gun, and I shot her twice in the stomach and chest. She fell forward, face down, onto the floor right in front of me and didn't move.

I breathed in, tasted the sweet burn on the back of my throat from the gunpowder, and for the first time noticed Agatha's quiet horror. She sat up in the bed, her blue eyes as wide as the Blue Willow plates, her claw-like hands drawn toward her robust pink cheeks. She did not move.

I said to Alex, "Help me." I gestured to Havinger's body atop Cyrus, who was slowly regaining consciousness.

We both pushed hard, aided by Cyrus's own squirming, to roll Havinger's large form of him. Cyrus huffed ragged breaths and rose from the floor slowly. He stumbled into the center of the room, clutching his chest. He put a hand smack dab on the side of his face that was painted with blood and pushed back, trying to wipe it away. All his attempt did was smear the red, and a fresh coat of blood flowed, trickling from his head wounds.

For a long while, he was silent. Cyrus gazed upon Mike and Evelyn. His breathing became less ragged, but he was nevertheless panting, and in profile his eye looked both furious and blank.

"Why did he do that?" I asked Cyrus, breaking the silence. "Why did he attack you?"

He did not answer. He held his palm out toward me and bobbed his head at the revolver. I lifted it slowly, grabbing the barrel with my left hand and placing the handle in Cyrus's palm. He gazed at the .38 carefully, checked its weight, and said, "Jack, thank you. I owe you."

He turned to Agatha and shot her through the head.

My jaw dropped. It was the last thing I expected him to do. Too much had happened for me to understand any of it. I looked at the bodies. Just seconds before, they had all been alive and healthy. Agatha and Evelyn had been happy, celebrating. Out of nowhere, Havinger had attacked and destroyed it all.

Cyrus, eerily quiet, looked at my gun and slipped it into his pocket. "Get in the car," he said.

I did. Alex followed. In seconds, he was taking us home.

Cyrus hit fifty miles an hour on the dirt road, and Alex and I were rocked in our seats so hard that it forced me to fasten my seatbelt. I peeked at Cyrus's bloody face; his brows were furrowed, his lips pulled back in what could have been a snarl. He bore down on the car like it was an animal he was riding, gripping the steering wheel with rage—a man with reins and a mission.

We returned to the house without sharing any words. As we entered the blue velveteen room, Roland asked from the soft silver divan, "What the hell happened to you?"

Cyrus did not respond. He retrieved his cell phone. For the next thirty minutes, Cyrus called people. Men trickled into the house, entering the large blue room.

By eleven o'clock, I counted twenty of them. I had seen some of them only once or twice before; others I didn't know existed. Their speedy arrival amazed me.

While Cyrus was calling the men, Roland asked me, "What happened?" I gave him just enough details to fill him in. We had arrived to help the Havingers, I explained, and then Mike had turned on Cyrus and tried to kill him. Now all three of the family were dead. Roland didn't respond except to grab a fleece blanket and wrap it around me. Then he found one for Alex and left for the kitchen. When he returned, he brought food for us. I sat and stared and ate a sandwich while the strangers arrived.

Cyrus had yet to clean his face. He looked like a demon that had crept from the shadows into the light. By the time all the men had arrived, he had had a few drinks, and the blood on his face had dried. Cyrus spoke with a cool and crisp anger.

"Things are going to change around here." He held a glass of liquor and sat on the solid oak table. He clasped the drink carefully between his hands, as if in prayer.

"From now on, the twenty of you live in this house, and, except for certain occasions, wherever I go, three of you will come.

"Tonight, as you now know, Mike tried to kill me. After I saved Agatha from her cancer, he tried to beat me to death. Why? I'm asking myself the same question." He took a drink. "I suspect that he did not believe I should be capable of what I am capable of.

"But I am. I am. And you all must accept it. Very soon, I will be able to achieve even more. When I *transcend*." He paused.

"Could Havinger actually have killed me?" he asked. "No. Of course not. Because I am much stronger than any enemy. And there is something in this house that will always save me." He pointed to his face. "I allowed him a few punches, and then I gave him a few of my own, and I killed him.

Let that be a lesson in terms of my...invincibility. Of my ever-approaching evolution."

As he asserted that he was the one who'd killed Havinger, a twist of childish jealousy rose in me, but I said nothing. I sat, confused as to why he would lie about what had happened.

"In case any of you doubt me, or perhaps were in on what happened tonight, there you have it. It doesn't matter who, what, where, when, or how you try to kill me. You will lose. Always."

He emptied his glass, slammed it down, and said, "No more saving you from your cancers, your cuts and scrapes, your sprains. I am not here to heal you anymore. I am only here to help you find more like yourselves and find more to kill. Tonight was the end of it.

"I will *never* heal anyone again. So...take care of yourselves."

He hopped off the table. "All right, you know what to do. Find the quick lime, and collect the bodies. You ten...you clean up. And don't worry. Whatever is on my side is on yours, as long as you're on mine."

"Yes, sir," said one man, and the others gave their vocal assent.

The men quickly filed out of the room. Finally, just Cyrus, Alex, Roland, and I remained.

Roland refilled Cyrus's glass, and he drank it down.

"How are you doing, Jack?" Cyrus asked, his good eye on me; the other was swollen completely shut.

"I'm fine," I said.

He sat beside me, and, to my surprise, he held me close. He pulled Alex to his other side.

Cyrus rested his head against the back of the divan. "Roland, can you dim the lights, and make it so it's not so damn quiet?"

"Sure." Roland spoke softly. A small dark dot marked him on the inside of his forearm where one of my bullets had pierced just a few days before.

Soon just the firelight glowed on the walls, and classical music played from the stereo on a wooden stand in the back of the room. A strange numbness suffused me as I replayed the events in my mind, turning them over like a Rubik's cube, not understanding how to twist and turn them until everything made the sense that it was supposed to. I had just killed two people that Cyrus would not bring back, not ever.

Cyrus shifted beside me and retrieved something from his coat pocket: the glass vial full of blood he had used at the Havingers' home. I was surprised it had not been crushed when Havinger beat him, but the glass was thick and not likely easy to break.

Cyrus uncorked the vial, and he held it to his lips. He tilted his head back, and his bloodied throat bobbed up and down as he swallowed the fluid inside. He set the bottle down on the coffee table in front of us and licked his lips. Cyrus's swollen eye deflated. He blinked, and the upper and lower eyelids no longer obscured his eyeball. They shrank back to normal. The cuts on the sides of his face disappeared. The puffiness in his cheeks vanished. Cyrus's breathing became soft and silent again, and he sat straighter against the couch and held me tighter to him.

"Whose blood was that?" I whispered.

He smiled a tired smile, not a smile full of cunning, though his slyness was slowly returning. The blood had renewed him.

"You know," he said, "whose blood that is. It belongs to the man in the basement."

Of course I knew, but I needed to hear it from him. I desperately wanted to speak of this creature, and I was almost certain, because of the night's events, that Cyrus might be more willing to do so.

"It heals people," I said softly.

Cyrus frowned and looked straight ahead. "It does."

Roland made a drink for himself and took a chair across from us. Cyrus said to him as he sat down, "The box didn't warn me about him. Why didn't it warn me?"

Roland's eyebrows formed a deep V. "Perhaps it did not know."

"It always knows." Cyrus bit the inside of his lip. After a time, he looked back at me and raised his eyebrows. "I think Jack has become one of my most trusted advisors, Roland."

Surprised at the compliment, I studied his face for any hint of sarcasm and found none. I smelled the sharp alcohol and blood on his breath. Everything about him was serious. He was not joking in the least. I smiled.

"What do you mean?" Roland asked.

Cyrus pulled my .38 from his pocket handed it to Roland. Roland twisted it in his hand and smirked thoughtfully, recognizing the gun he had given me the year before. "Jack killed Havinger and Evelyn," Cyrus said.

They exchanged knowing looks. Roland's eyes flicked to me. "You all right, Jack?" he asked.

I nodded. The truth, though, was that I wasn't quite sure *what* I was feeling. It was something new, different, and I could not yet tell whether it was good or bad.

Roland pursed his lips and glanced down at the gun. "God made all men, but Smith and Wesson made them equal," Roland whispered. "Just a child… Just ten years old."

I was suddenly tired. My eyelids were too heavy to stay open, and I let them close and nestled closer to Cyrus's side. As I began to drift, Cyrus hummed in time with the music—a soft piano piece.

I nestled deeper beneath his wing. Before I fell asleep, Cyrus whispered, "Swear to me, Jack, that you won't tell anyone you are the one who killed Michael and Evelyn."

Surprised he knew I was still awake—I was not even sure of that myself—I looked up at him sleepily with the smallest thread of surprise. His eyes glowed, reflecting the fire.

"I swear," I told him.

He smiled.

I relaxed against him again and very quickly fell asleep.

-

I woke with a start.

A sound—a bit like a gun—had roused me. The clock on the mantle said it was a little after two in the morning.

Beside me, Cyrus shifted. "What was that?" he asked.

"I don't know."

He scanned the room. Alex was no longer beside him. Roland's motionless form was prone on the sofa across from us. He was awake, though, and rose, thrusting off the blanket.

"Sounded like a gun," Cyrus said to Roland. He walked to the end of the living room and crossed the threshold. Roland followed Cyrus, and I trailed behind.

In the kitchen, on the other side of the safety gate, we found a mess of blood and fur; a little body was splattered across the tile.

My eyes widened as I stared at the limp form with a smashed face. My rage woke me fully. *My Rose.*

"Dammit," Cyrus said. He pressed his hands to his face, ran his fingers through his hair. When he spoke, he did not sound like his usual self. He sounded tired. "He has no self-control."

There was no question who had killed Rose. All three of us knew.

Roland spoke carefully, his voice moderated, without judgment. "He is envious."

I walked to the tiny furry body on the floor and stared at the blood. I'd only had the puppy a week, and there she was, dead. I mashed a hand to my face, squashing a tear.

Cyrus groaned in anger and rushed from the room.

Roland turned me to him and placed his hands on either side of my shoulders. He whispered, "I know it hurts, Jack. Let it hurt. You... You must be careful, hm?"

Tears dripped from my chin. The tangle of things that held everything back was coming loose. Something was breaking free—determined to, no matter what Roland said.

"I will," I assured him.

-

Two days passed before I saw Alex again. He had all but disappeared somewhere in the house. When he resurfaced, he was paler than usual and hungry. As he devoured a sandwich at the dining room table, I realized that he had been punished, like I had been when caught beside the mysterious being's door in the basement—that is, starved in his room for two days. The punishments were not equal. He had received the same for killing a dog as I had received for stealing a card from Cyrus's desk. No, things were not at all equal. And I had saved Cyrus.

I observed Alex, taking in his blond hair and blue eyes. His teeth broke down the food with animal ferocity.

This is the boy who tortures dogs, I told myself. *This is the boy who blew the head off a puppy.* My brother. He sat at the dining room table, relishing his food. It sickened me. I excused myself.

I went upstairs. Rather than go to my own room, I entered Alex's. I sat in the chair next to the bed and waited.

Perhaps twenty minutes later the door opened. Alex flipped on the light and shut the door behind him. After a deep breath, he turned. He jumped when he noticed me.

"What are you doing here?" he asked, wide-eyed. I was not moved.

I rose quickly from the chair. I raised my right hand toward him, palm side up. Slowly, he lifted his own hand. Right before he touched mine, I pulled back, squeezed my hand into a fist, and punched him in the face as hard as I could. The weight of my shoulder and body were behind the blow, sending him sprawling to the floor.

Both his hands rose to his face. Blood oozed from between his fingers and dropped, staining the carpet.

He lunged, pushing me to the floor. He tried to pin me, but he was younger, weak from hunger, and I easily shoved him off. I crawled on top of him, pinning his arms to the floor with my knees, and sat on his chest.

I reached into my back pocket and pulled out a firecracker and a lighter. I had retrieved these from Alex's top right bureau drawer.

"You enjoy hurting dogs?" I asked as he struggled to knock me off. "I enjoy hurting you." I leaned close. "And if you get to hurt dogs, I get to hurt you."

He yelled a series of useless and strange profanities that made no earthly sense.

I smiled. Alex was about the dramatic, whereas I was about the efficient. I unwound the large firecracker wick and dropped the cardboard tube into his mouth. I held my hand over his lips to seal it there. As I stared into his frightened face, the tangle of things inside me that held everything in place loosened another notch, becoming something hard and unrelenting—wild, raw, blinding rage had slipped out, and I quickly decided that I was not about to stuff it back in. I'd had enough of that, enough of a lot of things. I picked up the green lighter from the floor and lit the end of the wick.

Alex screamed against my hand as the brilliant light traveled up and down and around the fuse, lightning quick. It hissed like a cat.

I pressed Alex to the floor, my knees on his forearms. He kicked and pushed as hard as he could, but I was too heavy for him. Half the fuse was gone in a flash. The sparks bit my hand.

"The fuse wasn't nearly this long for Rose, was it?" I asked, bending close. The sparks bit my cheek. Their light illumined our faces in a fierce, hellish fire.

When there were only a few inches left of the fuse, I stood. I took a few steps back, and Alex spit out the firecracker. It sailed across the room and landed on the floor by the closet. He scurried backward until he thumped into his bed.

The explosion in the corner was loud, bright. Alex sat stunned, his breath rapid, terror in his face.

I walked to him and kicked his foot. He jerked back.

I held up my forefinger. "That's one. And I still owe you for Shakespeare."

He inhaled, fear in his eyes, and shrieked loudly for Cyrus.

-

Four days without food was my punishment.

When the four days were over, I was delirious, and Cyrus brought me a sandwich and water. He set them on the nightstand beside the bed. He told me as I devoured the food that the fights between me and Alex must end, that we were not to contact each other until he said we could.

That was fine. I had no intention of ever speaking to Alex again.

It was a day or two before the brain fog lifted and I could think clearly again.

I realized Cyrus had never once threatened to send me away. Though I had been punished for attacking Alex, he had not threatened me with exile, with being cast into the abyss with the other children. There was no mystery as to why—I had saved his life.

Most likely, that meant if Cyrus caught me down in the basement again, he would be more forgiving the second time, considering that I had helped him.

All I wanted in that moment was to be as close to the unknown being as I could. Even though we had never spoken, the idea of simply standing outside the old wooden door with the giant gem-like door handle, near him, made me brighten. I thought again of the dead rose hidden in a shoebox under the bedframe. Though the idea of resurrecting it rather than my puppy did not have the same value, I yearned for it. It meant much more than it had before. I was not about to deny what I wanted. I was done with denying.

The man I had never met was the only thing that could still lift my spirits after Alex and starvation and Cyrus's threats. He'd healed the rose, the blanched fabric. Perhaps, I thought, he can heal me so I do not feel this way anymore.

When the night was quiet, only the wind and the tree shadows remaining, even though I was more exhausted than I could ever remember being, I slipped out of bed and dropped to the floor.

I retrieved the rose and held it up in the moonlight streaming through the window. I pressed several of the petals between my fingers; they crunched like a bite of cereal.

Dead.

I carried the rose down to the basement again, and I carefully approached the familiar metal door. I stood, staring at it, and completely forgot about the key card needed to gain entry. I tried the door handle—it would not budge. I sighed and sat, too weary to stand. The key card lay miles away, at the top of a fake bookshelf that terrified me, and I could not walk miles. All I could do was sit.

As I slumped against the concrete wall, the sound of a click within the metal door beside me was unmistakable. Confused, I glanced up and reached high, touching the handle. I lifted myself until I could grip it firmly, and I tested it.

To my utter surprise, the handle dropped freely. My mouth opened in shock. I pulled, and the door opened.

Something was allowing me inside—or, rather, *someone.*

I set a bottle of wine at the threshold to prop it open, as I had done many times before. I walked to the first of two wooden doors in the hallway and knocked.

Though I didn't know why, I whispered to him, to whatever was inside. "I killed two people a week ago, Michael Havinger and Evelyn Havinger, in order to save Cyrus. Michael attacked Cyrus, and he would've killed him, so I had to shoot him. Evelyn was about to attack me, and I shot her, too. Cyrus is keeping it a secret, but he didn't save himself, like he told everyone he did. I saved him. I saved Cyrus." As I spoke, the weight in my chest blossomed and then relented.

Whatever it was did not respond.

"And Alex is angry. He killed Rose—my puppy. I want to bring her to you, but Cyrus would know if I did, so I can't."

The silence was thick.

Realizing I had not expected whatever was inside to speak, I dropped to my knees and slid the crumbling rose beneath the door. Within a few seconds, the stem disappeared inside, and I heaved a weary breath. "Thank you," I said. "I feel so confused and terrible. Something weird is happening in me." I pressed against my stomach, trying to staunch the pain.

When the stem reappeared, I—happy to witness yet another life renewed—pulled it gently from beneath the door.

There was, however, no bloom. In fact, there was nothing there at all. The tip was smoking hot and black. The petals were gone. The tip of the rose had been burned.

Tears welled in my eyes as a single tendril of smoke twisted under the clear, bright light from the bulb overhead. I slipped to the floor and pressed my hands to my face, smearing the salty tears across my cheeks into my hair.

"That's not fair!"

On the other side, the monstrous stranger began weeping along with me. He released a great moan that filled the entire basement. My heart quickened, and a burst of anger exploded in my chest. I thought, Good.

I rose to my feet as a shiver rolled down my spine. I clasped the black, smoking stalk as though it were an evil magic wand, turned from the door, and stumbled away, refusing him any other acknowledgment.

When the basement door shut, he cried loud. I cried too.

I did not return to that alcove for many days.

And then weeks.

And then years.

When Cyrus finished with healing and resurrection, so was I. The mysterious stranger had shown to me the worthlessness of taking pleasure in small things when all the world was dark and horrid and all the good in me was gone.

So, at ten years old, I cast the rose away.

And I learned to stop taking pleasure in small things.

And then larger things.

And then anything but death.

CHAPTER 8—LAWDENIM
AGE: 10 YEARS OLD

SEVERAL MONTHS AFTER I KILLED Havinger, I lay in my bed, unable to sleep. I stared at the tree shadows that crawled across the ceiling, my heart thumping as hard and steadily as if I were running. I was confused about what was happening to me. Something inside me urged me to scream as loudly as I could. It was becoming harder to squash that desire, especially at night.

There was a teddy bear on the floor of my closet, plush and brown, with big black eyes and a foot that had unraveled at the seam, a bit of shiny white stuffing protruding like white blood. It was propped up on a pile of my clothes.

I bit my bottom lip so hard that I drew blood and wiped it away. At last, I got out of bed and walked over to the toy. I snatched the teddy bear, held it to me, and returned to bed.

Beneath the covers, I clutched the bear to my chest, waiting for it to comfort me. As the seconds continued, though, my heart thrummed harder, and I began to sweat.

I sat up fast. My shoulders shook. I looked into the bear's beady black eyes, confused. The pounding in my head continued, unrelenting. Why wasn't this working? I gritted my teeth and threw the bear across the room as hard as I could. It landed with a soft thump against the wall and fell to the floor.

My heart quickened.

Boom! The sound of a gunshot reverberated.

I clapped my hands to my ears and looked around the room. I struggled to inhale, and hot tears tumbled down my cheeks.

The ghost of Evelyn was shrieking. It continued on and on and on, as did the image of her falling, landing at my feet.

I tried to scream but couldn't. My throat was too tight. When a breath came at last, a long, low moan arrived with it, as if from something foreign within me.

The door to my room cracked open. Light from the hallway spilled over me. The sound of the gunshots and screaming faded.

Cyrus stood in the middle of the light.

Our eyes locked. His expression softened.

"Are you all right?"

I shook my head.

His lips pursed. He opened the door wide and entered. He came to me and lifted me off the floor, held me and walked over to my bed. He settled me down and went to the wall to flip the light switch.

When light filled the room, my breath came easier.

Cyrus sat beside me. In his hands was a white plastic case, which he set opposite me on the bed.

"It's okay. These things happen, especially the first time. The only way to get over it later on is to get over it now." He smiled, as though what he was saying was obvious, but it wasn't.

"I can't stop crying," I told him, wiping a fresh flow of tears from my cheeks. "I don't know why."

"Guilt," he said. "It will eat you alive if you don't get rid of it. That's true for all of us."

He picked up the white container and set it on his lap. A large red plus sign marked the top. The words First Aid were also in red.

There were a variety of items inside: syringes, pills, gem-like things, various brown and clear bottles filled with liquids that shimmered like a lake on a dark night.

Cyrus withdrew one of the glass bottles and slid the open white case from his lap onto the bed. He unscrewed the top and then squeezed a black, rubber thing that protruded from the lid. When he finally separated the lid from the bottle, a long glass syringe-looking thing was filled with liquid. He held it up and brought it to my mouth.

"Drink this," Cyrus said. "You will feel better."

I opened my mouth. He doused my tongue in something that was simultaneously sweet and bitter. It sent shivers down my spine.

I clapped my hand against my lips and forced myself to swallow it. The liquid burned, glittering in my belly, the embers traveling deeper. Cyrus tucked the bottle back into the first-aid box. He turned to me, and the cool, sweet fragrance of his breath enfolded me. Had he, too, taken a dose?

"You'll feel better very soon. Any time you begin to panic, tell me. I will give you some medicine to make it go away."

I relaxed fully, trusting him.

"Now lay down."

I did. Once my head rested on the pillow, he picked up the teddy bear and placed it beside me.

"You did a good thing, Jack. Havinger would have killed me otherwise, and then he would've hurt you." I looked at him, completely surprised that he knew what I was thinking.

As I lay there, my speeding heart slowed. All the muscles in my arms, legs, jaw, neck, and chest relaxed. Something inside me turned liquid.

Cyrus gently kissed my forehead. "The power of laudanum," he said.

"Law...denim," I repeated. I liked the way the word rolled around in my mouth.

Cyrus smirked. "Yes," he said. "Law-denim." He stayed with me until I fell asleep.

When I woke in the morning, the night before was a distant dream; I could trust my senses again. I was in control of my own body in a way I had not been for months, and I was relieved, knowing that reality would not turn on me—not as long as I had Cyrus.

And lawdenim.

I ran my tongue around my lips, seeking just a bit more of the bittersweet. I discovered some in the right corner, where my top and bottom lip met, and licked it away. A sweet shiver came over me.

I had saved Cyrus.

He had saved me.

I was determined to ask for more lawdenim and use it to save myself, more determined than I had been about anything in a long, long time. I was in no place to deny my desire. I had needed a teddy bear, and I had found a version—liquid in a black glass bottle—and that was all right with me.

CHAPTER 9—DESIRE
AGE: 17 YEARS OLD

THE PROBLEM WITH CYRUS WAS that he seemed much more real than any other person I had ever met, more so than even he could probably conceive sometimes, and the problem with "real things" is that they can't be captured well with words. Cyrus was effective, of course. He was conniving. He was believable. He was a murderer. He was wealthy—he was *extraordinarily* wealthy. He was powerful. He was evil. Yet that wasn't all that comprised him. There was something about his personality— when he walked into a room, he was the room, he was the air, he was you.

Because of this, his followers loved him and praised him and worshipped him. They needed him to replace their rooms, their air, themselves. Reality was a bit like a funnel, and all of it led to Cyrus. While others revered him, I killed for him. Cyrus held a mental grip on me, just as he did on everyone, but I was one of the few who was not required to praise and worship him. That was not what our relationship was.

Watching others adore Cyrus did not look odd to me, and I never blamed followers for desiring him. After all, he had transformed them. He was charismatic, and he shared much of his wealth.

I had seen things I simply could not believe.

What became remarkable to me was that Cyrus had found his followers so easily, as if by fate. The universe was not at all random; rather, its darker aspects converged and met in places they were most welcome, places where they discovered a brother. Psychopaths recognized one another, murderers found murderers. At least in the Cyrus part of the world, some magnet attracted like to like. It all seemed impossible, dreamlike. Nothing about my world made logical sense; nothing was clear, no matter that Cyrus claimed otherwise.

Twenty or thirty times before I was seventeen, Cyrus would simply stop me, whatever I was doing, sometimes waking me up at night, sometimes planting a firm hand on mine in a hallway, and say to me with the weight of an anchor, "You know what's going on here. You know everything." Every time, I acknowledged that I understood, but comprehension slipped from my grasp like water.

"You know what's going on here, Jack.

"You know what *this* is.

"You know everything."

It stopped my breath every time.

If not for the fact I had been rewarded with Cyrus's deep trust for killing Havinger and Evelyn, that I was saved by my actions as a child, I might have ended up like a fading note on the old piano, lost with the other children in the great abyss, wherever that was. I did not ask about them. I did not want to know where I might have ended up. Even with his confidence, I was still anxious about Cyrus and other things in the house.

A man had visited one night, and in the dark areas of the mansion his eyes glowed. They did not shine brilliantly and were not red, but like a camera prepping itself to flash. He told me, "I've heard a lot about you." I was too embarrassed by this compliment and frightened of the man to talk to him, but he nodded as if he knew I appreciated the praise.

Almost every week, the floorboards would resonate, vibrating with the man's screams from the basement. I stopped listening after he burned the rose, but all the same I knew what I wasn't hearing. There was always something restless and tortured beneath our feet.

Sometimes a room would lose all its color. One day the velvet curtains would be ruby, the floor sapphire, the walls a dark green with gorgeous yellow flowers carved into the surface. The next day, the room looked filtered, boiled to white—much like the White Room, where I had met Roland. Soon there were too many white rooms for me to specifically identify the White Room. So, I renamed it the White Womb.

Moving through the house was like walking through a dream that had forgotten pieces of the normal world. Here was a room full of color, there was a room coated in white, the very air bleached. I began to wonder if Cyrus's hair was an unnatural silver for the same reason that many of the rooms were blanched.

I was not the only one who quaked before the red box. Everyone feared it. Cyrus locked people in with it many times, and they died within a few minutes.

Cyrus's abuse amid his generosity made everything precarious. Even my solid foundation as his savior wouldn't necessarily save me. The problem with being a "savior," or, rather, a killer, in Cyrus's mind was that its power didn't exist unless it was exercised. If I ever stopped killing—not that I wanted to, not that it ever entered my mind, but if I did—I would no longer be salvageable. Cyrus's "unconditional" protection was quite conditional.

Of course, this reality did not concern me in my childhood or early teens—certainly not at the age of eight, or ten, or twelve, or when I learned how to want it, wait for it, and then drink it. As horrible as living under Cyrus's rule was, it quickly became beautiful to me, as does everything thrust upon people who have no choice. When I dove in with all my head and heart, I blossomed, powerful.

In protecting Cyrus from Havinger, I had created an immense promise to fill, but what was so important was how luxuriantly I filled it. I loved seeing fear in the other followers when I entered a room, especially when they were twenty to thirty years older than me. I reveled in my reputation as "our little killer," and then "our Jack."

Between ages of thirteen and seventeen, my training with Cyrus and Roland increased and included more than financial lessons and acclimation to killing. During the day, private tutors arrived at the house to instruct me in all the usual subjects—mathematics, literature, music, history, biology, and chemistry. At night were target practice, martial arts, and weapons training.

The *repetition* of these particular lessons helped me—the time and effort I devoted to them. Winning a fight had nothing to do with an instantaneous surge of power and awareness but was about maintaining a sense of normality in the moment. It was about what I could forget. I got used to the sensation of a body against my body, of someone coming at me, the foreign twisting, pulling, and driving. When it became the norm, then it all fell away, much like a common denominator. Only the crosshairs, the target, the wind, the heart, the head, the veins were left. Training meant learning what one should remember and, more importantly, what one should forget. The winner is the one for whom the fight feels most like home.

In seven years, I learned how to narrow the scope, prune the sensations, and clean and dismantle guns. My aim became proficient enough that my .38 became an extension of my hand. The knife was no different than a pen.

I had a slight size disadvantage, and that made weapons all the more important. Cyrus and Roland made sure I was proficient with more than guns and knives. I learned how to use more unwieldy and extravagant items, like bows and arrows and swords. A tool could help erase any opponent's weight advantage.

Cyrus wanted me both intelligent and trained, and he made sure that my grades in all subjects were equal to what I studied in the evening. I read Plato and Aristotle and everything from Zeno's paradoxes and Theseus's ship to the brilliant economical play of George Soros. We went over the rhetorical methods of manipulation, the ethos, pathos, logos, and kairos of persuasion. I became so familiar with the amazing and unsubstantiated power of authority and symbols of authority—another item which, like everything during a fight, I learned to force away—that I was able to deconstruct their mythical substance, until there was no such thing as authority, excluding, of course, Cyrus.

I absorbed a full education.

In my midteens, I hit my peak—I was full-fledged, vicious. For a while, I murdered so beautifully that even I hated me a little for it. I was always the first person Cyrus came to with assignments. Upon his request, I killed an unknowable number of individuals. Nearly all of them were people who had once upon a time financed Cyrus's operations. Eventually, when the money dried up or when the individual began to back out of our great organization, I was there to give them a warm parting.

Eventually, though, I began to kill on my own, without Cyrus's command. At the age of fifteen, I started exploring. I chose who I wanted to put in the ground, and every one who went down lifted me up.

I killed anyone I judged might want to kill me—and would have, had Cyrus not been there. I stalked them in the alleys with my pistol and suppressor. I never waited for them to attack, but I could tell which ones would. I took my vengeance on those horrible futures that would never be if Cyrus had not been there. I made my choices carefully, and I've never been wrong.

I can only describe the experience as the perfect fantasy, the perfect... game. For me, every day was *the* day.

The first drops were always a flicker, a foretaste, of the raze that ensued chockful of chaotic swell. In another way altogether, the killing was short peace, like the silent gasp before a plunge, or movements deafened in the firsts of war. No matter what it was or how it seemed, though, men fell, and with them their lies and intimidation. Life was pandemonium, where the safety of my liberty lay. I found relief in the flares of uproar and shadows of exhaustive destruction. It glowed beautifully—in a smoky sweet break of ethereal, an atmosphere of eruptive disgust. It tasted like Cloves.

Often, I licked my lips in anticipation of each kill, awaiting the nip of cinnamon and smoke. I was an addict to that flash of past, with need to satisfy in infinite tastes that my victories could not be undone. Again and again, I made men fall, all vast cloaks and flayed souls; their bodies hit the ground like doll upon doll death, all fluttering eyelids and glassy gaze. I wanted to yell at them to crawl. Their weakness warranted misery—even more so their strength.

Yes, yes, murder is poetry...and I have written chapters with knives.

In less poetic terms, I killed men, and I loved them as they died. That was how I loved. Every human-gone-wrong was beautiful to me. This was life. This was life with Cyrus.

Those I killed were rapists, molesters, thieves, murderers, liars, psychopaths—sometimes women. Cyrus requested many of them. And the innocent...yes, I killed those as well.

Then I cleaned up the bodies—disposed and closed. Roland helped me without question, perhaps fearing me. Disposal was always the furnace or the quick lime. It became normal, this mobius strip. I began not to recognize where the beginning of the process was or how I had entered the arrangement. It was smooth, like an organ pumping along. I went out, I found a wasp, I pressed my thumb to it until it died, and then I took it home, where Roland helped me burn the antenna, the wings, the torso, the head—usually, anyway. Sometimes I knew I could leave the remains, and I did.

Though Roland never mentioned it, he recognized that some of the people I brought back Cyrus had never requested. There were too many. In this gray area, Roland helped me by keeping silent. Though it might have been easy to simply ask Cyrus to command me to kill those I wanted to kill, I relished in the spontaneity and lack of permission. I pursued these targets secretly, in the same way I had once sought the man downstairs.

As I grew into my role and expanded it, Alex became jealous. Killing did not seep from him as it did from me. It was not organic. Then again, he had abilities that I lacked—the dramatic and the painful. It just turned out that Cyrus had more need for killing wasps than causing them pain. It took me years to realize that I had little to fear from Alex as far as death. It was only the rest I needed to deal with.

In those seven years, Cyrus became more mysterious to me. He would not reveal anything behind the curtain he maintained around his operations. I knew him only through what he made of me. Considering how dark and creative I became under his guidance, he was just as dark and at least as creative, at least as addicted and obsessed.

The days during which I murdered were followed by nights when I injected heroin, a drug I discovered soon after my introduction to laudanum by Cyrus. When my tasks became rougher, the route by which I escaped from them became just as extreme.

I was regularly dosing with the drug so that those I killed actually *died* and did not creep into my mind to overtake me. It was interesting and maddening how little I could feel during the actual act and how much I could feel after, when I was alone. The universe would shift so suddenly, become so fierce. The cool opium liquid was one of the only things that could allay my misery.

No matter how dark the lines under my eyes became, no matter how wan my body waxed, no matter how hollow my cheeks might be, nobody said anything to me. Perhaps others hoped the drugs would tone me down.

They didn't.

One evening, I had finished killing a man, a loyal-supporter-turned-opponent. I sat down beside the body in the hallway and leaned against the wall. I lit up a cigarette, which made me sweat and swoon.

In a few moments I reached inside my jacket and retrieved the black zip case I carried around with me. It held the various items I needed to get the job done. I sat in the hallway and prepared the medicine. Soon, it was nice and warm in the spoon. I dropped the white cotton onto the liquid and put the needle into the pool to suck the it up and then injected the contents into my arm.

I slipped into the cool embrace, and the whole world seemed glorious.

Something in the hallway, though, short-circuited the pleasure.

A trail of blood stretched from where I sat across the hallway in one long expanse, toward the stairway that led to the first floor. Shoe marks smudged the blood.

There was no corpse. The man had vanished. Despite the drugs, my pulse made a little leap.

Shit. I groaned. Slower than a snail, I stood. The world swirled around me, dots flooding my vision like black flies on fire.

The fury tried to come. Its hand was just inches from my own across a dark, vast canvas, but then it disappeared, pulled down into my depths by chemicals as I slunk down the hall like a cat unable to wake from a nap.

Bumbling my way across the balcony that overlooked the house's entryway, I followed the trail of footsteps and blood. My leg knocked into a table on the left, and I fell numbly. I crawled through the muck and found my feet again. Soon I reached the edge of the staircase, and I grabbed the bannister and clung to it.

"I'm going to find you!"

My voice echoed around the house. When it stopped, I wished I had never spoken. Someone else might hear me.

When I reached the bottom of the stair case, a breeze of fresh air caressed my face and stopped me. The front door was barely ajar.

I walked to the door, swung it open soundlessly. I walked out.

Pain.

White-hot agony pierced my left shoulder. I reached, and my hand encountered something hard, familiar—the handle of a knife.

Something smack my face; I fell to the ground, landing on the knife, driving it deeper. I screamed. The pain drowned me. Something circled my right foot, and I was dragged several feet. I shrieked again.

Jim McAllister, my victim, stood over me, covered in blood, a maniacal, primal look on his face—a look that said he had won. He had a rock in his hands and held it above me.

I rolled over, barely in time; the rock pounded the grass hard, lodging deep in the soil.

I hopped to my feet, swaying uncontrollably.

Jim pulled a knife from his pocket and launched toward me.

He slashed my left arm, and when I grabbed my arm, he slashed my hand.

The chemicals wouldn't relent. All my cogs had broken down. My habit jammed.

I reached behind me to my wounded shoulder and searched until I found the hilt of the knife. I wrapped my fingers around it and pulled hard. The worst pain in the world poured over me as the blade tore free. Tears swamped my eyes, and my teeth locked together. The molars clacked.

I sucked in air, and I charged.

On contact, Jim fell straight to the ground, his head banging hard against a rock. He went still. I slipped to my knees.

A knife emerged surreally from my stomach—Jim's final act. Blood poured from me onto the grass. I pressed my hands against the hilt.

Don't pull it out. The warning came from somewhere deep in my mind, reminding me of my training. I released it. I forced myself to move one knee and then the other and then rise. I shuffled to the front of the house.

When I reached the brick steps, a low moan escaped me.

I managed to make it to the front door and leaned against the entryway, looking inside.

"Roland!" I called.

My voice was barely audible.

I made it a few steps inside before falling to my knees. I could not feel my legs or feet. The heroin had taken over again, and it was telling me to sleep.

I sat on the floor and leaned back against the stairs.

I blinked.

Roland's face was inches away. His expression was fiery and fearful, and he was yelling. He shook me.

"Drink!"

Something pressed against my lips. A coppery liquid spread over my tongue, filling my mouth. I swallowed, and the fluid traveled deep inside.

Roland grabbed the hilt of the knife that protruded from my stomach. He pulled. The knife slid out easily, followed by the sloshing sound of blood, but it rang distant and disconnected. Pain should have been there, but it wasn't.

Roland urged me to drink again.

More warm liquid, like molten pennies, filled my mouth, and I swallowed. And swallowed. And swallowed.

The black flies on fire no longer flickered in my vision. The high-pitched whine that cut off all communication no longer sang. Roland cupped my cheeks, and I was able to *see* him.

I coughed. The wound in my stomach had disappeared. My shoulder, too, fully healed.

I shuddered.

"Soon as I saw you," Roland said, "I went straight down to the basement. Got some blood. You're lucky he was weak. Otherwise, I wouldn't have been able to just go in and collect some."

Roland's dark, glorious face broke into a smile of relief, and I processed what he told me.

The blood of the creature—a creature I had not acknowledged for more than seven years—had been given to me. I was whole again. I ran my tongue across a smear of blood remaining on my lips, and I swallowed and grimaced. The image came to me of a dead rose sliding beneath a door and the same rose returning to me plump and red and alive. I inhaled and wiped my mouth with the back of my hand. I pulled from Roland, and I shook my prior thoughts, fears, and agonies from the night away.

"You can't tell anyone this happened," I said. "Promise me."

Roland looked me over once, wiping the tears from his cheeks. The dead man was lying just beyond the open front door.

"I promise," Roland said.

Looking around, I mumbled, "I've got to clean this up."

Roland helped me, and we worked efficiently. When we finished, I returned to my room and promised myself that I would never, ever use heroin again. It had nearly cost me my life.

I kept my promise for about twenty-four hours.

The following evening, I sat in my room, listening to the thumping of my heart. The shadows of the trees slipped across the ceiling as the sound of a hundred gunshots resounded in my head. My hands were wet with a decade's worth of blood, and a fresh hell descended upon me. I didn't understand how hell could feel so fresh when so much of it was old.

I rose from my sweat-soaked sheets and opened my case, revealing the paraphernalia of peace.

In desperation, I sought release, as I had done so many times before. Nothing would keep me from self-medicating, not even the threat of my death.

CHAPTER 10—LIFT
AGE: 17 YEARS OLD

NO ONE DISCOVERED MY MISTAKE with Jim. A few weeks later, Cyrus commended me for all that I had done for him, for my service to his following. He sat me down in his office and told me something that changed my world.

"I'm promoting you," he said.

My eyebrows lifted, and my mouth dropped. I sat straighter.

"You're a good assassin, Jack—I might even go so far as to say fantastic—but I am thinking it is time to move you to a more administrative role."

Roland watched me from the corner of the room. His skeptical look said that I might not deserve Cyrus's promotion. We both knew Cyrus wouldn't be saying this if he knew about Jim. Such a blunder would have created a roadblock between me and a new position, as well as all of Cyrus's praise. I would be, to him, an idiotic, drugged-up, egotistical, self-centered teenager with no self-control.

Ignoring Roland's gaze, I smiled at Cyrus, free of guilt and full of gratitude.

"Thank you," I said. "What is my new position?"

"Helping me manage part of the following…"

That made my heart swell, and I leaned forward.

"Eventually," he added. "That is a long way away, though. For now, I simply want you to observe behind the scenes the following's operations. There is so much you need to learn. Rather than telling you, though, it is better if I show you."

"I am ready," I said. I was. I didn't care how long it would take. I would do my best for him, and I would earn my place at his side.

"Normally, I would give Roland the task of filling you in, but he will be gone for a week or two. Some business needs to be conducted at one of our other locations, and it requires his presence. So I will be filling you in on much of it until he returns."

I glanced at Roland. "At one of our…other locations?" I asked. I had never heard that the following expanded beyond Cyrus's home.

"One of the many things you are going to learn."

His eyes probed me, and when he spoke next, his voice lowered. "It won't be easy, Jack. All that you're about to learn."

I shrugged, self-assured, and I leaned back in my seat. "It's never been easy."

Cyrus smiled widely and slowly, smug. He lifted his chin, and his mouth opened for a moment before he spoke. "All the same.

"You have killing down to an art. It is time for you to begin to learn more."

My heart summersaulted with excitement at the idea that our carefully molded habits were about to be overhauled.

"What more is there to learn?"

"How all of this works. It's time for you to see what I do—at the very least, how I deal with traitors. I don't necessarily need people like you to get the job done."

"People like me?" I repeated, my brow wrinkled.

"It is time for you to begin to understand why the others obey and follow me so very closely."

"All right," I told him. "So…show me."

He winked. "Just go about how you normally do things, and in a few nights, you will see. It will come to you. *It* will not harm you, so do not fear."

Slightly confused, I left Cyrus's office, wondering what "it" could be and what "it" would look like. Nevertheless, I didn't ask him any questions. Instead, I sought that surge of determination within myself I'd experienced when he first mentioned my promotion. It returned to me quickly, and it was enough; my resolve would carry me through anything. All that was left was to let the days play out as he'd told me to do.

CHAPTER 11—WATCH THIS
AGE: 17 YEARS OLD

A FEW DAYS LATER, AT twelve or so in the evening, Cyrus called for me to come to the Gillespie Hospital. One of his loyal supporter's daughters, Meredith, had been attacked. The attack, he said, was a message for him—two followers were no longer loyal. I told him I would be there as soon as possible and hung up. Over the next several minutes, I collected my usual weapons from the topmost dresser drawer—two guns and a knife—and then I went to the hospital.

I arrived, parked, and took the elevator to the second floor, where Cyrus and Meredith were. When the silver doors opened, I stepped out of the elevator. He was straight down the crisply pallid hall.

It was cold, mid-December, and Cyrus wore his black trench coat. He was stunning, with his silver hair and cold gray eyes, and his look reminded me that his coldness and calculation were equally matched with a strikingness and charisma that could have only resulted in him being what he was—the leader of a following. It was like a mathematical calculation. Beauty plus charisma plus cunning plus heartlessness equaled psychopath—equaled Cyrus.

I peeked in through the doorway near where he stood. Meredith sat in a hospital bed, crying, a green gown draped around her. The others inside consoled her. She looked rough, her eye swollen but not yet black, a jagged red patch on her lip, one more on her arm. Her hair glistened yellow, not white.

Cyrus touched my shoulder with his hand. "I want you to find them." He told me their names, where they lived, what they looked like. I memorized the information.

I looked at him. "Find them… and?"

"Just find them." His expression was lively and amused.

I had a hundred questions, but I pretended as if they did not exist. It was not my job to ask. I nodded. "No problem," I said, and I started on my way.

"Oh, and Jack…"

"Yeah?" I glanced back over my shoulder.

"It won't hurt *you*."

I did not know what to make of that.

The two individuals I was to seek out were Taylor Smith and Edward Burnett. They were best friends, known to always hang out together; the pair of them had recently turned eighteen about three months apart. Eighteen was a time of great uncertainty. It was when many of the followers' children suddenly believed they had a choice over what they would do with their own lives. They didn't yet grasp that their futures were already decided.

Taylor had red hair and blue eyes—easy to remember. He was tall and lanky. Edward's eyes and hair were dark brown.

I went to one of the addresses Cyrus had provided me—it belonged to Edward Burnett's parents. I knocked innocuously, but when Melissa Burnett opened the door, I forced my way inside, ignoring the bellows from her and her husband.

As soon as they realized who I was, they stopped.

I looked back and forth between them. "Where's your son?"

They both stared, silent, unwilling to give any detail away that might allow me to locate Edward. When I searched their faces, they avoided my gaze. That told me, most likely, he was near.

I glanced around the dingy house and quickly cleared each of the rooms, finding no one and nothing. Finally, I made my way to the back door. It swung open easily and banged against the wall.

I stared out into a very large property with no fence that led to a huge expanse of distant woods. Between the house and those woods, slightly to the right, was a rundown gray shack.

Locked on the shack, I stepped out, beyond the glare of the lights, onto the grassy land. Behind me, the door creaked closed. If it opened again, I would hear it.

The bright moon covered everything with a frosty glow, including the trees behind the shack, the shack itself, and the grass that crunched beneath my feet as I walked toward the ramshackle building. I approached the shed slowly, cautiously, my hand on the gun in my coat pocket as I scanned the perimeter.

The shack was small, about the size meant to store lawn equipment. Paint peeled from the old wood.

Instead of entering, I circled it. Neither Melissa nor Ronald had followed me out. They watched me through a window facing the backyard.

As I arrived at the shack's left side, something moved to my left. A branch swung back and forth at the edge of the woods. Two figures bolted.

I ran, navigating through the trees about thirty feet behind. One of them hollered something. I pushed myself harder.

We ran through foliage and long, thick, dead grass, dodging downed broken tree limbs. Now and then they'd look back and then bolt with a renewed burst of energy that lasted a short minute. I followed at a hot, fast pace, driving myself harder.

I clenched my teeth against the cold air. I heaved myself through the woods, powered by anger, the image of Meredith in hopeless tears.

Abruptly they stopped in the middle of a clearing and turned toward me. I could barely make out their expressions in the dark, but their harsh breathing echoed. Trickles of sweat glowed on their faces in the moonlight.

I was just as breathless as they, unable to speak, though I had nothing to say.

I sought the cuspate knife in my jacket, and when I found it, I slipped it out of my pocket and hurled it through the air toward Taylor's chest.

The young man with red hair levitated up through the branches; my knife passed beneath him and plunged deeply into the tree. He rose like an actor being tugged up on a pulley on a black stage. The bottom of his feet touched the topmost of the branches of the tree beneath him.

Edward's figure, too, shot up like a soundless rocket. The pair of them floated weightless in the trees, suspended like puppets held by an invisible hand. I reached out briefly, like I was trying to pluck them from the sky. Between shocked gulps of air, I whispered to myself, "What the *fuck* is this?"

In response, they disintegrated. Their bodies splattered all around me, splashing the dirt and leaves.

I stood in the woods, heaving, shocked. A shiver came over me suddenly, and I crouched down, afraid of the invisible claw that had clasped both boys. I was not alone in the forest—something else invisible and spindly was near.

Without wasting a second, I ran to where my knife was lodged in the tree. The smell of thousands of sugared pennies hit me. I jerked the knife free and nearly slipped in the blood. I steadied myself and flew back through the woods, faster than before, following the distant lights barely visible in the dark.

By the time I made it to the Burnetts' backyard, my legs burned, and my whole body ached.

I charged across the lawn, past the shack, around the Burnetts' house. At the car Cyrus had provided for my assignments, I jerked the door open, plopped inside, slammed the door shut, and locked it. The car's tires spit gravel, and I fled. I returned to Cyrus as fast as I could.

I did not wait for the appropriate meeting time; I did not care to go to the diner where we normally met after one of my assignments. I returned to the hospital, to Meredith's darkened room, and breathed. Cyrus was the only other person there. He was sipping tea and reading a book in a chair beside Meredith's bed.

Meredith was asleep, facing away, an IV dripping diamond drops in her veins. Cyrus's left hand rested on the bed rail. When he saw me, his hand moved to his face and slid his reading glasses to the top of his head.

"How'd it go?" The question sounded contrived.

I swallowed. "Something was there. It…scared me."

"Did it?" He closed the book in his lap and held his open palm out toward me.

"I got there. And…"

"And?"

I leaned against the hospital room wall, reached out with my right hand, gripped the door and shut it quietly. "Cyrus, do you ever get the feeling, sometimes, say, when you've just entered a room…" I looked into his gray eyes.

"Yes?" He tilted his head forward.

"That the Devil has just been there?"

He exhaled quickly and briefly. "Sometimes, after we do our work, I'd like to think he has." That made me pause, confused about how I could possibly relate the terror of my experience to a man who sought such experiences.

"Did you see the Devil, Jack?"

I racked my brain for words. "This was just…" I said, picturing it, and laying it out in the air with my hands. "I followed them into the woods behind one of their homes, into a clearing. They… disintegrated, Cyrus. Right in front of me. They shot up into the air and…" I looked up. I had said this loudly, as though it would amount to something, but I couldn't finish. "It wasn't real."

"But they are dead?"

"Yes, but I didn't kill them. *Something* did, but not me."

Cyrus never blinked. He just looked at me with his head tilted forward, waiting for more.

I stood there, thinking that it would make far more sense if I had developed some sort of telekinetic power that had killed those men. "No," I said, at last. "I didn't kill them." I pictured it all again and winced.

"Jack," Cyrus said, "go home."

I snapped back to the room.

"Drink something—something strong—or inhale something. Get the soul back in you. Take whatever you need. And, later, when you have color in your cheeks, I'll explain what you saw."

"No," I said, "tell me now."

The corners of his mouth pulled back, and his lips pursed.

"We've been working ten years now, together, and there'll likely be at least ten more," he said. "It can wait another night."

"Not this time." The pressure shifted. People didn't demand things from Cyrus. It simply wasn't done.

"I won't leave until you explain."

Cyrus lifted his hot tea and drank it down. The liquid twinkled with heat, but he poured it into his mouth like it was air. "Do you remember, when you were young, the first time you saw the red box? The one that looks like a clarinet case, with peeling velvet, that requires a key?"

I shivered. I could picture it clearly—the old velvet worn in places, underlaying wood peeking through—how deeply red it was. A foot long by half a foot wide, it was the perfect size for *holding*.

"Of course." I refocused on the hospital floor.

"And you remember Mr. Thornton, hm? And that box?"

I didn't want to think about that. "Cyrus, I remember everything about that box."

"Do you?"

"You lock them in with it."

"Well, Jack, it's safe to say that I don't always need to 'lock them in.' Not when I'm dealing with traitors. People of ours who suddenly...pivot. I don't need to lock anyone who pivots in with it. Do you understand?"

I thought of the word he used—an odd choice. He didn't say "betray" or "deceive" or "disobey" or "blaspheme." Pivot.

I nodded. I understood what he was saying, even if I didn't comprehend how it could possibly be true.

"For now, that's all you need to know."

"Where did you get it?" I said. "Where does a person get a box like that?"

Cyrus smiled and clasped his hands together. "I will tell you *later*, when you don't look ready to fall down. Go home. Shoot up. Sleep. Close your eyes for a while, and when you are rested, we will talk again."

He picked up his book and opened it. "Trust me, Jack," he said. "Days like this...heroin is surprisingly heroic."

He sat comfortably and began to read, at ease. Nothing at all was wrong in his world.

I pushed myself from the wall, opened the hospital door, and shut it quietly. I went home, wishing that Roland had not left for the week so I could talk to him about what I'd just seen. Instead, I did the next best thing. I went straight to bed and did as Cyrus suggested.

As I relaxed, enjoying the drug that coursed through me, I thought about the evening's events. There was something in the world that I hadn't known existed, and I had just witnessed one of the things it could do. It woke in me a new kind of terror. It was as though I were down in the basement with Roland again for the first time.

I closed my eyes and clutched my bedding, pulling it to my chin. Letting go of everything else, I allowed the only medicine that ever really worked to do its job. Slowly, I drifted into a dreamless sleep.

-

A few days later, Cyrus told me, "You're quite lucky. We've got another one."

"Another what?" I asked, standing in his office. "A traitor?"

He raised an eyebrow. "Money has a funny way of showing where a man's loyalties lie." He tossed something to me. "Observe."

I barely caught it. The object was cold and heavy.

In my hands sat the blackest stone I had ever seen. It was so dark, so incredibly dark, that my thumb disappeared into its surface. The writing on the top radiated in glittery gold. FREDERICK GAMMOND PIVOTS.

"What is this?" I asked.

"I'll tell you after this is over."

I thought of the two men a few days before, their rising up in the dark woods and their bodies unraveling. I hesitated. "How about you just tell me now? I've seen all I need to."

"I know it's hard. Here's something to make it easier."

He dropped something onto his desk. It was a roll of hundreds. I set the stone down and picked the money up. There had to be at least three thousand dollars. I looked up at him. "You've never paid me before. That's not how this works."

Cyrus nodded. "Things change."

I shifted my weight from one foot to another and back again. "Thank you."

"You're welcome."

I pocketed the cash.

"I hope tonight won't trouble you too much."

"No," I replied, already a few steps closer to his office door. The money'd had an odd effect on me, as if providing me a harder outer shell. "It's no problem at all."

-

Frederick Gammond owed Cyrus thousands, and he had not paid in years. Though, that was not why I was sent to him. The reason why I was sent was because quite suddenly he *had* paid. Every cent of the sixty thousand had arrived in Cyrus's hands that day, by mail no less. The crisp check had been on Cyrus's desk. I had noticed it immediately when I'd entered.

There was sixty thousand right there—no weekly or monthly installments, no reimbursement over a round of drinks or over dinner or after a soft knock on the door and a gentle nod. Gammond might as well have tied a nice red bow on top with a card that read, "Leaving now. Don't bother to follow."

It was as obvious to me as it was to Cyrus that Gammond had not paid Cyrus back to simply erase the debt but rather to break the tie, back out of the group. He wanted distance. Nothing owed, after all, meant nothing unified. He desired to free himself, stretch a wing between the bars and hope the rest of him would follow.

Someone needed to intervene. Cyrus could not simply sit there and watch as the bird heaved its tiny chest before squawking.

He was a small man. I had seen him once before. An easy kill.

After speaking with Cyrus, I went up to my room, opened my top dresser drawer, and retrieved my guns and knife. Within just a few minutes, I walked out into the night, knowing exactly where I needed to go.

Gammond lived in an apartment above his store, a perfumery called Spritz and Dash—and I went to him that night amongst the glimmering liquids to fix the situation, even though I doubted very much that I would get very far.

A thousand little vials of perfume twinkled beneath the store lights on golden wooden shelves. A thousand reasons Gammond had given Cyrus over the years for not having the money. Now, Cyrus had the money, and the man had a bigger problem. Me.

I stepped toward the shop and stood before its wood-framed glass door as the lights inside flickered briefly. They cast their glow upon me. Vials, test tubes, paper, and coffee beans decorated the store. The light caught in little flecks of gold in the wood shelves, flaring with the smallest movement. The interior was clean and minimalistic.

Gammond entered from a door on the left. He walked forward and suddenly noticed me. He looked me square in the eye, slowed his pace, and stopped. He was a short man, balding, with a dark beard and glasses.

I tried the knob. The door was locked. The man just stood there. A myriad of things passed between us that could never be put into words, but somehow he knew.

I retrieved the Five-seveN from my pocket and shot the window of the door. I kicked in the parts that did not shatter and stepped into the shop with a snap and crunch. The man dived to my left, tucking himself behind the counter. I wobbled on the broken shards as I took my first step.

I lunged toward the counter and slapped my left hand on its cool wood top, firming my stance and pushing with all my strength so that, with a jump, my legs were solidly on the counter. I stood, towering over him, my black coat swinging and nearly blocking my view. He looked up at me, like a cornered mouse, and I lifted the gun to shoot him. I pressed the trigger, but nothing happened. There was no sound, no spray of blood. It had jammed!

Gammond grabbed something from directly under the counter and swung it up. I ducked, leaped off of the counter, and waited for a boom. Moments passed. Nothing.

The perfume vials began to fall. They dropped slowly at first, one at a time and randomly, like flecks of a beginning snow. Some immense pressure had suffused the room. The perfume bottles cascaded to the floor. Whole shelves broke apart, and vials crashed like bombs. In half a minute, every bottle was broken. The piles of glass looked like hard candy in rum. The mist of hundreds of perfumes burned my lungs like noxious gas. I held a sleeve to my face as I carefully stepped around the counter, my Five-seveN dropped and .38 in hand, but there was no body.

A thick crimson mess coated the wood, swirled into the amber liquid, but that was all. Just like the two boys, Gammond had disintegrated.

For the first time, I didn't smell the blood.

I was tempted to storm to Cyrus's home, pin him in his office, but the more shocked I was, the less likely Cyrus would explain everything. If I appeared frightened or outraged, he would delay demystifying me until I became more accepting of whatever was happening. So, instead, I waited in the car on the side of an arbitrary road, staring at the steering wheel with a mixture of numbness and fear, until the usual time that I met Cyrus at the diner arrived. I placed the key in the ignition, turned it, and after a steadying breath drove to meet him.

Normally, after Cyrus sent me on my way to kill someone, when the job was finished, we'd meet at a diner—the same diner every time, usually very late into the night. Few besides us would be there. I'd order a meal and coffee. He'd order an Irish coffee. We'd switch. As I'd sip the smooth cream and bitter enfolds, I'd reminisce with him, glow for a while. It was our one-on-one time, our Cyrus-and-Jack time. It also partitioned those deaths like squares on a quilt.

Maria and Rebekah were our waitresses at the diner, and Cyrus gave them hundred-dollar tips every time. Almost every seat in the place was a booth of some sort, and the floors and walls looked like they had absorbed years of oil and food aromas. At the back of the diner was a silver owl wall clock. Its silver wings spread on the hour, and I'd watch for it to flutter those wings at eleven o'clock and midnight. Cyrus and I sat in the same red booth.

This time, when I arrived, Cyrus was already there.

"Well, how did it go?" he asked as I took my seat.

I sighed, weary of the game. "It was the same as before. I… didn't do the job because something else did it for me."

A smirk crawled across his lips. "And what happened?"

"Gammond just…disintegrated. Like the others."

His lips made a subtle movement. "Fantastic."

A cheery voice popped up beside us. It was red-haired Maria. "Good to see you two again. What can I get for you this evening?"

"Jack?" Cyrus said, motioning for me to go first.

I gave her my order, my gaze remaining on him.

Cyrus turned and smiled affably to Maria, ordering an Irish coffee and asking her to double the whiskey.

"Always do," she said, and she smiled at us and left.

"You promised you would tell me," I said, "so tell me."

He smiled. "All right," he said eagerly, and the words had a soothing chime of finality. He leaned forward and laid everything out for me.

"The red case was a gift to me," he said. "I received it just before I took you in twelve years ago. And it can do two wonderful, magnificent, beautiful things."

He held up his hand, the pointer finger slightly higher than the others. "The first service it offers is the naming of traitors. Anyone I know, whether a friend, a follower, or a family member, who desires and plans to kill me, it names. It warns me that the person has taken the first step toward trying to destroy me. That he has, for instance, selected his weapon."

"Traitors," I said.

"Yes. Over the years, it has named perhaps forty people. With each person, the box notifies me by making a noise. The particular sound is difficult to describe, but it is not unlike the sound of a rotary dial...or a marble rolling across the floor...or a coin spinning.

"In any case, after the noise, I open the box. Inside is a gold shelf that folds out, and beneath that shelf, deep within the box—far deeper than the frame of the case allows—is fire.

"On the gold shelf sits a stone. The stone is like the one you saw yesterday—black with gold writing. It states the name of the man or woman who has betrayed me, along with the word 'pivots.' When I get a stone, I have two choices.

"If I place it back on the shelf and close the box, nothing happens. If, however," and a blissful grin spread itself across Cyrus's face, "I drop the stone into the fire, the person dies...disintegrates, more specifically. Problem solved."

He placed a hand on his chest, pressing against his cobalt shirt. "When one is building a religion, there is no better gift. With this beautiful device I can know the name of any person who might destroy me, and I can kill him very easily. I can rid myself of *every* traitor before he acts."

"The perfect tool for building a following." I bit my lip, my heart doing a somersault in my chest.

"Yes." He smiled, almost giddy.

Maria appeared with a tray in her left hand. "A bottomless coffee and a very Irish coffee." She set both cups down on the table.

"Thank you, Maria," Cyrus said. "You are so nice."

Maria's plump cheeks burned rosy. "It's easy to be nice to nice people." She touched Cyrus's right shoulder, and she left. Her hips swayed as she walked; she disappeared into the kitchen.

Cyrus switched our coffees. The cups were unintelligible.

"I need never fear being one step behind the traitors," he said, his voice low again.

I drank my coffee deeply, hoping the alcohol would stop the slight tremble in my hands. "What is the second thing it does?"

He breathed deeply, and his hazel eyes gazed up into the rafters. "That box is...not exactly a living thing, but it is not exactly a machine, either. It is somewhere in between. And it craves something."

I looked him up and down, waiting. "What does it crave?"

"Souls."

I tilted my head.

"You heard me correctly. I feed it souls. I lock a man in with the box, and it takes a good bite. Each time, I become more powerful."

"Powerful...how?"

"I go about my business, and the world can never stop me. The more I feed it, the more I can get away with never, ever being caught. And *you* will never be caught. And, finally, none of my other followers will ever be caught, no matter what they do or where we go. We exist in the world, but not of it. We begin to have our own separate plane of existence—the flawless skin called anonymity.

"It is how you have been able to go out, night after night, and elude authorities, witnesses, and the hand of justice. To make your kills."

I began to protest that I never murdered unless at his request, but he waved his hand and said, "Jack, please."

Taking a deep breath, I let it go and instead focused on allowing this new information to soak in.

There was something in particular about his explanation that did not sit right with me. It took a long while for me to identify it. "Wait. What about Havinger?" I asked. "He was your follower. He betrayed you. But... you did not know beforehand."

Speaking of the man was strange, since Cyrus, Alex, and I had erased the fact I had saved Cyrus from him. For the past seven years, it had been our secret. It did not particularly matter to me, until now.

"I have considered that for a long, long while," Cyrus said. "And there is only one explanation I can think of."

"What?" I asked.

"That the moment Havinger tried to kill me was the same moment he decided to betray me. There was no delay between one and the other. I was simply...unlucky to be there the very moment it struck him what a wonderful idea it would be to do away with me.

"That is why I have never again gone anywhere alone."

"That night when..." I paused for effect, "*you* killed Havinger, when we got back home, was there a black stone in the box with his name?"

"Yes," Cyrus said, and his eyes flicked to the left. "Michael Havinger Pivots." His gaze distanced.

"Too little, too late," I said.

His attention flicked to me. "Almost."

I took another deep swig of the alcoholic coffee. "You said you have to feed the box?"

"Yes."

"But you have only locked in seven or eight people with it. And most of those were a very, very long time ago."

Cyrus nodded. "I was wondering if you would catch on. I don't need the souls of men and women anymore."

The vinyl cushion beneath me squeaked as I shifted. "What are you talking about?"

He smiled. "I..." he tapped the table with one of his hands, "have been strengthening this thing for years. And I have gone about it in a way no one else in the world has. Ever. It is paying off beautifully. Soon, very soon, I hope it will buy me my transcendence."

Cyrus sat very erect, and he cocked his head slightly. "The first time I did it," he made a swooshing sound with his lips, "I had never seen something so incredible."

I sat, nauseated. The smell of food sickened me.

"Roland and I fed it a long time on mortal men. The usual, inefficient way that others went about it." He sipped his coffee. "But when you were young, we caught someone...of a rare sort. We took him down to the basement, and I had every intention of letting him go straight to the box in one large gulp. But a wild idea occurred to me. I thought about the soul and realized that, perhaps, it did not have to be either/or."

"What do you mean, either/or?"

His eyes glittered. "The soul is not a zero or one. It's not existing versus not-existing. A soul is like a liver. A soul is like a lizard that can lose its tail. A soul grows back. No matter how small the fragment might be, it can return. I realized, with the being down in the basement, I had a bigger soul...or one of a different fabric to feed the box, a fabric that could be hemmed. And hemmed. And hemmed. Because it always returned.

"I didn't have to harvest Lutin all at once. I could keep stock, nick a sliver off just a bit at a time, and that is what I have done over the years to maintain a steady supply of food. Because Lutin's soul grows a lot faster than all the others. And it is thicker. And it is better food. I do not need human souls anymore, for I have something better downstairs than any man or woman. He has ensured my success in ways I never could have foreseen."

"Lutin?" I asked.

"Yes."

I thought back to when I had stuffed the rose and the piece of curtain beneath the door, how they returned to me in full bloom and beautiful color. I had never known who or what was on the other side doing it. I finally had a name. Everything in the diner came into hyperfocus.

"And...what of Lutin?" I asked.

Cyrus shook his head. "What of him?"

It was late, the magical hours when I shared much more than I might normally—the hours that made me both merciful and murderous. I dared to speak truthfully. "You and I both know I'm not the kindest person in this world and that I would do anything for you... But he isn't yours. When are you planning to let him go? Have some peace? Even if that peace is in death. You said it has been over ten years."

"You wonder that because you are young. When you have as many years of experience as I have, the only thing you eventually want to know is if keeping that man will give you more power. That is my only concern. Not the years. Not the pain. Not the objectification. The result.

"If the answer is that keeping Lutin in my basement will provide me with inevitable transcendence, if it will allow me to catch traitors before they catch me, if it will allow us to remain blanketed and unseen, then I will keep him chained downstairs. If need be, I will keep him there forever."

"I...see. I guess I'm surprised there's no other like him. No other to worry about that might come for him."

Cyrus inhaled and smiled. "There might be. But whoever, whatever it is, it's no match for the box. Or, it would have already killed me."

A nostalgic expression took over his face, and he leaned back in his seat, relaxing. "You know, you surprised me all those years ago," he said.

"Oh?"

"I told you to never return to the basement to see him, but I was almost sure I'd find you there again at some point in time. I didn't." He peered out the diner window. "You were the child for me, from the very beginning. You followed my teachings to a T."

My mind slipped to an image of Lutin's door and a charred rose. "I suppose so."

Cyrus nodded, and slowly his smile disappeared. "There is more to tell you. Much more, *child of mine*." He winked. "But for now, that's where we will leave it."

As he finished his coffee, my mind remained on the topic of Lutin.

The image of the burned rose, and the mystery of the creature downstairs, called to me as the perfect distraction from my new terror.

For the first time since I was eight years old, I wanted to see that man. I desired it more than I could remember ever desiring anything—to gaze at the *thing* that made it all possible.

I was not a child anymore. I could take what I wanted, and I could do so without being caught. Every lock could be picked.

Reality had made way for me for years, and so would the path to Lutin.

CHAPTER 12—THE MAN WITH STARS IN HIS BODY

AGE: 17 YEARS OLD

I CREPT DOWN TO THE basement that night, as I had done when I was younger. I stepped, completely unnoticed, down the stone steps to the cement landing, knife in my back pocket. The blended smells of moist earth and mold carried a cool, rotten undertone. There had been bodies in that basement—there might still be, in one of the rooms in the labyrinthian halls. In the quiet, in the dark, I shivered involuntarily.

I stepped forward, my footsteps obscenely loud in the desolate quiet. Every minute piece of grit scraping against the rubber soles of my black leather boots reminded me of an old western, where a stranger's footsteps in a bar introduce him. *THUD clink. THUD clink. THUD clink.* I could not pass unnoticed, even though there was no one there to notice anything.

I had already visited Cyrus's office and carefully pried the key card that opened the large silver door from between the two topmost books. When I withdrew it, the two books clapped together with a *clang* that sounded like a released spring.

Standing in front of the familiar stainless-steel door, I held the card just above the slot. With the finality of pushing a giant red button, I slid it through. Something inside the door clicked. I pocketed the card and slipped my left hand around the large cold handle, opening the door. Ten feet ahead, a brick wall curved to the right. I stepped over the jamb and into the walkway before shutting the door behind me.

The old brick was just as deep a red as I remembered; the years had not weathered the color. I moved to the first wooden door and its giant crystal door knob. The prism reflected all varieties of light.

I retrieved a small black case from my coat pocket and unzipped it, removing a few tools. I squatted low, cat-like, easy, slipping the metal tools into the lock and fiddling with the tumblers.

The tools jerked, and I jumped back. They moved on their own, jiggling slightly up and down. Something clicked.

My heart thrummed hard.

The tools dropped to the floor. The doorknob turned, and the door opened outward.

I stood paralyzed for a long time, my breath frozen. At last, I picked up the tools from the floor and returned them to their case. My long, silent exhale dropped my shoulders, and my chin rose. Nearly a decade's worth of weight, wonder, and mystery was about to be lifted from my shoulders. He was within—the resurrector. I pushed the door open.

The room had only one source of light—a fireplace on the left. The licking, lapping curls of flame shone against the cement and brick like a quiet pool reflecting moonlight. The cement floor was surrounded by dusty gray redbrick walls that, like the hallway, staved off any deterioration. Nearer the fireplace, they were redder. The odor of moist earth and mold were milder here. Something sweet was in the air, like the faint aroma of flowers. I took a deep breath and held it in.

Only one piece of furniture adorned the room—an old, orange-ish, 1970s velvet chair, the stuffing coming out through the arms and along the detachable cushion seams. The fabric was weathered and compressed by overuse. A man was sitting in it.

I stood straighter.

He reclined in the chair, looking tired. I stepped inside and approached him, moving to my left, nearer the fireplace to make him out more clearly.

He stared at a few tiny flames in the black fireplace. A dark brown blanket hugged him up to his neck; only his head was visible. Underneath the blanket, something glowed orange. My heart thumped, and my mouth went dry.

The man did not appear to have noticed me. I studied the dark shadows on his face and his thick, black hair, which looked like it had not been combed for years, interspersed with dusty grit.

I wanted to talk to him, but I wasn't sure how to start.

He turned and gazed at me.

I drew my knife reflexively.

The man was unlike anyone or anything I had ever seen before. He had moved like a statue, turning just his head toward me, the rest of him inordinately still. His thick black hair tumbled over his forehead. His eyes were so black they stood out against his pale skin like holographs. His cheekbones sat high in his face, and dark creases punctuated either side of his mouth, making him look gaunt and starved. A glow surrounded him.

"Hello, Jack," he said. His voice was low and smooth, like gravel and silk combined. He knew my name. My already thudding heart quickened.

"So you know who I am. You *do* remember me."

Firelight played on his lips, resembling a smile.

I tapped the blade lightly against a finger, feeling the sharp tip.

His gaze shifted to the knife. He cocked an eyebrow. "Has Cyrus come for another piece of me?" He moved his hands down, and the blanket slipped from his neck and fell to the floor.

The man's chest was bare, cracked like an old piece of pottery. The cuts were expansive, the width of a sword or knife, and covered his entire body, and they glowed. The gleaming light stretched every which way, like rivers of fire across his body, resembling the embers in the fireplace to his left. His interior was a furnace, and with each rise and fall of his chest, the furnace burned hotter, like he was slowly waking.

He was stunning—bright and dark simultaneously. He had lolled in the chair like an ancient being in need of resuscitation but now radiated strength, resilient and beautiful. The weakness faded. His presence pulled me to him, revealing something immense and gold, a brilliant shine filtered by what appeared to be hot coals.

Realizing I had not answered his question—whether I was there to take a piece of him—I shook my head. "No."

I would never.

"Do you know who I am?" he asked.

"I...I thought I did," I replied, my mind just then barely letting loose of all the brilliance inside of him and rising to his face.

His dark eyes slipped to the weapon in my hand, and I stopped sliding it across my palm.

"You've come without a thought, then, in that head of yours to kill me? Even if I'm something you've never seen before? Ready to thoughtlessly murder a miracle. Just like a machine?" The way he asked the questions, he was prodding me. There was no fear in his voice.

If he wanted to know, I would tell him.

"Perhaps," I said. I turned to the door and shut it behind me. It was largely a pointless gesture because the large, vault-like door blocked us from the rest of the world, but I didn't like an open door at my back. When my attention shifted to his dark and brilliant form, I prodded him in turn. "What does it matter if I've come to kill you or just look at you? I can do whatever I want."

He bobbed his head once. "That you can. Whatever you want. It must be marvelous—to do so much and feel so little. You get credit for being wholly alive at the cost of only half of that." As he spoke, the giant cracks in his body fluoresced. When he stopped speaking, they dimmed.

Despite my awe, I nearly rolled my eyes at the insult. "I've seen many people in my life I've never encountered the likes of before or since, and I've killed them. That is normality." I flicked the knife out to my side with a half shrug. "If you want...I *could* kill you. Perhaps, after being down here, tortured for so many years, you've been waiting for it. To finally have some peace."

"You're wrong. I don't want to die. I want *out.*" He leaned forward. The sharpness of the last word startled me. "You don't realize," he said, "but even if I allowed it, you couldn't kill me. Not tonight, not ever. Not even," he raised a hand with a lightning strike buried in it, and he gestured toward me, "with all your experience, your expert coldness. No, not even with that. You're not the type who is able to stop me."

My stomach soured. The room blurred. I pinched the bridge of my nose, thinking it was my imagination. It wasn't.

My knife gently clattered to the floor. I, too, dropped to the cement, barely feeling the impact. I rolled over, grabbing my head, trying to rid myself of the blackness that obscured my vision. It would not relent until I stilled completely. I lay there, staring at the gray cement ceiling and the light flickering across it, consciousness slowly returning.

I went to call out for Cyrus, for anyone.

Before I could yell, the man's luminous form rose above me, his body glowing through his black pants and naked chest and arms like tribal hellfire.

"Cyrus has his plans, and I have mine," he whispered.

I tried to call out, to squirm, to crawl, to turn, but I could only lie immobile and breathe. I was paralyzed.

"Don't you realize, Jack," he said in that smooth, low voice, "that you are not a member of the only team playing in these games? That you never have been? No. No, I don't think you have. You are so...what's the word? Inbred."

The man, so sickly before, was now as thick with life as any human I had ever seen.

He lifted the bottom of my shirt, baring my stomach. I tried again to sit up, to crawl away, but I could do nothing. A childlike fear gripped me, spreading from my heart outward, making me tremble.

"I have been waiting for you, Jack. I have been waiting for years. Cyrus plans and strategizes, and he is very good, yes. He owns his part of the world, just as he planned. But he is not everything, and though he tries, he never will be." He traced his hand along my stomach. I shivered. "I do apologize for this, but trust me. It's for the best. Things for you could have turned out far, far worse."

"What do you mean?" I asked, forcing the words out.

He reached for my knife, dragging the tip along the red brick floor until it was next to my arm. He gripped the hilt in his hand.

"I won't let you feel the pain," he whispered. "That's not what I'm about." He studied my stomach, and his eyes narrowed. The blade pressed against my skin. "You would be smart, though, not to tell Cyrus this happened."

I gasped in panic. "What are you doing?"

He slid the knife across my naked belly. I gaped at him.

"I am giving you what you want even more than killing, though you don't know it yet. I am granting you the *ability* to provide your own cure."

The knife sliced into my skin, gentle but firm, without pain. Though the knife was cold, nothing was physically horrific. He worked inside my deadened belly as though I were a machine, tinkering close to my heart. Nothing had ever been so close to my heart.

After a shifting pressure, something warm blossomed inside me. I thought it was his hand, until he told me he was done. The warmth remained.

My blood spread over the white skin of his hand, and he wiped it off on his pants. When he finished, I could move again.

I stretched my right hand gingerly, testing my muscles in the cool air. I hugged my bare stomach and pulled myself to my knees, moving quickly away from him. There was hardly any blood on my belly, and what remained was nearly dry. There was no incision, no wound at all. Nevertheless, something was in me, heating me, heating my heart.

"With barely a whimper," he said, "the whole world has changed. I give you a week at most."

"A week until what?" I hissed. My knife, covered in my blood, rested on the cement floor nearby. I lunged for it.

It slid across the floor into the fireplace, burying itself into a chunk of blazing wood. Flames crawled over the metal, engulfing it, flaring bigger and brighter.

"I give you a week before you see the truth about what Cyrus is. What I've placed inside you will help with that, but not only that. Look at me," he said, and without a second's thought, I glared at his ethereal form, his almost holographic eyes.

"What did Cyrus teach you? Think back to the very beginning, when it all started. What did he say to you the first night you understood Roland had returned? In that white room. Yes, you remember. You've chanted it your whole life."

The fact that he knew what Cyrus had said to me made me wonder if he knew *everything* that had gone on in that house.

"You have no right to ask me."

He winced. "I know it hurts to remember. But I am not here to wound you. Go back to that experience. Tell me. What did Cyrus say to you, all those years ago?"

Persuaded against my will by something I could not understand, I did as he asked. My mind returned to the dark night when it had all begun, in the white room, and the resurrected man, the man I had never met until that night—Roland James.

Roland sat in front of me, wearing a brilliant blue suit in a white room. He smiled, his thin face creasing in the multitude of lines that gave it character. Cyrus's face broke into view. He opened his mouth and spoke to me, and then I opened my mouth and repeated the words.

"I'm not really killing them," I said. "I'm just not bringing them back."

"Well... Now, Jack, you can."

I shivered. I stepped away, ready to bolt from him and that basement forever. I crept toward the door.

"You have something to put you on equal footing now. All that matters is that Cyrus does not realize what I have given you." He held his hand with its glowing strip to his lips. "So, shh. Don't end up down here with me. I make for very boring company."

"I don't know what you're talking about." The warmth near my heart increased. I pushed my hand against my chest, wishing to squelch it.

Lutin was right, though. Whatever he had just done, if Cyrus found out, the repercussions would be unfathomable.

"Why did you do it?" I asked, at last.

His words softened. "To wake you. So that you might realize that Cyrus cares very little for you. That the box would have you dead in an instant. That you have no allies here. No one wants you.

"But that is fine," he whispered. "There are others who do."

CHAPTER 13—LUCID
AGE: 17 YEARS OLD

I RETURNED TO MY ROOM trembling and alone. My heart beat at a terrifying pace as I showered, washing the blood from my body. I hid my shirt so I could burn it later.

I sat beside my bed in the quiet, small hours of the morning. The trauma of what had happened fell fully upon me, saturating me with numbness. Something inexplicable had befallen me, and I had no friends to tell this to, no one to confide in who might help me.

I couldn't allow Cyrus to know I'd gone down to the basement, or why, or what had happened to me while there.

I sat on the floor, shaking, until I no longer trembled.

Reaching between my mattress and box spring, I retrieved a shrunken, brittle stalk, once thick and green, once bearing a red hat.

I twisted the stalk in my hand and clasped it hard. I licked my lips and then gave it a small try. I willed the burned rose to life—not intensely but tentatively, tickling it with my mind.

A strange, heated sensation trickled from my core to my fingers. The rose grew, shifting, until in full bloom, healthy and vibrant, as though bloody puddles shone on its petals. The stem appeared freshly clipped, a bit of moisture on the tip. The flower's scent was healthy and strong.

That's all it took—a blink, a nod, a bite of the lip. It was like breathing, bringing that rose back to life.

"Holy shit," I whispered.

It was easier than killing, absolutely effortless.

I caught sight of myself in the mirror hanging on the back of my door. For the first time in my life, I really *saw* myself.

I walked toward my image, entranced. My skin was pale, the color of milk splashed in tea, my eyes obsidian. My hair was so black it was almost blue, and it swooped to just above my breasts, framing my face in an oval. My body was tall and lanky, like a scarecrow.

To an outsider, I could have been anyone—a sister, a daughter, a friend, a lover. Nothing about me betrayed that I had killed anyone. I was young, thin, one might even say darkly pretty. The scar on my right hand signaled nothing. The nick above my left eye was silent. My shadowy eyes revealed no words.

There were men, women—children, even—who looked a hundred times more savage. In that mirror stood an average teenager.

I lifted the rose from my bed and twirled its soft petals across my palm.

I could have been anyone.

CHAPTER 14—NAUSEA
AGE: 17 YEARS OLD

THE NEXT DAY WAS SUPPOSED to be one of my practice days, but I sat in the gym in sweat-wicking black capris and a tank top, sick to my stomach. I punched the bag, but the sound and the sensation reminded me of the night before, when Lutin slid the knife into me.

I sat in one of the chairs against the back wall and observed the equipment—the bright blue power spring floor with its Dollamur carpet and foam underbelly; the gray weights on two shelves by the long row of mirrors that reflected the cloudy sky; the punching bag hanging across from me near the two Bob punching bags; the foot targets and bag mitts; the rubber knives and plastic guns on their shelves. These tools had brought me into being, carried me out of myself. None of that, though, could compare to what had happened the night before. Thirty seconds had beat ten years. How was I supposed to prepare for those thirty seconds?

Footsteps sounded from the hallway. They were not simply walking but trudging, abnormal for the halls of Cyrus's home. I stood, still woozy, and crossed the vast expanse of the gym to the door. Beyond it, a file of young men marched. Man after man carried cardboard boxes down the hall, taking a right, out of view. I asked one who passed me to stop. He did, and I lifted the folds of his box.

Inside were red and black wires and metal parts. I ran my hand across them. "What is this for?"

The man shook his head once to the left and once to the right. He stepped back in line and continued, turning right at the end of the hall, like the others. After several more individuals marched past, I went in search of Cyrus.

He was standing in his office, with its solid oak desk and metallic rows of books on a fake bookshelf behind him. He pinned red tacks on a map.

His nails were impeccable, shiny, almost opalescent, his skin flawless. His thick silver hair shone like mercury beneath the gleaming windows as he bent over his diagram. It was late morning, and the clouds had parted. The sun released its invisible hot arrows, and the heat in the room became oppressive. Cyrus, of course, was just as cool as he always was. He punctured the paper with a pin, and I shivered. He looked up.

"Are you all right, Jack?" His silver eyebrows rose.

"Yes. I just caught a chill."

His focus narrowed. "There are circles under your eyes. What happened with Gammond didn't keep you up, did it?"

"What?" My mind searched for what he was speaking of. "Oh. No."

"Because the box only identifies traitors," he added, "and it would never, ever..."

"No," I repeated. "I'm fine." I motioned toward the map. "What are you doing?"

He returned to the chart. "Planning."

"Is that what all the men are doing downstairs, with all those wires and metal parts—whatever you're planning?"

"Yes."

I drew closer and pointed to the little pins on top of his desk. "What are those?"

Cyrus's shoulders relaxed. Slowly, he sank into the black leather chair behind his desk. He looked at me keenly.

"I am so very glad you asked. It's the next item I was going to introduce, after you understood how the box works and saw what it can do." He indicated the map with his right hand. "These are all the executions that will take place in two weeks."

I peered down. I had never heard of any such thing. Many people in the house, however, were already preparing for it. Then again, I reminded myself, just because they were acting on Cyrus's behalf didn't mean they knew what they were doing or why. They could have simply been told, "Pick these boxes up from there and bring them here." He kept much hidden from everyone.

"What executions?" I asked.

Cyrus bit a corner of his lip and leaned forward. "My largest project so far. Each of these are cities where one or two bombs will be placed."

I tried counting them. "Must be over a hundred."

"Nearly two hundred. And plenty of people for the job."

"Why haven't you told me about this before?"

He shrugged. "You weren't ready. You've been lost in your own world for quite a while, having your own fun, and I thought it best to let you stay there for a bit. I didn't mind. But you're seventeen now." He smirked. "It is time we have these discussions. You will be eighteen soon."

The magic number: eighteen, the age when he and I kept watch on the other young followers—like Taylor Smith and Edward Burnett—in case they decided to blaspheme and leave. I cocked my head, wondering if there was a veiled question or threat. Perhaps there was no strategy, just fact.

I perched on the edge of the chair across from his desk and took a steadying breath. "You're right," I said. "So tell me. What do I need to know?"

He leaned in. His eyes blinked languidly as he pointed toward large swaths of individual locations.

"I am very close to my transcendence. One more giant move toward the destruction of innocence should help me get there. That is why I have orchestrated the bombings," he said. "To create the right amount of chaos. A new, public chaos. Just enough, maybe more than enough, to cross the threshold."

He waved his hand over the map. "Schools here, and churches there." The way he said this, it didn't seem to necessarily matter what he targeted.

"This," he said, displaying his artwork, "should be enough to fill that last little gap. The idea for what might vault us to the next level popped into my head just over a year ago, and I have been working on it ever since with many followers spread all over the country."

"Is that why Roland is at some other location? To ensure that this plan runs smoothly?"

"Yes," Cyrus said. "There were a few problems in one of the northern communes. He is taking care of it."

How could he have kept this concealed from me so long? Perhaps he was right. I had been in my own little world. Then again, perhaps he had kept the whole picture obscured.

"How many communes do we have?" I asked.

"Two hundred and forty-one." He smiled. "And what we have created together will tip the scales. It will be my fiery entrance into an altogether new world. It will complete my transcendence. And, after considering it a while, I do believe it was set up this way on purpose. I think *he* wants the entrance to immortality to be marked with a bang."

"Who?" I asked.

"My boss."

"Your...boss?" I asked. I nearly choked. "Do you mean...there's someone higher than you?"

He chuckled abruptly. "No. No, I am the top of the mortal chain—the hand that holds the hammer, if you prefer. I manage all the other pieces, bring them together, spread them apart, fine-tune them. I manage all the groups. I do it all.

"My boss is from the other side of the veil, the one I serve and always have. I've helped create the chaos and pain he has needed, and in return he will grant me a place beside him. In less than a month, I will grow beyond this human form. And I will help you and Alex begin your journeys toward immortality as well.

"Nobody will be left behind."

He put me in awe, in spite of the fear. "What's his name? How did you find him?"

"I will never tell you," he said. His voice dropped low. "You can only know him if he wants you to. I didn't discover him. He discovered me," Cyrus said. "You kill enough, and many things find you."

I suppressed another shiver. "After you bomb these places, you are supposed to transcend?"

He nodded.

"And I am supposed to transcend, too, eventually?"

Another bob of his head.

I pressed my hand against my stomach. "What happens before then?"

He clasped his arms and sat on the edge of his desk.

"You will begin learning the elements of the following. You will prepare to, eventually, take it over—at least a portion of it. Alex will handle another portion. But to do so, you need to know about how everything, and everyone, is formed, how it all works."

I nodded, forced into the motion to keep the conversation humming along. The remnants of the day—Lutin making me nauseous, making me fall, slipping something inside of me—had blocked the significance of my interactions, no matter how revelatory. Cyrus was providing me with a place in the world, but my heart shrank from it.

Eighteen. The number echoed in my head.

I forced myself to smile. "Of course."

"We could begin today."

"Today?"

"Why not?"

I was being carried to and fro by things beyond my control. What was I to say, though? I couldn't tell him no. "All right."

"Come." He stood and gestured with welcoming arms. "Let me show you the basis of the following. The foundation on which all is built."

CHAPTER 15—THE OTHER CHILDREN
AGE: 17 YEARS OLD

I STROLLED BESIDE HIM FROM his office to the garage. As we left the house, a few orange leaves blew inside the doorway, and I stepped on one with a crunch.

The sky had shifted. Fluffy patches that blotted out the blue sky were darkening, threatening to expand. Occasionally, the sun peeked out again, an unmuted melody, before the clouds again concealed their light.

We settled into the car. Cyrus backed down the gravel driveway. He took a left and circled in the grass near the garage before he drove the car toward the road. The hum of the engine, the smooth leather seats, and the fresh smells usually comforted me, but not then. I gripped the seat, grappling with nausea. I swallowed back bile as Cyrus drove the car over rocks and dips and then up a small incline.

"When one boils it down," Cyrus said, "there is just one necessary element to transcendence for me, for you. It is the creation of followers and the use of those followers to create the total and utter decimation of the world, of innocence. That is how I will evolve beyond this human existence, how I will slip beyond the veil."

The pavement shifted, became smooth. I relaxed my grip on the seat and took a deep breath.

"When I do transcend, you must keep the manipulation of followers in the forefront of your mind, for that will help you work upward the same way I have. This is the way it will be for you. Over the years, you will use the following to rise, and then once you have risen, you will pass it on to the next one."

We had only traveled ten or so blocks when he turned left into another drive.

A large red structure met us. "Here?"

"Here," he said. "This is, technically, where it all begins. This is where the followers are created."

No. That didn't seem right. I had seen the red barn before, but *I* had never been inside. "*I've* never been here before."

Cyrus smiled. "I do not mean that the leaders are made here. The followers are. This is where the other children go."

It was the first time in many years Cyrus spoke of the others. At the mention of them, a sharp tingle crawled down my spine. I was ten years old again, caught in the basement beside Lutin's door. I had never known where these children were located, where they were raised. I had never wanted to. Distancing myself from them had been my highest objective. As it turned out, they lived a lot closer to home than I had ever guessed.

"There is a vast difference between you and them, which you will understand once you have a look inside."

The structure in the yellow grass loomed. "All right," I said.

The large barn must have been at least as large as Cyrus's home and was pristine. I had passed the edifice many times on the way back from the cafe, the midnight killings. Electric lights shined out front in the dark. Adults occasionally speckled the lawn. Children, though, I'd never seen.

Cyrus opened his car door and stepped out. I followed and breathed in the crisp air as we walked to the front of the barn. He retrieved his keys, unlocked three dead bolts, and entered. After a deep, steadying breath to suppress a swell of queasiness, I walked inside.

Cyrus shut the door and locked it.

The foyer was quite small. The interior was not structured like a barn; it resembled a doctor's waiting room. It extended twenty feet left to right. Perhaps ten feet ahead was a waist-high counter. Cyrus and I slipped past this and met a golden brown door with two locks.

Cyrus slid a key into each of the locks and turned them simultaneously. Inside was a long corridor with white tile floors and cream walls that shimmered in the light. Several doors lined the hall. At the end, the hall took a sharp right. Together we walked and reached the last door on the left, which Cyrus opened. He made a swooping inward motion. We stepped inside.

The tile floor was white. The cream walls had faded to an old, discolored cream. In the center stood one brown desk and two wooden chairs. The only thing worth remarking was the large rectangle of dark glass that stretched across the wall. It looked entirely out of place. I wondered what was on the other side.

We took a seat in the chairs.

"I intend to show you something," Cyrus said, "but it is important that I preface what you are about to see with an explanation."

He retrieved a gold cigarette case from his pocket, set it atop the table, and opened it. He offered me a cigarette. I took it.

"My name is and has always been Cyrus Harper, and my business is and has always been to breed murderers." I noted how he didn't use the words "make" or "create."

"I have done so for the sake of chaos, for the sake of corruption—but, as well, for our protection. If a group is to survive, several must be willing to go to any lengths to ensure that survival. That is why you exist, why Alex exists, and others, like Roland.

"But it is more complicated than that. The people I bring into the following can't *all* be ruthless. I trust only those at the top of the hierarchy—like you, for instance—to lead. The rest are followers, and I form them here.

"They are people who *believe* they are murderers, and that is a completely different thing. I am going to show you just what I mean.

"In this particular facility are thirty children."

I tilted my head, looking to the walls, wishing I could see through them. Thirty children… I had never even suspected their existence so close to Cyrus's home. He must have kept them locked up tight.

"The ones here now are fresh recruits. I take in as many as I can manage at one time."

"Are their parents here?"

He shook his head. "These boys and girls are cared for by the group of people I entrust them to. Most of these children were rescued from unwed mothers, poor mothers outside of the group. Some are from foster homes. And others—well, others we simply take.

"I bring them here, and I form them into devotees—totally and completely obedient. How I accomplish this, you are about to see." He rose from his seat and went to the door. He swiveled on his left shoe. "There are two distinctions between how I work with them and how I worked with you. Two. But they make every single bit of difference."

He left, telling me he would return.

My heartbeat threatened to become thunderous as I smoked, waiting. I sensed I wasn't ready for what I was about to see.

A small click sounded, and a movement flashed.

The black glass wasn't black anymore. It had transformed into a window.

I walked to the glass. There was a room beyond of equal size to the one in which I stood. It was sparse. A metal gurney waited in the center of the room. A small table and metal chair sat beside it.

Cyrus entered the room accompanied by a stranger. The new man was tall and thin, with blond hair and blue eyes. He resembled Alex, except he was taller and thinner, his face not as round.

This blond man lay down on the metal gurney. An image of Roland flashed; there was a butterfly needle in my hand. I plunged needle into Roland's neck. Blood poured out.

I stretched and popped my neck, forced the image to disappear. The room, though, similar Cyrus's basement, begged comparison, begged remembering. I pressed the back of my hand to my mouth, trying to swallow everything back down.

Cyrus carried the chair next to the man, and then the two of them spoke inaudibly. Cyrus walked back to the door and flipped a switch on the wall.

"Can you hear me?"

His voice arrived through a small dusty speaker above the glass window.

I dropped my hand from my mouth. "Yes," I said, trying to sound as normal as possible.

"Good. This is Julian." He pointed to the man. "He is going to help me today."

Cyrus told me to wait a moment, and he left the room. Julian lifted his head off the table, looked through the glass, and winked.

The image was uncanny, and I took a few steps back and sat on the large desk. It wobbled beneath me. I grasped the edge and willed it to stabilize, and when it did, I couldn't release. Something uncurled inside me, and I became increasingly ill. I wished I were back in bed with a needle in my arm.

The door on the right reopened. Cyrus entered, and he wasn't alone. A short boy, young, with brown hair and brown eyes, entered alongside him, wearing a worried, sheepish look.

"No one is going to hurt you," Cyrus assured him. "Come on." His hand circled in the air.

The boy went to Cyrus, who lifted and set him on the chair beside the gurney. My heart jumped to my throat.

I wasn't watching the boy anymore. I was him.

I stood on the chair, staring at the brilliant blond hair and the man's pale skin beneath the electric lights. His neck pulsed.

Cyrus said, "We are going to do this as simply as possible."

He clasped my hand gently and placed the handle of a scalpel against my palm. He guided the point of the blade to the pale man's neck. A chill ran through me. I resisted, but Cyrus said, "One little incision. That's all." The sharp point of the knife slid into the skin and pressed down.

Bile rose to my throat. I couldn't look away. My hands gripped the scalpel with white-hot fear. A blanket of blood coated the metal gurney and dribbled to the floor.

I jumped back. Cyrus caught me and returned me to the chair, holding me, placing his hands on either side of my face. His slow, steady pulse assured me that this was the most ordinary thing in the world. The body twitched, the legs and arms jumped, splashing the blood just a little; the gurney wheels slid. The blood sloshed down the drain, swirling like a cherry glaze.

I cried, and Cyrus held me.

Suddenly, I wasn't the boy anymore.

A microphoned voice high above poured down from the speaker, sobbing, sniffling. "Make it stop."

Cyrus held the boy close, and I sensed his comforting hands on my arms, his breath on my face.

"Would you like him to come back?" he asked.

"Yes. Yes!" the boy cried. The word was in my own mouth, the burning need in my chest. The young boy rested his head on Cyrus's shoulder as he wept.

Cyrus tapped the blond man's shoulder, and Julian's eyes opened. He sat up, and Cyrus told the boy, "Look...look!"

Julian's face illuminated. It was not resurrection. It was facade.

The blood was fake. Though moments before it had fooled me, it was now far too bright to be real. The man's movements had been too flamboyant. He was not paler. His body revealed no residue of death.

To the child, though, it was real. Magic had happened. To him, it was no facade. It was as Cyrus stated. The man had been brought back to life.

As the blood dripped less and less, the boy's sobbing diminished to a few choked whimpers.

"It's a good thing I am here," Cyrus said. "To clean up your mess, hm?"

The child looked up at him in wonder.

"I said, it's a good thing I am here, isn't it?" Cyrus asked more firmly. The child nodded.

"You are too dark. You need me to help you. You don't know how to handle what you've done—thank goodness I'm here. You are so evil. Thank goodness I am here to keep you from your evil self."

The child clutched Cyrus's arms, pulling my mentor toward him.

"It's all right now. I'm here to clean up the mess. You killed a man, but I am here to help you. You are too dark to be on your own."

Cyrus held the child. How small and fragile he was. There was no one for him to run to, no adult to help him. Any pain he suffered during Cyrus's teachings Cyrus would claim was due to the boy's evil nature. Doing this would create a deep and irrevocable wound, and the boy would naturally need to depend on others for stability. That was how the boy became Cyrus's. That's how it all worked.

My mentor lifted the boy, held him close, and carried him out of the room.

I took that moment to wipe away a small tear that had formed at the corner of my eye.

Julian, bright red blood smeared around his neck and body, toweled the paint off. He peeled the false wound from his neck. A large piece of fake skin fell to the floor. The fake skin was connected to a tube concealed down the front of his blue button-up shirt; it fit into an inside pocket that held an empty bag that had once been full. He had squeezed the fake blood out of the fake wound.

"Another one down," he said, his words grainy in the overhead speaker.

I wanted to hurt him. If things went well, in due time I would simply make him disappear. It didn't soothe me like heroin might, but nevertheless, the more I thought about it, the more I liked the idea.

Julian smiled at me, and I mimicked his expression back. After cleaning, he left the room.

I collapsed into my chair. I dropped my face in my hands and sat on the edge of an emotional abyss. What all of this meant for the child and me swirled darkly, my thoughts tumbling like rocks that might become polished in the process of a brutal fall.

Cyrus would soon enter the room. I sat straighter, pushing my emotions down, putting them back on their shelves. I needed to think, to ask the necessary questions.

CHAPTER 16—ECHO
AGE: 17 YEARS OLD

WHEN CYRUS ARRIVED, SHUT THE door, and took his seat, I said, "He didn't really kill that man. Not like I killed Roland."

Cyrus nodded, his thin lips spreading into a proud, avuncular smile.

"You told him it was his fault. You never said that to me."

"Very good, Jack. No, I didn't. Because I did not want you to feel like a murderer. But I want him to."

"Even though he hasn't committed any crime?"

"It doesn't matter if he has or hasn't. I need him to believe he has. I need him to feel like he has very little worth."

"Why?"

"Because then he'll need me to validate him. To solve his problems. This is how the game is played. With him. With everyone. What I needed from you was an emotionless murderer. What I need from them are emotional, sensitive, unstable innocents.

"When they believe they are dark, unclean, and unworthy, all they care about, and what I assist with, is that I help them *feel* better. Better put, I help them feel they and their future will be brighter because," he pointed to himself, "I am here to right all of the wrongs, heal all the scrapes, patch all holes."

"But not actually heal all the scrapes," I said. "Since you are the one who causes them."

"Correct. That is the key to manipulation. Inflict the wounds and provide the salve. The salve is, of course, more wounds. The key is that you are seen as *the provider*."

I took a drag on my cigarette and tried to imagine going down the steps to the basement, stepping into the room with Cyrus and looming over Roland. I tried to imagine what it would have been like if Cyrus had told me, after Roland's blood had poured out and he died, "Thank goodness that I am here. You are so dark. I'll clean up your mistakes."

I wondered how much it would have changed me. Infinitely, I suspected.

"What did you tell Alex?" I asked.

He shook his head. "Alex was never down in a basement. He never had to be. I taught him that there are two ways to kill a man—two deaths each of us die. One occurs while we are still living, and that is the one he is interested in. Death of the spirit, not of the body. That is why he helps me with Lutin."

"What? What do you mean?"

"Lutin is the enemy," Cyrus said. "From the other side of the veil. I trim off pieces of his soul every week. He feeds the box, and he will never die." Cyrus smiled. "I have an unending supply of soul. With him, I have been able to do so many things, and so has Alex.

"Roland taught you how to kill down in that basement. Alex was never interested in killing. You know that."

"Yes."

"So I tutored him in something he does enjoy. My son is very good at trimming."

That gave me pause. I had never quite put everything together. Alex helped Cyrus cut away pieces of Lutin's soul. The very idea made me writhe. Alex shouldn't have been allowed to breathe the same air as Lutin. So Cyrus would not sense these thoughts, I shelved them and returned to the issue at hand.

"In just one moment," I said, holding up my finger, "you gain entrance to the rest of our lives."

He leaned forward and rubbed his hands together back and forth. "Yes. And it's all through pressure. Death is simply pressure, and with death—real or otherwise—I can mold them.

"I don't need the death to be real, for it's not about the death itself. It is about the pressure that death and murder exert upon the living. The fear and hate it instills. Everything becomes meaningful under pressure." He nodded toward the door. "Come on. There is more to see."

I paused, thinking. At last, I stood and followed him out of the room and down a long hallway. At the end was a door and beyond that a stairway. I followed him into the stairwell, and we climbed three flights before he opened another door. We stepped into a hall decorated with the same white tile and cream walls.

We walked through the hallway until we reached a door on the right. My jaw dropped.

A large rectangular room with many, many tables broke into view. On the tops of the tables were small corked vials. Attached to the bottles were tiny blue tags, and on the tags were names. Inside each bottle were three pills, one yellow, one white, one pink.

The geometrical uniformity of the bottles on the table was astonishing. Everything was pristine and the bottles themselves striking, like seashells in a glass jar.

"I tell you," he said, running his hand over the tops of the bottles and catching the labels, "it's so easy to manipulate people. The human psyche is so fragile."

"What are these?" I asked.

"LSD. A mild muscle relaxant. And Synthroid—a thyroid hormone. Lock a child in a dark room on an acid trip right after he has killed someone—or believes he has—and his mind produces the most interesting things. Sometimes they're too interesting. Sometimes you need the yellow pill to calm them down."

My throat clicked as I tried to swallow. The world around me expanded. I could not imagine what these children had experienced. I myself had barely managed to climb my way back to a semblance of reality after what Cyrus had done to me. The others didn't stand a chance.

I bit my bottom lip. "What is the thyroid hormone for?"

"Did you know," he said, folding his arms, "that before a person can be diagnosed with paranoid schizophrenia, he must be checked for hyperthyroidism?"

I shook my head.

"Too high a metabolism makes you feel and act very similarly to a paranoid schizophrenic. It makes your skin crawl. That's useful. Another kind of...pressure. Like death. Like murder. All of this," he said, "is used to break down their grasp on reality. So that, again, they need us to supply reality to them. The reality we supply is whatever we desire."

The bottles stood like soldiers at attention. I picked one up labeled "Greg." The white, yellow, and pink pills clinked as they slid down the glass. I wondered how well Cyrus himself would do facing such "pressure." I returned the bottle to the table.

He motioned toward the door. "There's just one more thing."

We retraced our steps, and I trailed his dark form.

"You might be asking yourself, 'Why children? Why not adults?' And that is because one of the ways I accomplish chaos is to unravel the pure. Every bit of innocence I devour *he* devours. Adults are rarely, if ever, innocent."

His eyebrow raised, and I nodded.

We took a left, and a woman appeared. Her long hair was pulled into a ponytail, her eyes starry. When she spoke, her pupils didn't focus. It was not unlike looking at an individual whose cruelty ran deep, her intelligence inadequate to keep up.

"Can I help you, Cyrus?" Her voice emanated saccharine.

"Hello, Kay," he said with a warm smile, slipping behind his familiar disguise. "We are here to take a look at the children."

"Of course," she said. Her gaze shifted to me momentarily. "They're deep in their reading at the moment. Would you like to speak with them?"

"No," Cyrus said. "Just see them."

"Well, there's a perfect room for that," she said, her voice airy. "Just this way."

"Exactly where we were headed."

I took a deep breath and followed him and the woman named Kay along the hallway. We took a right and entered a door at the end of the corridor. Within was a room with several chairs and a glass window through which sat thirty or so children.

Kay dipped her head sweetly and then stood at the back of the cream room. It took some effort to turn my back on her. I didn't like the sensation of her standing so near. I barely managed to meet Cyrus beside the one-way glass.

The children were at their desks, going over some mathematical figures, and all thirty of them silently looked up at the instructor.

They wore identical uniforms—light blue shirts and dark blue slacks. Dark smudges were like bruises under their eyes. They did not look at the instructor with the abandon children should have. Something terrible had happened to them. Cyrus observed them, expressionless.

"This is where they stay?" I asked.

"Yes. Where they learn." He inhaled deeply and spoke low, tilting his head toward mine, as if imparting a secret. "If you combine your followers, you can manipulate them more effectively. That is because, in a group, they relax into each other and become one. Look at how uniform they are. That never changes."

I counted them, thirty children total—fifteen boys, fifteen girls—the lost children, stolen children, children who were not his.

"Was I ever here?"

"No, no. You were part of a culling."

My heart softened, my body stilled. I had never heard that word before. "What are you talking about?"

He looked me up and down.

"You don't remember?"

Heat crept up the back of my neck to my face. I wanted to run.

My mentor inhaled deeply.

"The culling," he began, "doesn't happen often. Sometimes, one of my followers will ask me to take his or her child under my wing for tutelage…"

"Why?" I asked.

He paused, thinking. "Responsibility," he said, "can be frightening. Many of my followers believe that I could do a better job ensuring their children have the right start in life than they can. They feel...incapable in raising their kids. Sometimes, I receive requests for aid in the development of people's children. Lately, I have received many. And when I say 'development,' I mean my personal tutelage. Bringing a child into our family.

"Right now, I receive requests because rumor of my ascension has gone around, and the idea of having one's child raised by the above-human is alluring. This year, there have been fifteen requests so far. Over the past decade there have only been seven."

My mouth was terribly dry. Something was coming.

"Considering the process, I don't immediately accept a request, and even if I do, I don't immediately accept the children. But Jack, you should know all of this."

"I should?"

"Yes." Cyrus's eyes held mine. "Do you not remember the berries?"

His words pulled me back, way back, to a place I had never visited because it had not seemed as remarkable to me as the other parts of my life. Bringing the memory to the surface was like hauling a chest up from the bottom of a deep, dark sea. When the heavy thing floated to the top of the water, ready to be opened, I feared what was inside.

I did not want to remember.

-

"Jack."

Cyrus said my name. His tone was purposeful, heavy. I was just seven years old.

We were in a smoking room with red velvet floors, wooden walls, and gold molding. The ceiling was blue, covered in angels. My dry tongue stuck to the roof of my mouth as I swallowed, but I went to him.

The room, with its portraits and crystal, swayed out when I stood beside his chair. It disappeared when I looked into his eyes. They were silver, fickle, and cold.

"What does your mother tell you?" he asked, staring straight through me.

I did not understand. "What?"

"What does she tell you about, say, me?"

He took a sip of a velvety brown liquid in a beautiful glass. The glass sparkled in the dim light.

"Nothing," I said. This pleased him. He ran a hand through a strand of my long dark hair. He smoothed a wrinkle from the shoulder of my dress.

His thin cream lips pursed meaningfully. There was something more there beneath his surface than in others. I both liked and disliked it.

"What does she say about our church?"

"It's everything."

"It *is* everything." He smiled, setting his glass down on the table before he took my hands. One of his palms was moist and hot, the other cool.

"And what does she say about you?"

I did not reply until he encouraged me and kissed my hands.

"That I don't belong here."

"That's quite dark."

I giggled because I didn't know what he meant.

"Let us see what God has to say about it, hm? Or, at least what *something* has to say about it."

He called another man over, who reminded me of a waiter. In a few minutes, he returned with a square silver plate. He set the plate beside Cyrus's glass and left. Arranged in a circle on the silver platter were ten white berries that reminded me of eyes.

"I don't think you should live with your mother anymore," Cyrus said. "Do you understand?"

I nodded, even though I didn't. I was so wrapped up in the moment, I couldn't consider his questions.

"However," he continued, "I do not know if you should live with me. So this will be our way of deciding." He held the plate out to me. "I want you to choose one, and just one, of these to eat. If you choose appropriately, you will come to live with me. You will be like my own daughter. Alex, my son, will be your brother. With luck, you'll grow with us, be better, stronger. If, on the other hand, you choose incorrectly, you will not come to live with me. Understand?"

I drank him in and slowly nodded. I didn't question, pout, cry, laugh, or smile, because this was Cyrus. This was *Cyrus*.

The berries on the plate all looked the same—sparkling white; black dots decorated the tops of their heads. All of them were relatively the same size, and they circled the angels reflected in the mirrored plate.

One, though, appeared slightly brighter. I studied him. I liked him. He was prettier than the others, different. I picked him up and looked at Cyrus questioningly, but he gave no response. He simply stared at me, interested but contained. I peered down at the fruit and, after a time, smelled it. I wanted to eat him. I did.

I crunched through it, swallowed despite its bitter soap taste, and was proud of myself. I looked back at Cyrus, confident. Without smile or frown, he set the plate on the chair-side table and motioned for the waiter to come and take it.

"Did I get the right one?" I asked.

"Oh, let's give it a few minutes," he said. I watched him as he smoked. He gazed at me.

-

I swallowed, not knowing what to say.

Cyrus sighed, placed both of his hands on my shoulders.

"My dear, you are like a daughter to me now. But twelve years ago, I was unsure if you could mean anything to me. So you went through the same process as all the other children who were offered to me.

"I sat you down, and I offered you a plate of ten white berries. The same ten berries I have presented to every child I might accept. Nine of the berries were *actaea pachypoda*—also known as doll's eyes, one of the most toxic flowering plants in this area. It immediately sedates the person who eats it and kills him or her quickly. One of the berries, however, was *symphoricarpos albus*—the common snowberry—with a black dot painted on its stigma. This berry is not as sweet, but it is also not fatal. I asked you to choose one of them, and you chose the snowberry. You survived the culling process. Most children—in fact, every one except for you and one other—have not."

"One other?" I asked, my voice barely audible. "Do you mean Alex?"

Cyrus shook his head, but he would not tell me who the other person was. "That was a long time ago, and he does not matter, anymore." Cyrus's hands gently squeezed and released my shoulders. "The point is that you needed my help, and you were fated to have it."

The anger that rose in me threaded from my heart to my marrow. I bit my tongue, and as I did, something caught my attention through the window. I was ready to scream at Cyrus, but somewhere, in a distant part of my mind, a red flag rose, and I shut my mouth.

I stopped so close to the window I nearly hit it.

"What is it?" Cyrus said.

All the children appeared sickly, unhappy, disconnected, but there was something else. I tried to decipher what I was seeing, like decoding an ancient script. I missed it again and again. My focus began to fail as I observed the group. These children would soon be going to their deaths. In very little time, they would be marching with bombs on their way to churches and schools.

Cyrus placed his hand on my shoulder comfortingly, as if I were in pain, not on alert. "Let's go."

I shrugged him off. I wasn't about to leave. I was on the edge of something big.

A small silver twinkle shined across the room. It wasn't particularly bright, this sparkle around one of the girl's necks, but it stood out. Unlike the others, she wore a necklace, which looked rather familiar.

The tip of my nose brushed the glass, and my breath fogged it. "I want to go down and see them."

Cyrus went on edge. "Why?"

I pointed. "I need to see that girl's necklace."

Kay and Cyrus exchanged a look. At last, Cyrus shrugged, his face pensive. "All right."

Kay's smile widened, still empty. She was on edge, too, perhaps fearful that she was about to be accused of something. She tapped her fingers nervously against her leg and turned quickly, leading us out of the hall and down the stairs to the door that opened into the auditorium-like room.

I entered. Every face turned in my direction. The instructor, who had long, wavy brown hair, stopped speaking. She appeared utterly shocked to see both Cyrus and me. "Sir. Is there, uh, something I can help you with?" She tugged a hand through her hair and pulled her cardigan tighter around herself, ensuring everything was in its proper place.

"Just taking a look," Cyrus said, his voice comforting. "Letting Jack observe the students."

I walked between the rows of children. Each of their faces peered up at me with empty, hollow expressions. I reached the girl whose necklace had sparkled.

The girl was fearful, but it was not a new fear. I bent toward her and said, "It's all right. I just need to look at what you have here." I took a deep breath, and she let me inspect the jewelry.

Roland's cross hung around her neck—the one I always kept in the nightstand drawer beside my bed. I reached down and touched it. The girl watched, silent.

I undid the clasp and lifted the necklace from her. The rolled-up little ball, the withered windowpane, tumbled in my hand. Impossible.

"How did you get this?"

She did not speak at first, but after a little prodding from her instructor and Kay, she eventually replied, "He gave it to me."

"Who?" I asked.

I knew what she would say before she answered.

"Alex."

The carefully constructed web that kept my emotions in check came loose. I pocketed the cross, a fury rising inside. I took a deep breath and surveyed the other children. "How many of you have received things from Alex?"

Almost half of them raised their hands. My heart leaped. Alex was giving them my things.

The hands dropped, one by one, as I looked at the faces of those who had raised them. I walked down the row, taking each of them in. I stopped.

The puzzle clicked into place. It was torturous.

I turned to Cyrus. When I finally spoke, it was like someone else had crawled out to talk to him, the reptilian part of me who killed for him but never dared speak to him, the part of me who survived and survived, the unstoppable part. "*Who* chooses these children?"

Cyrus frowned, and he opened his mouth to speak, but paused.

"*Who* finds them and brings them here?" My voice filled the room. The children shrank from me. Kay grimaced. The instructor stared at Cyrus and backed away.

What was obvious to me was becoming obvious to Cyrus. Each little girl who had raised her hand had black hair and dark eyes, pallid skin. Some faces were a little rounder than others, but the resemblance was unmistakable. Once I saw it, I couldn't unsee it. Each face I peered into was like looking into my own. My child-self sat everywhere I turned.

Alex. He was the one who chose them, the one who supplied Cyrus with his child army. He had chosen these girls because they looked like me.

He had given them my things.

Cyrus's eyes closed, and he raised his hands. "Jack, I will speak with him."

The words flew out of my mouth before I could think. "The fuck you will!"

CHAPTER 17—ZEROES AND ONES

AGE: 17 YEARS OLD

"I'm going to *kill* Alex." I paced back and forth in the driveway.

"No. You're going to sit out here," Cyrus said pointedly. "I don't want you doing anything rash."

"How could you not notice?" I said. "As soon as I walked in, I knew there was something off! He stole things from me. Your son gave one of the girls Roland's cross. I had to *take it* from her."

Cyrus held his hand in the air. He gritted his teeth.

Once again, Alex had proven himself to be beyond Cyrus's control. It was obvious that Cyrus was on edge, but he wasn't angry enough to let me loose. For fifteen minutes, he tried to manage my unrestrained, fierce emotions instead of considering Alex's bullshit actions.

"I said I would speak to him, and I will."

"I don't care if you speak to him. I want you to show him that his plan isn't going to work! I don't want those girls going anywhere, doing anything, much less carrying bombs. He wants to see girls who look like me die."

"Jack." He pressed his hands together, in silent prayer. "I won't stop this plan simply because the children look like you. I said I would talk to him, and I will. But this *must* happen. For my ascension."

I shook my head. I almost couldn't believe his lack of reaction. "Alex slipped this past you."

"Yes, he did. I will speak to him."

"What is there to say? He knew you wouldn't stop it from happening, and he strategized. He *strategized* so that he could make a Jack after Jack after Jack march to her death."

"If you refuse to see it that way, it isn't that way."

I jerked back. "What?"

He didn't elaborate. "I will talk to him, I promise. But you—you must control your reaction to what he has done. That is what matters, now." Cyrus placed a hand on my arm.

"No," I said, pulling away. "It doesn't matter how *I* react. It matters that there are fifteen girls who look like me in that building. And it matters that you won't show Alex that what he has done is unacceptable.

"For how many communes did he select children?" I asked. "Was this the only one?"

Cyrus took a deep breath. When he looked at me, his expression was hard, but also slightly apologetic. He knew the situation was fucked. He simply wouldn't admit it.

"That's what I thought." I burst into hysterical laughter. I had never laughed like that before, maniacally giddy over the absolute ridiculousness of what Cyrus was versus what he claimed to be. I stopped abruptly. At last, I backed away.

"Where are you going?" he asked, his voice on edge.

"I've just… I've got to go think."

Cyrus winced. He motioned towards me as if to say something and then stopped. "Go for a while, if you need to, but not far. I'll speak with Alex. I'll punish him. Trust me."

I shook my head and turned away. "There is no such thing as punishment for something like that."

For the first time, Cyrus appeared lost.

I left him and went down the road, away from the house and the barn and the children.

As the barn faded from view, I ran. Exercising in the piercing cold air might soothe me, help me calm down after the devastating scene and Cyrus's lack of reaction to it. I adjusted to the cold air in my lungs and the speedy beat of my heart, but the insult of my discovery resurfaced again and again and again. After a couple of miles, I slowed down and plodded through dry orange leaves and twigs to lean against a nearby tree and catch my breath. I thought again of Alex. He had been choosing Cyrus's followers for *years*, and I hadn't known. Not only that, but he'd helped Cyrus with Lutin. Perhaps Alex's plan to become better than me, at least in his father's mind, had come to fruition. He had been entrusted with much, much responsibility.

Those children… Everywhere I looked, they stared back at me.

They were me.

Every new thing I learned about him made me loath him more. Alex had not started out in a dark basement, not like the other children had— not like me, not like Lutin. He did not know what it was like.

I tore my glove off with my teeth and reached into my coat pocket to retrieve my cigarettes. I savored a good, long warming smoke in the cold to chase away my queasiness. It wasn't the drug I wanted, but it was the drug that would do.

I pulled the long necklace from my pocket and examined Roland's cross. It was, perhaps, the only object ever given to me out of kindness. I remembered sitting beside Roland on the couch beside the fire, right before he played the piano. He had dropped the necklace into my palm and shared the strange story of the man playing the violin on the water. It made me smile. Knowing I'd nearly lost the gift sickened me. I returned the cross to my pocket.

When the cigarette embers drew down to the filter, I wasn't any calmer, but a wonderfully insane image had entered my mind, something raw and cruel, something that Cyrus could never have sculpted. The inspiration came from a maniacal fever, a fury I could not squash. A part of my mind arrived at an answer before I had formed the question. I had figured out a way to hurt Alex without I myself inflicting the pain.

I tossed my cigarette to the pavement, my breath steadier. I jogged the two miles to the house without another break.

-

Very late in the evening, I went to the mansion's garage and found a shovel. I laid it over my left shoulder and walked to the tree line to the west of Cyrus's home. There was no one there. It was cold and quiet, and after several minutes of prodding with the flashlight, I located the right spot on the ground and stomped the metal edge into the dirt.

I dug down again and again, until I was sweating in the cold. Finally, the hole was deep enough. The presence of the corpse tingled the nerves of my spine before I hit the bone.

Dropping the shovel, I bent low to the ground and brushed the soil from the cream skeleton as best I could. My fingertips slid over and between pearly teeth and rough ribs.

As with the rose, I tentatively pushed the warm sensation in the pit of my stomach down. A hot tickling sensation slid from my belly to my hands. The ground pulled it from my fingers.

I blinked.

The dog was alive again.

In the dirt was black and brown fur, muscle and tendon, beautiful sinews and corpuscles. There, a muzzle and wet nose. I sensed the stomach, spleen, colon, heart, lungs, and liver deep inside. He licked my hand, and I drew my right palm across his chest. Beneath his thick fur was the quick and sure beat of a refreshed heart.

"Shakespeare," I whispered, and the old but eerily familiar dog sat up. There were flecks of gray in his black and brown fur. His body looked haggard, but he was alive.

"You got anything left in you?" I asked, my breath visible in the cool night air. I looked at him, disappointed that I couldn't grant him youth. Though he was large, I picked him up and stroked his head. His brittle fur smelled of cold earth, and I pressed my nose deeply against his neck and breathed. "Yeah," I said, "you've got something left."

He sat beside me as I filled the grave, heaving hot breaths into the dark, and walked with me as I returned the shovel to the garage, as if he knew what he was there for and was ready.

When we entered the house, I carried him so that no one would hear his four-beat steps.

Alex had never really liked this dog.

I carted Shakespeare up the north stairway. When we reached the second floor, Alex's door was closed, his light off. I kissed Shakespeare on the head with pleasure in my dark heart and said, "Tonight is your night." He looked at me keenly and closed his mouth. He tilted his head and then leaned closer to me; he licked the side of my face. I kissed the side of his muzzle, breathed in his scent one more time, and set him down. He stood in the hallway quietly and stared at Alex's door, instinctive.

I gently twisted the cold metal handle, and it revolved silently. I pushed the door forward quickly enough so that the hinges didn't squeak. The room was black. Shakespeare padded into that darkness, and I shut Alex's door behind him.

I tip-toed to my own room soundlessly, quickly dressing for bed. When I threw the day's clothes, covered in dirt and sweat, into the laundry hamper, it arrived—the intense and frightening snarl of a dog, a young man's scream.

I leaned against the wall by my door, filled with the exhilaration that can only come from a secret, apposite retribution. Soon, several pairs of footsteps rushed down the hall—Cyrus, and a few men, I presumed—and then I left my room, playing my role, appearing quietly surprised and confused.

Cyrus opened the door. The screams were deafening. Blood pooled everywhere.

Alex's face revealed dark, deep marks. Ragged, horrific gashes slashed his neck and arm.

Cyrus fired his gun at Shakespeare and dropped the dog with a single shot.

His lips frozen in a snarl that looked rather like a grin, Shakespeare collapsed in a pool of his own blood.

Cyrus observed that dog for a long, long moment. At last, he helped his son staunch the bleeding.

CHAPTER 18—EVOLUTION
AGE: 17 YEARS OLD

THE FLAMES DIDN'T CATCH FOR a while. Little tendrils of fire started, stopped, started, stopped, until finally the fur was alight, like tiny matches. The yellow flames gathered in clumps and shifted to orange, orange to red, before Shakespeare's entire body was burning in huge twists of light.

Cyrus and I stood in the basement, staring into the furnace. His looming form was quiet and still beside me. His black coat was snug around him, buttoned. Large gray protective gloves stretched up to his elbows.

Moments before he had lifted Shakespeare's body, placed it on the grate, and slid it inside the coffin-like door to the furnace. Once the fur, skin, muscle, and bone caught, Cyrus remarked, "He won't return again."

The warm, flickering light on his skin contrasted with the cold, metallic color of his hair.

"How do you know?" I asked.

"I have experience." His voice was low and pensive. "With things that can and can't be brought back. The burned and the scattered cannot be resurrected."

That was good to know. My attention returned to the burning body.

"It might not have been Shakespeare," I said.

"It was."

There was no doubt or lilt in his voice, no need for reassurance.

After a lengthy pause, I speculated, "That wouldn't make sense unless Lutin had somehow...I don't know...snuck out of the basement, dug the dog up, brought him back to life, carried him to Alex's room, and then returned to his cell. It's impossible. I mean, unless Lutin's blood itself could bring something back to life. Maybe someone could have gone down to his room, drained him, and used that blood."

"It wasn't Lutin."

The heat flowing toward us from the furnace was suddenly unbearable. I blinked against it. "Who was it?" I asked, studying the scar on the back of my right hand, my heart thrumming hard in my ears, sweat beading along my left temple.

He was quiet. "Me."

I nearly choked. "What?"

"It was me."

He took a deep breath and leaned forward, his weight on the toes of his shoes. He clasped his hands together, the sound of his leather gloves sliding together above the *whoosh* of the furnace.

"Why would you think that?" I asked.

He shrugged. "I knew, at some point, I would become something more. That I would evolve beyond my humanness, like I am supposed to. When I was given the box, I believed it would be soon after that," he said, looking a bit haunted. "And now it has finally happened. I was angry with Alex. For choosing children who look like you. I must have done this... without realizing it."

Thrilled at the idea that Cyrus did not suspect me, I made sure to keep that thrill from my voice. I chose my next words very carefully. "Are you suggesting that you left the house, dug Shakespeare out of the earth, resurrected him, and placed him in Alex's room?"

"I don't have a memory of the event, but I might have...I might have done it, Jack." He clasped his hands together, his brooding eyes sending an uncharacteristic glance my way. "It is about time, after all, that *he* gave me something more. Perhaps this is it, and I simply can't remember—or can't control—what I'm doing. Maybe I'm possessed."

Pieces of Shakespeare dropped into the fire.

I'd decided to be brazen, no matter the consequences. But if Cyrus had discovered it was me, well…that would be the end. Resurrecting the dog was a stupid, immature decision, but I nevertheless made it. I had never imagined that Cyrus would blame himself, but he was doing just that. His focus was on himself, as always.

There was a good chance I was going to get away with it. I could, maybe, get away with more.

"There could, perhaps, be another explanation?" I said.

"No. There is no other explanation. I am beginning to ascend. To the other side of the veil."

His gaze met mine, hard and unyielding and certain.

"All right," I told him. "All right. You are…ascending."

He took a deep breath. "I need to better control my emotions. Please, allow me some time to digest what I should do with Alex regarding the girls. There are more important things happening."

He was using what had happened as a way of brushing me off, of not having to punish Alex. Even if he truly believed he was responsible for Shakespeare's resurrection, he was taking pleasure in it. He was delighted there might be evidence of his metamorphosis, not haunted. And he was simply using this moment as a way of saying Alex had suffered enough for now, as a way of placating me and my desire that he be punished.

"The culling will proceed in the meantime. It will occur tomorrow. I'll tell everyone to come to the house to celebrate my ascension. We can gather and toast."

I said nothing. I didn't want to push my luck.

We left the furnace and the basement together. Cyrus placed his hand on my back gently. "How lucky you are," he said, "to be here at the moment I advance. To be at ground zero. To witness the end of the old world and the beginning of the new."

I placed my arm around him; we ascended the stairs together, side by side, our strides in equal measures.

"Yes," I said. "I wouldn't have it any other way."

CHAPTER 19—VANISH
AGE: 17 YEARS OLD

IF I HADN'T BEEN so wary of Cyrus, I would have already murdered Alex.

While I'd slept, my so-called "brother" had sought girls who looked like me, planning to send little Jacks to their deaths. I was now determined I would not see any children die, whether by culling or bombing. An illogic captured me. I had to protect myself—all versions of myself.

The impromptu celebration for Cyrus's ascension began early evening the next day. As I approached the main hall, dressed in normal clothes, boisterous sounds and music filtered out toward me. The chatter of perhaps twenty individuals, then thirty, and then maybe a hundred, rolled down the hall.

Cyrus had decided it was only fitting to mark his ascension by hosting a masquerade—fitting, he said, for the metaphor of peeling off humanity's mask—on the same day that the culling would commence. Everyone would wear a costume except him.

Cyrus's followers filled the ballroom. The gargantuan powder-pink space always featured the spicy-sweet smell of wood, and now that aroma mixed with the heavy perfumes of the participants. The ballroom was filled with streamers and rose petals and dry ice. Masks were hung throughout the corridors, and a million smiling, false faces greeted me. Colors—cobalt, maroon, black, and clementine—exploded around me. The white rooms brimmed with boiling colors. I walked among women wearing ball gowns the color of pastel cupcakes, some in black and gray. Some wore slim, bright silk sheaths. The men dressed in red and black and bright white. Everyone wore masks. It was nearly impossible to guess who was whom.

Champagne flowed, and every room was filled with ice statues, fruit pyramids, candy bowls, and towering cakes. In every hall, music soared, but it did not seem as if anyone was listening to it. Rather, they were chuckling, guffawing, sighing their own symphonies. It was over the top, and I was astounded that everything around me could have been arranged in such a short period of time.

Cyrus perched like a hawk on the second-floor balcony that overlooked the ballroom, sipping a drink while he watched the crowd below. The red box sat behind him on an old oak table by the wall. I climbed the stairs.

The people below gathered, swayed, danced, and drank.

"Having a good time?" Cyrus asked, when I reached the top.

I shrugged.

"I know. Not your kind of entertainment."

The music changed to something in a minor key, soft, smooth. Cyrus handed me a mask, and I—unwillingly—put it on to appease him. He smiled. He talked to me like we were in his dining room, drinking coffee, smoking, as he explained our dark world.

"I want to be there. Tonight. When you cull the girls," I said to him as I looked down at the others below.

"Why?"

I shrugged. "I just want to see what the process looks like…from the other side."

He pressed his lips together and scanned the crowd below. "After my speech," he said. "Meet us in the smoking room."

"I'll be there."

I descended the steps slowly and weaved among the mingling individuals.

Someone clearing his throat and a bell rang. Then several bells. It was the sound of spoons tapping against crystal glasses filled with what appeared to be pink champagne.

The crowd quieted. People from the other areas of the house flowed into the ballroom.

"Ladies and gentlemen," Cyrus called from the balcony. "Thank you so much for joining me on this glorious evening so I may share my ascension with all of you."

A few hands clapped before the entire group joined in. The sound was muffled by evening gloves, and most people were also holding glasses, but soon the percussive applause echoed around the chamber.

When the clapping slackened, Cyrus spoke again.

"I started my life like most of you. I was lost and frightened. I was exceedingly unhappy. My wife had left me. I was penniless. I had no family to speak of, no one to call on to guide me. Until the day *he* arrived, the man who made everything make sense. He goes by many names, but they don't matter right here, right now. What matters is that what he has given me I can hand down to you.

"I have brought each of you in to *heal* you. Everyone remembers. Darla," he pointed toward a woman, "you lost your job. You had nowhere to turn." The blond woman nodded. "Samuel, you hadn't eaten in, what? Two days?"

"Three," Samuel said.

"And Kay, I gave you a home away from home. Away from the husband who abused you."

The woman who had been at the commune with the children stood in the back of the room. She smiled, her eyes still remote, her smile too wide, like it was glued in place.

"I came to heal all of you," Cyrus said. "And I did. I never let you go. You are my flock, and I am your shepherd. We have traveled a great distance together, and you have aided me as much as I have aided you. I put my trust in you, and you have never failed me."

A murmur of assent swelled. I looked around at all of them, never unsurprised at how moved others were by my mentor. Cyrus descended upon them in times of great duress or pressure. He'd waited until life itself beat them down, left them open to his will, and then he *took* them in.

"Tonight, I am going to heal you again. Take a look at the glasses you hold. When you toast to my ascension, you swallow the blood of one beyond the veil. It will heal your bodies, as well as your spirits. Drink with me and heal yourselves. Drink with me and know that I will always be there for you. I once swore I would never heal another again. The ban is lifted. It is time for communion, faith, and celebration."

Excited gasps erupted, and everyone raised their glasses to their lips, wide-eyed, watching the liquid go down.

As people chugged the fluid, total silence reigned. They closed their eyes, pressed their glasses to their chests, and swayed. The ballroom floor was filled with silent, swooning people. The lines on the woman's face nearest me softened. The man next to her smiled; his dry, pale lips became moistened and pink. Bruises disappeared, spines straightened, and eyes glittered. Lips were parted in silent ecstasy.

"Let me heal you," Cyrus called in a sing-song rhythm. "Let me wash away your pain. Let me eradicate your misery. Let me *heal* you."

He shifted into an entirely different man as he surveyed them, sang to them. This Cyrus would never think of harming a child, let alone poisoning one, or sending hundreds to their deaths.

As the audience swayed to the sound of his voice, I walked to one of the carts holding several drinks.

"Let me fulfill you. Let me bring you the happiness you once thought was lost." He seemed right beside me.

I picked up one of the glasses. The drink was redder at the bottom than at the top. I sniffed. It was indeed champagne. It had been spiked with blood, though... Lutin's. Bitterness, far more than I had expected, flooded my chest. My grip tightened, and the glass cracked. Gently, I set it back down.

The crowd raised their hands toward the man wearing no mask, pressed closer to the balcony overlooking the room.

A rising cloud of whispers sounded. "Heal me. Heal us."

I left.

-

I waited beside the smoking room with its ruby floors, the ceiling painted with angels, until Cyrus arrived. I attempted to rid myself of the needy energy in the ballroom. I straightened and nodded to him kindly, pretending I thought as highly of him as everyone else did, and then I followed him through the doors.

Three girls sat inside in three velvet chairs, side by side, their long hair perfectly brushed, their dresses without a single crease. They appeared about seven years old. Two of them had dark brown hair. The other was a silvery blonde. Their eyes were abnormally large. One girl's nose curved up into a point. Another's cheeks revealed dimples. None showed any sign that they knew what was about to occur. Then again, how could they?

A few lights in the corners dimly lit the room, and Cyrus's and Alex's forms were coated in shadows. A few others hovered over the buffet in the corner. Two men with brown hair were spooning something from the dark mahogany buffet onto three square silver plates.

I struck a match to light my cigarette and inadvertently breathed in the sulfur, stinging my nostrils. I pressed my hand to the bridge of my nose, where the pain was greatest. My eyes watered. Through the shimmery film, Cyrus approach the girls.

"What are your names?" he asked them.

One by one, they said, starting with the girl closest to Cyrus—Donna, Maranatha, Sybil.

"And what have your parents told you about me?"

The three girls looked at each other and shrank back, evidently embarrassed under his intense gaze. None answered.

"That's all right," he said soothingly, and he patted the leg of the closest girl. "The only important thing now is that you are here. Today, we are going to decide if all three of you will stay."

His words were so familiar, so calming.

"If so, I will become like your father, Alex and Jack your siblings. And you will be wholly welcomed into this family."

Alex strode over to the buffet, where three silver plates waited on a tray. He swiveled around and carried the tray to the three girls. He kneeled and offered each girl a plate, which contained a ring of white berries with black dots.

"Just choose *one* berry to eat," Cyrus said.

The three girls looked at one another briefly, and then their little pink fingers grasped random berries. They lifted the fruit to their mouths and chomped down.

I took a heavy drag on my cigarette.

Alex disposed of the rest of the fruit into a barrel at the buffet. Then he approached me. I stiffened as he neared; a desire to strike him on the bridge of his nose and strangle him nearly overpowered me. It took all my restraint to stay still.

"Feeling nostalgic?" he asked.

I didn't respond.

After a moment, he plucked the cigarette from my hand and took a long, hard drag. He handed it back to me. I put it out in a nearby ashtray.

He smiled and whispered, "So, tell me. How did you feel when you visited the commune? What was it like when you figured it out? Part of me wanted to walk in there with you, see your reaction, but I thought it best to leave you to it." He pulled away. "Are you ready to admit that I am the winner of this round?"

I gazed at him and said nothing.

"Not going to answer?" He smiled. "That's fine. I have all the time in the world. I think Cyrus is more impressed by my stunt than anything else." He turned toward the three girls and waved at them. "Do you think any of them will survive?"

"No."

He smiled. "I don't think so either." He breathed deeply. "Look at them. They believe they are safe when they are not. That's always thrilling."

I chewed the side of my lip. "Kind of like when you thought you were safely asleep in your room, before Shakespeare appeared suddenly? 'Thrilling' like that?"

Alex froze. He looked like he had just been chewing and had slipped and bitten his tongue.

"Careful, Jack. I might be the next to transcend," he said. He walked away.

None of the girls survived. They dropped to the velvet floor, caught in a deep and fatal sleep. Cyrus checked their pulses, checked them several times, until he was certain.

"Better luck next time," Alex said to me as he headed toward the door.

Later, as Cyrus, Alex, and I stood in the woods that night and watched several hefty men shovel through the dirt, the bodies nearby, I asked Cyrus, "Are girls always brought to you?"

"Usually."

I had thought that might be the case. "And when I passed the culling, were nine of those berries doll's eyes?"

"Yes."

"If it had been Alex, would the ratio have been the same?"

Cyrus blinked. "I don't understand what you mean," he said. The way he looked at me told me he did know what I meant, but he wanted me to drop it.

"You do your best," I said, "to stack the odds. Nine to one. But you don't do that with everyone. That's how Alex got away with finding those girls. I wonder what else he's gotten away with."

Cyrus stood there silently. At last, he left.

-

At three in the morning, after the others had gone to bed and only the wind could be heard wailing against the windows, I lay in my sheets, full of burning rage. The children in the barn were me. The girls in the smoking room who chose the wrong berries were me. Cyrus's system killed me everywhere I turned. That truth poked at the already plump pocket of rage inside, until, finally, the pocket burst.

I got out of bed.

I slunk through the dark, shadowed halls, the marble cooling my feet, before I reached the door. Out in the night, wisps of chilly air licked my skin like metal tongues. Barefoot on the grass, I festered over Cyrus's self-centeredness and coldness, but the breeze washed him away. It was just me and the grass, me and the dirt, me and the night.

I arrived at the place, a quarter of a mile into the forest behind Cyrus's home, where the girls had been buried. He and the following, for once, were hardly a speck in a distant universe.

One of the men had left his shovel leaning against the mansion near the front door, and I had grabbed its gritty handle before trudging alone to the shallow graves. I braced myself, popped my neck, and pitched the shovel into the earth with little resistance. The dirt was as soft as cake; the single grave had been dug just a few hours before. Less than six feet deep, the bodies were revealed in a couple of hours. I freed all three of them.

The girls' cloudy pupils watched me, looking like old film frames stuck in a projector, beginning to burn away in the golden moonlight. The dirt that powdered their clothes glittered like black snow, hematite, or ebon spinel. It was all over my hands and their faces. It littered my clothes.

I dropped the shovel and jumped into the shallow grave. I crouched and crawled forward, taking a deep breath. I touched one of the girls' cold faces.

The first tendril of that warm, inviting, tingling sensation coursed through me, and the eyes of the first dead girl focused, her pupils narrowing, and turned toward my hand. She had no pulse or warmth or any other sign of life, but her corpse knew that I wasn't just any person capable of just anything. It knew I was there for it.

Something beyond that time, that place, filled me. What I was about to do I truly wanted. Resurrection called to me deeply. I desired to complete the circle, like the first time with Roland; it had always been part of me. I imagined digging up all the people I had ever killed and filling them with life. One by one, I pictured their compressed bodies as plump, though these bodies were quite unreachable.

I moved my hand around the first girl's face. Her dead eyes followed me. Tiring of the trick, I refocused on the cool night air, the moist earth, and the task at hand. I gingerly closed her eyelids with my fingers. One of the three pieces of cloth in my pocket I tied into a makeshift blindfold for her. I touched her cheek.

I released the warm power in my stomach and brought her to life. She twitched, her mouth parted, and a deep, rattling breath escaped. I told her to sit there, not to remove the blindfold, so that I could help the others.

I blindfolded each of the other two young girls, and then I brought them back to life.

Their limbs trembled, but they were as supple and alive as before Cyrus culled them. They said they had no knowledge of what they were doing there, on Cyrus's property, covered in cold moist earth. That was a blessing.

They sat quietly as I refilled the shallow grave, not packing the dirt.

One of the girls asked if I would take her back to her parents. I had no intention of returning her to them. I responded I was going to take her somewhere safe, that she should not say anything else because sound traveled surprisingly far on a quiet night.

Finished, I laid the shovel over my shoulder. I told the girls to take each other's hands. Silently I led them, still blindfolded, back to Cyrus's garage. I was glad to see that the overhead door was open. I replaced the shovel where I had found it.

I had the key to the Lexus, and I opened the car doors quickly and silently and helped the girls into the backseat.

The wheels compacted the gravel in the driveway, and then we were on the road. The closest fire station was seven miles away. I chewed my lips, urging the miles and minutes to pass more quickly.

"Who are you? Where are we going?" one of the girls asked. When I didn't answer, she demanded, "Are you kidnapping us?" Her voice trembled.

Before I could reply, the middle girl said, "She's not kidnapping us, *obviously*. She's an angel. Aren't you? That's why you won't let us see you."

I looked at her in the rearview mirror, noted her tiny bones, her frailty, her humanness.

"I'm not anything," I told her.

There were no such things as angels. There was only Cyrus, those who followed him, and those who snuck around him. Everything was a backward dealing. As for good works—they were dangerous and impossible.

Yet I was doing the impossible.

"It's okay," the girl said. "I'll keep your secret."

I smirked, despite myself. "Thanks."

When I reached the fire station, I dropped them off in the parking lot. One of them—Maranatha—reached toward me, trying to hug me, and I indulged her for a moment before pushing her away. I quickly climbed back into the car. They removed their blindfolds and walked toward the doors. I took a right, leaving them behind.

Then I did something no angel would do.

I found the parents of those girls, and I killed them.

I did not just want to resurrect all the mutilated dogs in all the world and unleash them upon their monstrous masters. I did not just want to resurrect dead children and lead them far away from poisonous berries. I wanted to *be* one of the mutts, I wanted to *be* one of the youths that took the masters down. I would unite with those in their second life.

If I had been good, truly good, how could justice have been done?

Drip.

Drip.

Drip.

That's how it rang that night—the bell of liberation.

CHAPTER 20—FERRIC
AGE: 17 YEARS OLD

AFTER MY VENGEANCE ON THE resurrected girls' parents, I carefully parked Cyrus's car in the garage and turned off the engine. With a deep breath, I stared at the garage wall, the tools hanging on nails. As the engine ticked and cooled, except for the crickets, the night was eerily quiet.

I opened the car door, stepped out onto the dark gray cement, shut the door, and locked the car. I peered out into the night, into the woods where I had just been, and watched the fog roll in. Little tufts, like loosely woven cotton, swirled through the trees. When it broke through the perimeter of the forest, the fog splashed down the hill in a silent wave, altering the surrounding appearance and atmosphere. I bit my bottom lip. When everything was misty and glowing, I turned from the fog, made my way into the house, and headed toward the kitchen. There, I gathered fixings from the refrigerator and cupboards to make two turkey sandwiches. I retrieved a few other items. When my collection was complete, I crept to the basement. Key card once again in hand, the backpack on my shoulder containing everything I'd thought to bring, I swiped the card through the black slot, listened to the large metal door click, and opened it. I entered the brick hallway and stopped beside Lutin's door. After steadying myself for several moments, I knocked. "Can I come in?"

For several seconds, there was no response. Then, something metallic clicked, echoing through the red brick corridor. The door opened wide. Warm air fell upon me like a wolf's breath. This basement room emitted no damp scent, nor was it cold. It did not feel like a basement at all.

The man I had come to see sat in the lone worn chair, in front of the fireplace, a blanket pulled just above his stomach.

I took a few steps inside, and the door shut behind me on its own. I didn't jump.

Lutin turned to face me. His coal-black eyes, the dark shadows in his face, his black hair, and the vibrant glowing branches gleaming through his chest and arms were beautiful.

"Well, look who has returned," he said, his voice soft, weak, unwell. He had overtaken me in an instant the last time I had visited him. He could likely do so again, but his drawn, fevered face made him look sickly and in need of a warm bed.

I dropped the backpack from my shoulder onto the floor. "I don't know if you eat, but I brought two turkey sandwiches, water, and a bottle of wine for you, if you would like them."

He sat motionless. His mouth parted.

I sighed, figuring my preparations had been pointless. "Do you not eat?"

"I do. I'll take it." He rose from his seat quickly, and the blanket dropped to the floor. He approached, his wide eyes fixed on the backpack. He was practically salivating.

"How long has it been since you've eaten?" I asked.

"One month."

I looked at him, shocked.

"Cyrus does what he can to keep me weak."

We both knelt, and I withdrew both sandwiches and handed them to him. He ripped into the first one greedily with giant bites. He finished the first sandwich before I could get the wine open, and then he guzzled the water. Glittering drops fell from the corners of his lips.

After opening the wine, I sat against the door and smoked while I watched him.

He ate like a boy, careless about making a mess, and he rushed through the second sandwich as quickly as the first. When he finally finished, he released an audible sigh and breathed deeply. He placed his hands behind himself, rested against them, and closed his black eyes. The bright lines along his body burned brighter.

"You know why I'm down here," I said.

He nodded, wiped the crumbs from his dark lips. "I know."

"Then I'd rather not say anything more about that than we need to. Something in this house keeps an eye and ear on everything, and I'm not ready to make specific decisions."

Lutin nodded.

"But I do want to know what...and *who* you are. How did you come to be trapped here?"

"How much time do you have?"

"Let's keep it short."

He swallowed. "There are many names for what I am. *Noir étoile*. Fear séanadh. Blazing man. Ferric."

"Ferric," I repeated. "And what do you do, exactly?"

"I unstrip the drained items of the world. The humans and animals and objects that are emptied. I fill them in, again."

I waited for him to explain.

"For instance," he said, "Cyrus's red box strips objects and men and animals. Do you know how the brick turns white? When Cyrus and Alex bring the box here and chip away at me?"

"Yes."

"When the box opens, you see the material for what it is. What you are seeing is the stripping of the illusion. Color is merely light reflecting and absorbing in different ratios. It is not real. Color is an illusion, and in the face of the red case, illusion is stripped. Like all things are stripped."

"All right," I said.

"I unstrip them. That is who I am. I bring everything back. I fill in the lacks, the gaps, and I coat the world in the fantasy that keeps life livable. I return positive illusions to the world. The things that make this dark place a tad brighter."

I looked up at the ceiling. "I'd say you're falling down on the job."

He smirked. "I apologize."

"How did you end up here?"

"I am here because there is one other job that I and others like me do, and I failed. We kill men like Cyrus, and we destroy their tools of power. Sometimes, destruction is the only way to fill in the gaps and the lacks.

"One night, years ago, I and four others came here to do what we had done thousands of times before—destroy a box that has no place in this world."

"What happened?"

He shook his head, looked at the ceiling. "Cyrus is a special one. You really were, believe it or not, raised by one of the best."

"I believe it."

"He made a habit of sleeping with the box open. I have never in my thousand years encountered anyone who could do that. He knew, somehow, maybe unconsciously, that we were coming. And he made the appropriate preparations, took the appropriate risk. To sleep with that thing open, though..." Lutin winced. "Have you ever witnessed it?"

I shook my head.

"You will never see anything more frightening. Cyrus was relaxed with it, at home with it. I had never seen a man like that before."

He paused, slowly sliding his tongue across his bottom lip. "As soon as we walked into his bedroom, the other four were dead, and I almost was. It knocked me out. I woke in this room. For a reason I could not comprehend at the time, Cyrus kept me alive. He kept me down here, spoke to me as I slowly recovered, and then he waited until he knew it was safe to cut me down again, and again, and again. After the first couple of weeks, it all came clear to me.

"That box performs two tasks: it protects, and it reports. To do so requires a certain fuel, the soul of men and women. When it fed on the souls of my four brothers, its power grew incomprehensibly, and I became trapped here, beneath its invisible shroud, bits of me fed to it every week, keeping it strong.

"There was a time when I hoped another group of us would arrive and save us, but I have come to understand that in my weakness, and in its strength, the box has been able to hide me from my own kind."

He brought the wine bottle to his lips and drank heavily. Without a breath, he emptied the bottle and set it on the brick floor. I wondered if wine was like water to him, simply for quenching his thirst. He wasn't the least drunk.

I leaned forward, a cigarette poised midair. "I have just one question."

His black, almost holographic eyes flicked to me.

"Where do you think your four brothers are?"

"I don't know."

"You can't feel them here?" I said. "Do you think their bodies have been burned?"

"They cannot be burned."

I paused for a moment, wondering over that.

"Our bodies cannot be destroyed by any earthly tool."

I did not dare say what I was thinking, in case it gave him too much hope, but it was obvious to me where in the house his brothers might be.

I was picturing the room that was the farthest from him, here in the far east corner. The room I was thinking of was in the west, on the second floor, just beneath the library. I considered the clang of metal books. I thought of the ironic key card location. It had occurred to me years before that the pretend shelves with pretend novels might be the gateway to a room—a room holding something terribly important to Cyrus.

Before becoming too entranced by these thoughts, I brought myself back to the present, storing them away for later.

"Well," I said, "sounds like you're one lucky bastard, surviving, unlike the others." I inhaled deeply on my cigarette and leaned back against the wall.

"Right. I have been so lucky."

I gazed around the dingy basement room, without any windows, only a fireplace, a chair, and a door. He had lived here for more than a decade and had remained sane. "I'll find them," I said.

"Perhaps you will," Lutin replied. "But I wonder what the use of that is, when there are eyes watching and ears listening to you and your intentions. And there is a box you cannot race to the finish line. It will always be at the end before you begin to run. It is built to be.

"If you persist with this, at some point, it will name you. Cyrus will know."

I smiled at him and winked. "You would be surprised what a child of Cyrus's can come up with. I wouldn't have come today unless I thought there was a second option."

He didn't reply, and I wondered if he remained silent out of faith, doubt, or despair.

"Didn't you give me the power to resurrect in hope that I could find their bodies and return them to save you?"

He shook his head; the denial was genuine. "I gave you that power to awaken and aid you, to fill in something you desperately lacked, to allow you to realize there are others who will help you."

I lifted my eyebrows. "And with no intention of me, in return, aiding you?"

He smiled. "I never believed this would end happily. I simply wanted to help you before the final blow, before I was gone. I allowed you to experience something beyond all this monstrosity."

"Yes," I admitted. "You did…that."

"You're welcome."

I glanced at my phone and then looked back at him.

"Time for you to go," he said.

I nodded slowly.

"Here." He pulled something from his pocket and slid it across the brick floor to me. I recognized it immediately. It was my knife—the one he had used to cut into me and share his gift of resurrection. He had sent it into the burning fireplace. It smelled of soot and blood.

I ran a finger across a charred section of the blade. "Thank you for returning what is rightfully mine."

"Any time," he said. "Wouldn't want Cyrus to find it down here."

I paused, gazing into his eyes and then at his beautiful, ethereal body one more time before I stood. I gathered the remnants of what I'd brought and placed them in my backpack. "All those years ago, why did you have to burn that rose? We could have spoken sooner. Things could have been different. More efficient. You frightened me when you did that."

His eyes narrowed. "Why did you have to save Cyrus from Havinger?" he countered. "You frightened me when you did that."

I stared at him. He had a point. "We have to move beyond our fears," I said, staring at the cement floor, seeing the young girl's face again, the one whom Alex had given my necklace. "Because there's more on the line now. Cyrus has collected children—I don't know how many. Hundreds, near a thousand maybe—and they're going to be carrying bombs for him in a few nights so he can 'ascend.'"

The information made no impression in him, and that deepened the sinking sensation in the pit of my stomach.

"Everyone knew but me, huh?"

Slowly, carefully, Lutin said, "I have known for about a year. Cyrus likes to taunt me with the things I cannot stop."

I bit my lip, ripped a piece of dead skin off, and chewed. I stood straighter. "Those children are not going to die. No bombs are going to explode." Before he could reply, I left.

CHAPTER 21—AGREE
AGE: 17 YEARS OLD

THE NEXT MORNING, ROLAND RETURNED after completing his unnamed task at one of the northern communes. His face appeared worn, his energy radiated tiredness. His clothes were wrinkled, and he was hunched over. When he closed the front door, bag in hand, and discovered I was sitting in the living room, he smiled kindly. The lines in his face had deepened, and he had paled. I smiled back and nodded. He turned away slowly, like an old man, and went up the stairs. I let him alone for several hours, gathering my thoughts and letting him decompress, but I needed to speak with him as soon as possible. We were on the verge of Cyrus's "day of ascension," and what I had in mind would be impossible without Roland.

About midday, I visited him in the armory, where he was alone, sharpening a knife. Sparks flew as he pressed the metal against the grinding wheel. A loud ring reverberated throughout the room. Some of the sparks landed on his clothes, threatening to set them on fire, but he didn't flinch. He sharpened several knives before I approached and tapped his arm. He stopped and looked up at me.

"What?"

I shook my head. "It looks like you've learned just about as many things as I have over the past few days."

Roland frowned and set the knife down on the workbench and removed his gloves. "So you understand everything now, hm? Cyrus told you how it works?"

"Yes. How were things up north?"

"I don't want to think about it."

I leaned in very close and whispered. "We need to talk. But not here." He eyed me carefully.

"Outside?" he asked.

"Yes."

A few minutes later, we were outdoors, alone together, near the woods' edge. I nipped my lip a bit too hard and settled my hands into the satin-lined pockets of my coat. I wasn't confident about how he would react to what I had to say, but I had to say it.

The only way a person *wouldn't* question Cyrus was if they were blind or nuts. Roland was neither. He did not look at Cyrus as a savior, nor did he regard anything having to do with the following with passion. He was there; he participated, but I suspected he did not want to.

"Cyrus is insane."

The uncharacteristically bright fall sunlight lit Roland's face. His expression never shifted as he studied me, confirming I meant what I said.

"Yes," he finally responded.

I pulled my hands from the warm pockets and pressed my fingertips together. "I believe I have a potential solution to our mutual problem."

His gaze circled the empty land around us. "That's a dangerous thing to discuss, as you well know."

"Yes. But...my idea only requires one discussion. And then..." I sliced the air with my hands, "it will be the end. If we walk into that forest, and I tell you what I have been thinking, all of this is gone."

Roland was silent for a long while. He was thinking something. "You feel...*certain* you have a solution? You *want* a solution?" His voice lilted, sounding skeptical.

"I do."

"Nobody has ever proposed a solution and lived, what with that box upstairs."

"I know," I said. "And it may be hard to believe, but I've been considering that problem, too."

Roland's kind gaze narrowed, and he lifted an eyebrow.

I walked ahead to the line of trees and glanced back, inviting him to follow. Slowly, surely, he did. "Only because you're you, Jack," he said. "Only because you're you."

We walked for maybe a mile, past a few small streams and hundreds of bare trees, before I stopped by a large moss-covered stump that looked aged.

Roland pulled his jacket snug around his thin frame. He settled onto an overturned tree trunk. "All right, tell me. What is your solution?"

"First, I need to know about the bookshelf in Cyrus's office."

Roland did not blink or move. He remained unearthly still, like a living statue, before he took a deep breath that reminded me how tired he had appeared when he arrived home. "I can't tell you about that."

"I already know what's behind it. Or, rather, who."

He blinked and cocked his head. "What?"

"I *know*, Roland. I just need to know how it works. The books are metal. When they come out, they don't go back in. It's some kind of mechanism, isn't it? How does it work?"

A few words low and sketchy emitted from his throat.

"How does it work?" I repeated.

He sighed and threw his hands in the air before he succumbed to the question. "It's like a password or a combination. Only one of the books opens the mechanism. The others lock it for about..."

"Two hours," I said, considering.

Slowly he nodded, clearly surprised.

"Which book opens it?"

"I don't know. I've never known. No one does but Cyrus."

I was distraught, but I'd expected that answer. "It may not matter."

"What, exactly, may not matter?"

"About three days ago, I went down to the basement to find out what I could about Lutin. I was jealous that Cyrus trusted Alex with him, and I wanted to see the monster myself."

"Oh, Lord, Jack," Roland said, turning away and putting a hand on the crown of his head. "Are you insane?"

"Wait," I replied. "Lutin gave me...something while I was there. A kind of power."

"What are you talking about?"

"He cut me open, placed something in me—it was as though I had never been stabbed. Roland...I can resurrect the dead now."

Roland's eyebrows arched in a deep V.

"The dog that attacked Alex? I'm sure you heard about it..."

"Cyrus told me."

"It *was* Shakespeare. But it wasn't evidence of Cyrus ascending. *I* brought Shakespeare back from the dead."

"That was...*you*?"

"Yes."

He shook his head vehemently. "No, no, no. Oh, Jack, no."

"I knew you wouldn't believe me, so..." I placed my hand on the dead tree beside us, releasing that familiar warm tickling sensation. The bark vibrated briefly; in a matter of seconds, a full, green tree rose beside us.

Roland's eyes flicked left and right as he trembled. His mouth parted.

"I resurrected three girls who were culled last night," I confessed. "Sacrificed. This is why I'm asking you about the bookshelf where the other...étoiles *noires* are. I'm planning to bring them back. I can do it. And the only reason I haven't already is the same reason you have not attempted to kill Cyrus all these years. You and I both know that with the very first step I take to resurrect those four ferrics, the box will name me. It would name you, if you were to reach for a weapon to eliminate him."

He plucked a leaf from the tree and smelled it.

"But I've figured out a way we can work around this problem, if we work together."

The robust tree fascinated him. "Tell me."

While I explained my plan, he folded his arms and leaned against the fresh, clean bark.

I asked him what he thought, and he closed his eyes for a long moment. When he opened them again, he nodded. "That should work."

We hugged twice and walked back toward the house in complete silence, the only sound our footsteps and the bright red birds chirping overhead.

Before we reached the house, Roland said, "I'll do it tomorrow."

Despite my best efforts, tears came to me. Roland frowned and wiped one of them away.

"It will work," he said. "I have faith it will work."

I winced. "I do, too."

CHAPTER 22—GONE
AGE: 17 YEARS OLD

THE NEXT DAY, I SAT in my room, trying to read a book and failing. Inevitably, Cyrus arrived, just as I had expected. He knocked, and a lump formed in my throat.

Outside my bedroom door, Cyrus announced, "Jack, I need to speak to you."

Forcing myself to breathe normally, I rose from my bed and straightened my shirt and hair. I walked to the door, swallowed, and opened it. Cyrus stood in the hallway, his hair glinting brilliantly. "Please follow me downstairs," he said.

Involuntarily, I shivered and hoped he hadn't noticed. "All right…"

We walked through the living room on the first floor and didn't stop there. We strode to the basement door.

The hinge creaked as he pulled the white door wide open. He beckoned me. "After you."

I thought of Roland and of our plan. A sense of fear, and also resignation, washed over me. Glancing down the stairs, I asked, "What's this about?"

"Please," Cyrus said, unsmiling, pointing.

I descended, and he followed. His energy was like bottled lightning. When we reached the landing, he took the lead. To my relief, he did not choose the hallway to the left. Instead, he led me straight ahead, past several doors, to an open one on the right, revealing on an empty red brick room. He waved toward the room, his hand wide. I stood at the threshold, hesitant.

I feared that he was leading me down there to trap me, just like Lutin. Had he found out about my power, what I'd done? Was he was leading me to my own prison?

"Please," he said, the word sharp.

I swallowed, took a deep breath, and remembered what Roland had said about having faith in our plan. Tentatively, I entered. Cyrus followed. He shut the door behind himself. It was just us and the silence.

He stared at me pointedly. Heat spread from the back of my neck to my face. I ignored it. He was watching me for a sign that I knew something, more than I was letting on, a sign that I understood why he had led me down to the basement. Perhaps he didn't find one; before I could ask him what we were doing down there, he spoke.

"I received another name from the box this afternoon."

"Oh?" My heart roared in my ears like fat rain pounding against metal. "Who?"

As soon as Cyrus revealed the name on the stone, I would counter that the box was a liar, was wrong. I would suggest he test it. I would ask if he had ever tested it, ever tried to ascertain whether or not it was delivering the truth.

"Before we get to that," Cyrus said, "I want to know if you know who it might be. If anyone, any person at all, has expressed doubts to you. If maybe you *shared* doubts about me with someone."

"No," I responded, immediately, certainly. In the back of my mind, though, a sudden and irrational fear that perhaps Roland had betrayed me flashed.

"Are you sure? Maybe you have doubts about my right to ascend? About whether I deserve to gain the power I'm gaining?"

"No, never."

"Or perhaps about the culling."

"No."

He cleared his throat. "The name the box delivered to me was Roland's."

There. It was out. He said it so quickly that I stood for a moment in legitimate shock.

"That can't be right."

"The box is never wrong, and it has given me Roland's name."

I laughed, the sound dripping with disbelief. "It must be wrong. It has to be."

Cyrus's jaw muscles revealed themselves as solid lines at the perimeter of his face. "Never."

"Okay. Well, you're certainly not thinking of actually killing Roland, are you? I mean, you can talk with him, ask him what's going on—why his name was written on one of the stones."

Cyrus shook his head once to the left, once to the right. "That's not how this works. I won't be doing that."

I stepped closer. "You're not seriously considering..."

He looked at his phone briefly, checking the time. "Yes."

I stepped toward him, but he held his hand up. "Don't." One word. "I knew it would be hard for you. That is why you will wait down here until it's finished."

"*What*? That *man* has lived his *life* for you! He has done every single thing you've asked. How could you...kill him without questioning the box? Have you ever tested it?" I swallowed. "Have you ever waited to see if it showed the future? Or just revealed what it wanted to show?"

Cyrus frowned. "The box is truth. It has never been wrong, and doubting it is blasphemy."

"How could you possibly know that?!" I asked. "I mean, you could at least show him some mercy," I sputtered. "F-find out why he has decided what he's decided, if he has actually decided it. Or...or let him go. You could just let him go! This one time."

"No. I've never suffered a traitor to leave me. And I don't particularly care why it happened. Only that it did."

"But..."

He raised his hand again, cutting me off.

"You don't realize how he has changed, Jack. He has been changing for many years. He is not the same Roland you once knew. You will stay here, until it's over. I'll make it quick. He'll never feel a thing."

"But this is Roland!" I yelled, and my words boomed in the small chamber.

"It's hard on me, too," he said kindly, even though there wasn't a kind bone in his body.

Before I could blink, he opened the door, slipped out, gently closed it. I slammed my hand on the door right as it locked. I desperately jerked the handle, but it refused to move.

"Cyrus! Come back here!" I screamed. His footsteps became distant, and then nothing.

I paced the room and took deep breaths. If he killed Roland, I could just return him. Just like with Shakespeare and the children. What's done can be undone. Nothing is cemented. All is erasable.

I thought of Roland and wished I could be there, could hold his hand, as though we all were in that basement room again.

Even though I wasn't the one killing him.

And Cyrus wasn't the one promising to bring him back.

-

Time passed, enough that my stomach growled, and still no Cyrus.

Lutin was in a room far from me. There was no speaking to him or anyone.

I laid down on the floor and listened hard for any sounds from above. I promised myself that things were not so bad; I could resurrect anyone or anything. Even if Cyrus had delivered Roland's name to the box, I could bring him back to life. All was fixable. Yes, all was mendable.

Eventually, the click of the latch turning got my attention, and I stood quickly, brushed the brick dust from the back of my coat. Cyrus stepped into the room, and I asked, "Did you do it?"

"Yes."

I gritted my teeth and lifted my chin. "Fuck you."

He reached me quickly and silently, his nose nearly touching mine. "Careful," he warned. "Do not say anything you will regret. You feel betrayed now, but when you are older, you'll understand."

I shook my head and walked around him. "Where is he? Where did you put him?" I asked as I stepped beyond the threshold of the door. "I want to see him."

Cyrus beckoned me toward him, and I refused. He finally came to me in the hallway, and he hugged me. I tried to push him off, but he held me close.

"I know this is hard for you."

"*You've never known* how hard anything is for me!"

"Shh..."

Tears welled. "Where is his body?" I whispered. A tear dripped from my cheek onto the shoulder of Cyrus's jacket. "I want to see him. Where is he?"

"There is no body. We took him down to the furnace."

I tried to swallow but could not. I jerked back. "What?!"

"Jack, calm down."

A hot, panicked fury expanded in my chest. "You couldn't let me see him? You couldn't let me...let me..." The world suddenly unraveled around me. There was no point in finishing my sentence. He had just told me there was no body. Without a body, there was no Roland for me to return.

It was impossible. Absolutely impossible. Roland had come back to life so many times, he was veritably invincible. Yet there stood Cyrus making sure Roland would never defy death again.

I pushed him backward, hard. I turned from him and flew past the basement rooms, up the stairs, and beyond the floor.

Cyrus called after me, but it was pointless. Everything was. There had gone my plan, and Roland with it.

CHAPTER 23—MARGARET
AGE: 17 YEARS OLD

DISORIENTED AND NUMB, I ABANDONED Cyrus's mansion. I could barely understand where I was or what I was doing. I had no thoughts. I was... blank.

As I drove through town, I had no sense of ever having been there before. The street signs all looked unfamiliar, the buildings were alien, and there was no sound.

I stopped in a graveyard far from the rest of the town, thousands of graves shaded by hundreds of trees. I'd visited this place many times. I usually went there for the scent of the cherry blossoms and to watch the cottonwood puffs that drifted like snow in the night.

I walked through the graves numbly. When I found an empty tomb, I sat on the edge, facing a stone angel.

From my inner jacket pocket, I retrieved the only medicine I knew how to administer when the world was collapsing. In my hands was the familiar black case. I opened it. Inside was a syringe, lighter, spoon, vial, tourniquet, cotton. I boiled the contents of the vial, pulled it up into the needle, pressed it into my body, and went down, down, down, far away from the alien town and Cyrus and Roland and Alex. I did not think of them at all. I said good-bye to murder and resurrection and anything else resembling the life I knew. The syringe slipped out of my hand, into the tomb. I reached for it and lost my balance, dropping inside. Sharp pain burned my shoulder and hip. Lying there, too dazed to move, I accepted that was where I would stay. I stretched out on the blanket of cottonwood seeds.

The moon shined down on me. In front of it, movement. The stone angel's face appeared, faintly luminescent. She bent down, clasped the ledge with her hands, her hair transformed from stone to silver threads, her eyes a bejeweled green instead of sparkling white sand. Her pinky lifted, then the rest of her hand. She held it out to me inquisitively.

"What are you?" she asked. I wanted to tell her my name, but the drugs took over, and I passed out, dreaming that I was in a catacomb, not a tomb, and there were hundreds of me in the vaults.

I did not wake for a long, long time.

-

"A vampire! Wouldn't that be wonderful? Finally caught one in the cemetery! We can come back at night and take it home."

"How ridiculous!"

"Indeed. I've been needing a pet. A vampire would fit the bill perfectly." Laughter followed.

Three voices? Four voices? I couldn't tell. There were too many giggles. I moved slightly, trying to figure out where I was. Everything hurt, and my joints popped loudly, painfully. Gasps replaced laughter.

"Shh! Your vampire is waking!"

Someone else cleared her voice. "Had a little bit too much to drink last night, dear?"

I was lying on my right side. The first thought that entered my head was, *Too bright*.

Someone patted my arm. "My dear," the same voice said, "do you need some help getting out of there? I know it must be the most comfortable and lovely of places to fall into when drunk and disorderly, but really, one must eventually rise and shine again, especially by two in the afternoon. Come on. Fresh air will do you good." A hand tugged my arm gently. I lifted my head and looked into the face of an older woman with auburn hair, dressed in a 1920s-style flapper dress, pearls swinging from her neck, a cloche hat firmly on her head. I peered up past the ledge. The pair of women beside her were dressed the same. One of them said, "What a very sturdy bed. I must try it once it's free."

I pushed myself upright. Hands tugged me to my feet. I sat against the edge of the tomb, rubbing my numb and sore face, trying to wake. My stomach churned like it was full of gravel. Sounds of music, very distant, filtered the air. Why was I hearing such notes in a graveyard?

The one they called Margaret said, "We came from the little church across the way. Beatrice's daughter got married, and we were having a wonderful little gathering afterwards. The weather was so nice, the peacocks so beautiful. So we came outside, sort of chased the birds a little—or they thought we did. Then decided to take a little walk through the graveyard. There really are some beautiful tombs and statues. Plus scampering off through the graveyard is interesting, don't you think? Birth and death, wedding and grave—oh, I probably sound crazy. I do that."

I was not entirely sure where I was, what day it was, or who I was. I studied her again and peered at her dress and the dresses of the other women. "What's with...?" I pointed up and down.

"Oh!" she said, "Yes! Well, the wedding was themed for the 1920s. It really was a marvelous time. Simply loved the idea. I feel a nostalgia for that era, though I wasn't alive then. Isn't that strange? How you can be nostalgic for things you've never experienced?"

The other women giggled.

"Have you ever felt that way?"

"I don't know," I answered. I barely knew what she was talking about. I was nauseated. "I need a cigarette."

"Oh yes," she said, "I think I see them right there." She bent down to grab the pack in the tomb. Then she paused, her hand inches from the syringe I'd dropped. She stared at it before she turned to me, suddenly inordinately still.

I returned her gaze and whispered, "What can I say?"

The other women paid no attention to this awkward and dramatic moment. As they chattered behind her, she placed two dainty fingers along the top of the plunger, lifted the syringe, and handed it to me. I placed it in the inner pocket of my coat. She bent and grabbed the pack of cigarettes before she straightened and acted as though nothing had happened.

She spoke cheerily. "Used to love the things, but I quit...oh, I think twenty years ago. Still enjoy the smell. Cloves! How wonderfully dark." She smiled at me and winked. The other two women were absorbed in their own discussion, chatting in the background. Margaret handed my pack and lighter back to me. I lit a cigarette and savored the first draw.

She gestured toward the hill. I knew the church stood some yards off. "I bet you haven't had anything to eat. Rachael—the woman getting married—she and her husband are serving tons of cake balls. Chocolate, red velvet, vanilla. As well as hors d'oeuvres. Plus tea and champagne and water. You should have some. We'll introduce you to Rachael. She doesn't know you, but she'll pretend she does. She doesn't know half the guests there."

She didn't wait for a response. Having decided what I should do, she now attempted to help me out of the tomb. I willingly stepped over the side. Vertigo threatened to make the earth spin. I drew again on my cigarette and steadied myself. "Do you do this for all the dead?" I asked.

"I do whatever I please."

She marched me forward, arm in arm, as the pair of her friends followed. The woman was insane.

"My name's Margaret Wilhelm. That's Emily Brown and Sarah Moulder. I am pleased to make your acquaintance...?"

"Jack," I replied.

"Jack! That reminds me of London and Burton at the same time."

I had never taken the time to visit the little wooden church. Now I beheld it with wonder. It seemed more a park than a religious building. Peacocks, their feathers brilliant with different blues and greens and golds, paraded, their tails brushing against the ground like their own dresses, long and thick and full. Along the lawn were little ponds with stone edges and bright green lily pads. A few were habitated by dark spotted frogs. The surfaces were covered with downy flakes of cottonwood seeds, a few more landing after their journey through the air.

The church's double doors stood open. Facing the back porch were rows of white chairs with light blue ribbons tied in bows on each arm that trailed to the ground and kissed it in the breeze, imitating the peacock tails. Dark-leaved trees lined the lawn and swayed dreamily, stirred by the wind.

The guests were inside the church. A familiar jazz clarinet riff played behind the *tinks* and *clinks* of dinnerware. The fast swing echoed within the little church, which seemed to me in my uneven state to rock gently to the rhythm. A soprano saxophone sprang into a solo, replacing the clarinet's smooth, perfect notes. The raspy saxophone reminded me of playing on a brand new reed, the inevitable raspiness before it was broken in. That, of course, made me think of Roland. Tears threatened. So I shut the music away.

The four of us silently climbed three wooden steps. The first room we entered was completely empty, as was the room beside it. The other rooms were separated by one wall; a fireplace opened to both. The floor was light brown, the walls bright white. Everywhere was the odor of spicy wood. I took a deep breath.

In both rooms, large and complex crystal chandeliers hung above us, each covered with hundreds of tiny stone drops dangling from six gold arms. We did not linger there long, though. Soon Margaret ushered me to my left, through another room, where we arrived at a hall. A table at the other end was covered with fruit and delicious-looking food and several cakes. We passed through a set of French doors to arrive at the loaded large table.

"Here, dear," Margaret said, handing me an antique china plate. "Pile it up. You're skinny. That's a shame great enough to kill you in itself if hunger doesn't. Eat. Eat! Let's see if we can put a pound on you."

More confused than hungry, I let her select and plate a few pieces of piercingly orange cantaloupe, as well as honeydew, red grapes, vegetarian potstickers, cheese and spinach quiches, spanakopita, bruschetta, baby brie, and white and cream crackers, among many other delicacies.

She picked out a china cup for me, filled with cake balls. "You get to keep the cup," she whispered. She winked. "I chose a good one for you."

The guests stood in groups, chatting and eating. The room featured ten windows; the wooden floor was painted a nice blue. There were fifteen tables, with multiple chairs at each one. A picture of the bride and groom smiled from every table top, which also supported a vase full of peacock feathers and paper flowers. The petals were rolled pages from books. On the table I was eventually led to was a picture of the couple standing on a lawn, staring at each other adoringly. Rachael was blond, a lily in her hair.

Margaret and I sat at the table and observed the many guests, wearing fedoras and pin-stripe suits and loose black dresses, conversing. No one glanced at me twice. Margaret sat across from me, sipping a glass of champagne she had acquired, watching me in silence.

The aromas from the plate began to clear my head, and the sense of the surreal lifted. Roland was dead. Yes, he was gone. Cyrus had burned him, and, most likely, I could never bring him back again. There was nothing, after all, to be brought back. I could have cried right then. I swallowed the memory with the first bite of food.

I looked up at Margaret. She seemed knowing. When I finished, she asked, "Feeling better?"

I nodded, and I knew what was coming. She would want to know about the syringe.

To my surprise, though, she did not bring it up. Instead, she carried on without pause. "Jack, I know you must only be fifteen or sixteen, but have you ever experienced postmodern art?" She looked at me with inquisitive green eyes.

I softly answered, "No."

"Ah," she said. "Well, some people say it's shit." She paused and looked out across the room full of guests. I wondered if she was speaking about anyone in particular. "They say that it lacks the beauty of classic art and has no meaning. Others say that it is too human-centered. Then there are others, people like me, who absolutely, positively disagree. I mean, I admit that the postmodern is repetitious and does not focus on beauty alone, and yes, okay, it does place a lot of emphasis on the human, but does something matter to a human unless it addresses the human? There's no acceptable reason to hate it.

"What I—and many others—believe postmodern art does is what all art is supposed to do: create a frame in which that which cannot be presented is presented. The vastness of space, for instance, cannot be fathomed." She swung her arm out and slammed her hand down on the table, startling me. "If you even try to grasp it, your mind gets dizzy. You feel a pain from the immenseness. You start to swoon. Art is supposed to provide the occasion to experience it. That is what the postmodern does. Do you understand?"

I did, and I told her so, but I was also confused as to why she was telling me this.

"Wonderful," she said as she flicked her wrist. "Now, now. I heard a poet by the name of Anis Mojgani one day. He has captured this idea of art quite well. 'I want you,' he said in the poem he read to us that marvelous night at a wonderful retreat, 'to draw me a picture of what smoking a cigarette feels like.' Well, now. What a great example! Presenting that which cannot be caught or bound! Purifying into a drop the complicated amalgam of the human condition. And I, my dear Jack, have a question for you, like Anis Mojgani. What, pray tell, would you choose to represent the soul? Of all the things in the world, what would you choose?"

My jaw might as well have dropped. I stared at her. I did not know what to say. This woman, with one simple question, had opened up a new world to me. She was like smelling salts, generating a tingling sensation within my skull, like hundreds of red roses were suddenly blooming. Their petals brushed against the roof and walls of my mind.

I suddenly began to wonder if perhaps we shake hands with God, agreeing to the lives we'll live, before we are ever born. I wondered what I might have agreed to.

I didn't know what to tell her. I was small under the weight of such a question.

When I didn't respond, Margaret said, "As an example, I picture a lung. A healthy, working lung. Just a few years back—oh, perhaps ten or so—a doctor friend of mine showed me interesting pictures of cancerous black lungs, as well as pictures of healthy, pink ones. He thought I might learn something from them." She stopped and winked. "I used to smoke." That made me smile. "But he was right. I did learn something. For some reason, the healthy image stuck with me. When I thought of the soul one day, I just...associated it with that image. I'm still not sure why, but there it is, my dear. The soul is a lung for me—a healthy, vital, living, expanding, supporting lung. And...I stopped smoking." She laughed. "As for you, though—what do you look at that screams soul? What do you imagine to present what can't be presented?"

The second time, to my surprise, the answer came to me, and it did so in the form of images.

The answer was dinoflagellates. It was diphenyl oxalate. It was luciferin. I pictured a liquid sapphire plasma.

"A glowing cobalt-blue plasma. That would represent the soul to me. The liquid. I mean..." I thought for a moment. "That's what the blood of a soul must look like. It would have to be something brilliant." I sat, somewhat stunned that I could have come up with that idea so immediately, when it was so outside my world, when I was in such pain.

Margaret smiled.

The only reason I came up with an answer so quickly might have been because we were unknown to each other, anonymous; she did not know me, nor I her. Speaking with her was almost like thinking to myself.

"That is very beautiful, Jack," Margaret replied. "Very beautiful indeed. You surprised me. Most people don't say anything. They never think about these things. Why, I don't know. Have you thought about this sort of thing often? Are you a philosopher already?"

"I have never thought or heard of anything like this in my life."

"You should do it more," she said. She smiled reassuringly. "These questions are life itself. Art is life itself."

Margaret lifted her champagne flute and took another swig. Laughter and tinkling plates surrounded us, which made the glass globe of our own making all the more noticeable. The snow was awhirl.

"I did not see a syringe down in that tomb with you," Margaret said in a lower, but still kind, tone. "But if I had, why might it be there?" She pursed her lips.

I looked into her green eyes, and I wasn't sure just how far the safety of anonymity would cloak me.

"Has the glowing plasma run out for you, Jack?"

I looked around the room at all the celebrants wearing 1920s attire. Cyrus could have wiped all of those people out in just a few seconds. Still, they were all there, alive—the sort of people he would loath. It was unfathomable. "I don't understand this world anymore," I told her. "That's why you didn't see such a syringe."

She closed her eyes. When she opened them, she asked, "In what way?"

I shrugged and moved my hand like I were pouring the meaning out on the table to dissect. "I don't think that it matters if there are any souls. The idea of them is nice, but that niceness runs out."

"I don't understand."

"The world's evil," I said, my voice harsh. I forced myself to breathe. "There's nothing redeeming about it, nobody meaningful."

"Oh?" she said skeptically. "Have you been to Venice and seen monsters there?"

I raised my eyebrows questioningly, but she did not elaborate. "No," I replied.

"Did you go to Paris and see vampires on the streets draining the blood of the innocent?"

I shook my head, perplexed by her question. "I've never been to Paris."

"Well then, have you gone to Japan and seen witches harvesting the children?"

"Of course not."

"Then what have you seen?"

"Worse things than that."

"Oh? Where are these worse things?"

"Home."

She inhaled. "When it gets that bad, then that's not home," she said.

I rubbed my face, livening the capillaries. I shook my head, not knowing what to say. "I'm so tired I could sleep forever."

"You look it."

Another silence stiffened between us.

"What is so bad about where you live?" she asked.

"Even if I told you, you wouldn't be able to help me."

"Why not?"

Because even I can't seem to help me, I thought.

"That is not your place in this world. If it were, you would have already helped me," I said.

Margaret smiled broadly. "But I thought we just agreed that you don't know the world. You know your 'home.'" She used air quotations. "That's all."

I bit my lip hard and thought about that.

"Are you fifteen? Sixteen? I do apologize for being so blunt, but you don't know a damn thing about what's out there." She grinned, revealing her perfectly straight white teeth. "What you think you know...it might be true for the one square inch where you are, but there are millions of miles out there to explore. Trust me. What's true for one moment or place isn't true for another. Whatever or whoever's king or queen of the castle at 'home' can't be everywhere. What if all you needed to do was take a step out of the kingdom? Just one. To the left. Hm?"

"And if I trip?" I asked.

"You'd nevertheless still land farther from where you started. And you'd dust yourself off. And you'd keep walking." She planted her fingers and tapped the table with every word. "Just. Like. Everybody. Else. We all have our monsters, Jack."

She threw her hands in the air and shook her head. "I do not know your position or problems, but I guarantee you that a portion of the world exists out there where they will disappear. Poof!" She waved her fingers, as though she were dispersing glitter and dust. "Well, maybe not *disappear*. Some might stick with you. We all carry our scars, after all." She touched the upper right side of her face, just above her eye, where a horizontal scar wandered within her eyebrow. "But people and things are often tied to locations. When you leave those scenes, more than likely they will never follow you. They don't know how, because they don't normally travel that far."

Inside myself, something was propelling, tumbling, bouncing, and running again.

"Who are you?" I asked.

She shook her head and looked around at the wedding guests. "Just your average person." She placed a hand on her chest. "I like to think I'm special." She laughed. "But truly, I'm like most."

"No one has ever pulled me out of a grave before."

She nodded and shrugged. "Most teenagers don't literally fall into graves.

"Goodness isn't that sparse, Jack. You should know this. In my one square inch of the world, at least, it has free rein. I would dare say you might find a whole square foot out there filled with it. Maybe it flickers occasionally, like a lightbulb not screwed in tightly, but goodness is there."

"Why wasn't I born into it?" I asked.

She cocked her head to the side.

"Like everyone else. Why wasn't it given to me?"

She reached across the table and collected my hands in hers. Her look of pure compassion was both refreshing and unfamiliar. Her skin was thin and washed soft, like lotion had been massaged in. With one hand she gently held my wrist; with the other she pushed my sleeve up to my elbow and inspected the bruises. I didn't pull away.

"I can't tell you why you are where you are," she said, stroking my hand, resembling a gypsy analyzing my life lines. "All I can tell you is that where you begin does not make you what you are. If things are so bad, you should leave. Know there's something better for you in the unknown, not more of the same."

She added, "Don't worry about where you started off or why. Life is all about breaking habits, getting away from your origins, no matter what they are—breaking ties to what you love that holds you down and back, sometimes simply because they are what once was rather than what will be. Trust me—the more habits you can break, the better off you are."

"There's no loyalty," I said, "in that."

"No, I suppose there's not. But maybe that is for the best." She lifted her shoulders questioningly. "Loyalty is tricky. It's often the last thread, the one we fall back on when all else goes. It is only needed when no reasons remain. Sometimes it's necessary to just cut that thread."

Margaret frowned. "At some point, you realize there are things in the world that make you more you than your origins. It's a powerful understanding. You're just too young," she smiled, "to have experienced that yet. But I hope you do."

I inched forward. "Did you have anything to run from when you were my age?"

She paused and shook her head, the pin in her hat reflecting the light from above us. "No, I did not. I mean, nothing terrible. I had a good home. A bad husband, later on, but a good home."

I slowly slipped my arms off the table. "What did your husband do?"

She shrugged. "He was abusive."

"How?"

"Oh, in all the ways. Verbally. Physically." She sighed, her eyes darkening ever-so slightly. "The problem is, you don't see abuse at first, and by the time you do, the connection is so strong it's hard to let go of the loyalty." She smiled directly at me. "You're not dropped into boiling water. You're dropped into a lukewarm pot, and the temperature slowly rises. Sometimes it takes a while to notice you're cooking, and, well, even then it's hard."

"I understand," I said. "I just wonder why that is."

"Learned helplessness," she replied. "You forget how strong you are. You're blind to the proof. And then you become attached, loyal beyond reason, because it's easier, a habit, a beautifully automatic thing you dare not touch. Of course, you're dying inside all the while. The last thread is strong, so strong, until finally...finally..."

"Snip," I replied.

"Snip."

-

Margaret drove me to my car, parked not too far from the church, in her limo, the likes of which I had only seen Cyrus navigate. It was like traveling back to reality in a cruise ship—a clinking, sparkling, soothing cruise ship, with music and whiskey and a very nice leather interior.

I opened the door and thanked her for everything.

Margaret laughed, an innocent, womanly sound. "Jack, dear. Hear me now. What you are makes up for what you're not. Do you understand me?"

"Yes," I said. "I think so."

"No matter what you've done, or what has been done to you, you *can* step away from it."

I peered at her.

She smiled. "Look, here's my card." She handed me a business card the color of bone. On it was her name, number, and address. "You call me," she said, "No matter the time, no matter the day. No matter if you feel like you're in too much trouble for me to handle. You call me, or you stop by. Okay?"

"I'll keep the card. In case."

"Really," she said, "there's no reason not to."

I slipped her card in my inside jacket pocket and said good-bye. I stepped out of the car into the bright world. The limo drove away. I did not trust the wealthy, but they nevertheless found me. Margaret, though, in every way, had destroyed my assumptions about the rich. Not only that, but she had destroyed every way that I knew the world worked, just by happening to be there.

It was...a different kind of murder.

CHAPTER 24—INSCRIBED
AGE: 17 YEARS OLD

When I returned to Cyrus's midafternoon, he was calmly waiting for me. He rose from his chair near the garage door and asked me to follow him to his office. Tentatively, I did. We stepped inside the house and walked quietly to the third floor. When we took our respective places on either side of his desk, he heaved a large sigh.

"Do you know what name the box has delivered now?" he asked.

Before I could answer, he placed a black stone on the wood with the words JACK HARPER PIVOTS.

"You are the first person I have ever shown her name. And you are the second I have not simply dropped into the fire in the bottom of the box and been done with. Do you want to know why?"

"Because you do not need the box to kill me?" I asked numbly.

"That's not the reason," he said. "I expected your name might arrive." He cleared his throat. "I know you are in pain. And I know you do not believe that Roland would betray me. And because of that, for the first time, for the very first time, I'm being merciful."

He stared at me. I didn't say anything. There was no point. He would decide whatever he decided, and anything I said wouldn't change that.

"For once, and only for you, I am going to give you time to come back to me. To adjust, recover, and learn that I truly have your best interests in mind. Not only that, but I have sent Alex away, for a long while. The fact that he selected girls who look like you to be sacrificed is...more than I ever expected of him—and grievously unacceptable. I made that apparent to him. Part of his punishment is exile. For the next two years, he will not visit here. I will not stop the bombing, but I have sent him away. Do you understand all that I am doing for you?"

I sat in the chair, a bit shocked by what Cyrus had told me. Of all the things he would choose to do, I wouldn't have expected he would send Alex away. At the same time, he probably would not stick to that promise. He was simply saying all of this because he wanted me to believe he was making a sacrifice for me.

I looked up at my mentor, remembering Roland in the forest, the absolute rapture with which he stared at the resurrected leaves.

"Do you understand?" Cyrus asked again.

Roland disappeared. Cyrus's cold eyes and silver hair replaced him. I regarded them bitterly and nodded.

Cyrus held up his pointer finger. "Just once."

CHAPTER 25—SNIP
AGE: 17 YEARS OLD

THE MORNING WHEN CYRUS PLANNED to bomb multiple cities, he sat with me in the living room, smoking a cigarette. I stared at him quietly. Since the box had named me, he had kept a close and persistent eye on me—the kind of supervision that was like constant accusation.

There was a toddler in the room, a boy two years old with black hair, and Cyrus was pushing around alphabetic blocks on the floor with him. The boy's name was Jamie, and Cyrus had taken to him. He said that Jamie's mother was considering allowing him to be culled.

Cyrus talked about the bombing a lot, explained he would only be gone for one day before he returned. I didn't say a word to him.

In the absence of conversation, Cyrus began a monologue about the importance of destroying his followers' imaginations, which was easy to do. He insisted he had made me differently, made me a murderer with imagination. I was one of the few followers worth knowing. He absolutely drenched me in compliments. "You see things for what they are. You have open eyes. You are no fanatic." He tried to compliment me into loyalty.

As soon as Cyrus realized this tactic was not working, he tried a different one. Sitting among the child's blocks, he withdrew something from his pocket and placed it on the coffee table. I stared at the words.

JACK HARPER PIVOTS

"Would you like to talk about this?" Cyrus asked.

I shook my head. "Only if you plan on bringing Roland back."

"You and I both know how impossible that is. I can't control my newfound powers, and Roland has been burned."

The rims of my eyes stung, and I swallowed my grief down. It threatened to overcome me; grief was becoming more and more difficult to control.

The child on the floor made a strange bubbling sound. He should not have been there. No child should be in the same room with Cyrus.

"What a mighty fine replacement you've chosen. Hope he will be able to keep up," I said. It was obvious why the child was there—to show me I was replaceable.

Cyrus's gaze swept up the length of me and settled on my own. He rose from the floor and strolled to the couch, hands in his pockets. He sat next to me and placed his hands on the sides of my face before he kissed my forehead. "I would never, ever replace you. Ever."

Liar.

I made sure to smile just a little. He wasn't the only one who could lie. I thought of Roland as I stared at the man who could have simply dropped the stone with my name on it into the box's fire and been done with me. Cyrus could not see what went on behind my eyes. He could only guess, like everyone else. That was going to be his downfall.

-

On the day Roland and I were in the forest, he absorbed the resplendent resurrection of the tree. The tips of his fingers touched one of the green leaves. His lips were parted. While he inspected the greenery, I spoke of Cyrus. "I've figured out a way we can get around this problem, if we work together."

"Tell me." His words were urgent, and they moved me.

"One problem is that anyone who has ever tried to stop Cyrus has acted alone. Planned alone. Been named alone. Died alone."

Roland's brown eyes absorbed every bit of me, as though I were speaking about saving the world rather than merely surviving it.

"One advantage we have is that we can work together. And there is one more advantage."

"Which is?"

"Though the box names traitors, the box does not say *why* a person betrays."

Roland glanced at the base of the tree for a moment, thoughts whirling in his head. "Go on."

I swallowed, and my throat clicked. I opened my mouth and continued.

-

Cyrus leaned back, sighed, and gazed at the child playing on the living room floor. He rubbed the scruff of the silver stubble along his jaw. "I never told you about my father, did I?"

He had not.

He withdrew his pack of cigarettes from his coat pocket and lit one. He exhaled a stream of smoke that almost reached the tip of my knee. Cyrus placed his hand on top of mine, lowered his head toward me, and lifted my hand to the back of his skull. My hand had never been in his hair before, and the strange intimacy put me on edge.

He pressed my fingers beneath his smooth hair. I touched a hard ridge beneath his scalp, protruding perhaps a centimeter. Following its edge, my fingers made a circuit through Cyrus's hair. On top of the protrusion streaked a white scar. "Is that...?" but I didn't finish.

"That is my father."

He bent his head away from me and drew on the cigarette. "Metal plate." He smiled at me. "You think you're the only one who has suffered?"

"No," I whispered, privately admitting it was hard to imagine Cyrus had ever been weaker than anyone. In fact, it was hard to imagine that Cyrus had ever been a child. He was too perfectly unreachable, untouchable.

"You are probably thinking right now about why Roland might want to betray me. Why I killed him. Why you had to end up with someone like me, forced into this life. Don't deny it. I can see you're thinking of him. I just want to say something. I hope you'll listen."

He faced me, placed his cigarette between his middle and forefinger and blew on the tip before he set it down on the tray. Jamie gurgled and slammed some blocks together. We looked at him briefly.

"My father beat me," Cyrus said. "Almost every day."

-

The wind barely grazed Roland and me as we stood in the cool, pure forest air. A short rain had fallen several hours before, cleansing the atmosphere. The colors around us were vibrant, magnified.

"Do you believe that Cyrus is completely cold and inhuman?" I asked Roland.

Roland gazed up at the leaves that shaded us from the uncharacteristically bright autumn sun.

"I think he is close enough it is impossible to tell the difference," he said.

I nodded. "I think he *wants* to be."

Dropping the leaf to the ground, Roland folded his arms around his torso. "All right."

"That's what his transcendence is about, in part. Becoming more. Becoming powerful. Becoming invulnerable. But he is none of these things. He believes he is transcending, that he will be beyond human, above weakness, above pain and pity. *Will* be."

"Okay," Roland said, squinting at me, telling me to get to the point.

"I think, in his dark heart, though he might not love you, or any of his followers, there are two of us that he does, at least in part, feel a shred of something for. Alex is one. I, at least I think, am another.

"It may not be one hundred percent love, but it might be twenty percent, or fifteen percent, or even ten percent. It may not even be love. It might be habit that he feels for me. It might be pride. It might be tradition. Loyalty perhaps... Even so, he feels something."

Roland studied me. "I agree," he said. "He feels something for you that he doesn't for anyone else."

"We can use that to our advantage."

Roland gazed at the tree again. "I'm listening."

I took a deep breath and began to explain.

-

There was not a shred of sadness in Cyrus's voice. He might as well have been reading from a book. "And not like most adults reminisce about their parents beating them. This wasn't the kind of beating you talk about; it's the kind you try to forget forever. And then one evening, in the midst of this abuse, there was an island of calm.

"My father came home fuming. I stayed in my bedroom, expecting him to come in and find me. He didn't. Later, I sat throughout dinner, wondering why. I went to bed wondering why.

"The next day, the answer came to me." Cyrus's eyes lit up just a little. "The news," he whispered.

"The local news reported a colossal catastrophe. I remember it perfectly. Thirty miners were stuck in a mine after the exit collapsed, more than two thousand feet below ground. Everyone was afraid they weren't going to be able to get them out in time. They did, but it took a month. It was horrible news, absolutely awful. The evening it was first announced," Cyrus said, "my father was angry, but he didn't beat me. I began to put two and two together.

"Those miners, stuck down in the ground for a month, maybe saved my life.

"They were finally rescued, and the news coverage switched to a lighter subject." Cyrus licked his lips. "The rescue crews retrieved the last miner, and that night, things at home went right back to the way they were. The next day, my entire back was bruised.

"The world turns to shit, I am saved," he said, winking. "The world resolves, and I'm looking at another visit to the emergency room.

"That's when I started killing."

His voice was emotionless, and his expression revealed no despair. "I started targeting those I knew would generate the most news coverage. When I became more intelligent about it, I killed those who looked like my father. So he could relate to them, you understand. So he could feel for them, feel for himself, and forget about me.

"I made the world turn to shit and saved myself.

"If I'd ever tried to heal the world, I would have died. I'm sure of it."

"Cyrus," I whispered. I placed a hand on my forehead. I didn't want to hear any of it. I didn't want to hear about him or his father or his family. I didn't want to learn anything new about him. I wanted to be done.

He cleared his throat and retrieved his cigarette. "I'm not telling you this to make you pity me, though that would be nice. After all, when you have someone's pity, you have *them*. No, I'm telling you this because I want you to know that even after my father died at the ripe age of seventy-three, I kept killing. Because I enjoyed it," he said. He smirked. "I never considered killing him—getting rid of the problem at the source—because I wanted a reason, you see. I desired a reason to go forth into the world and murder.

"We do not do these horrible things," he said, "because something spurs us to do them. We do these things because we want to do them, and we find a reason, the blame, necessary to excuse them. Generally, we blame the past. That's usually where the pain resides.

"You might want to believe that I'm drawn toward chaos because as a child I assumed chaos was the only way to live safely with my father. You might think, 'So that explains him. He got in the habit of sacrificing the minimal amount for the sake of his sanity, and he simply never stopped.' You might want to believe that, but it's not true.

"The story of my trauma will not explain me any more than the story of yours explains you."

He smiled at me fondly. "Do you understand?"

I nodded, slowly. "I understand." It wasn't a lie. I was putting the pieces together. What he said made sense, and I knew where he was going.

-

Roland clasped his hands together and paced a circle along the cold earth. "So you believe he feels a shred of pity for you, or comfort with you, or pride for making you." He turned back to me. "I would agree with that."

"I think we can use it."

"How?"

I swallowed, gazed down at the ground.

"How?" Roland asked again, his voice warm, gravelly, a voice that sounded like it had sifted through the earth, a voice that sounded like it had known death many times.

"This is the part you are not going to enjoy," I said. "Because I'm not sure that it will work. I can't guarantee it, but it's the only route that I can see out of this place."

Roland blinked knowingly, and we both stood there in complete union, understanding that what I was about to say involved nothing beautiful, nothing pretty, nothing certain, only sacrifice.

-

I leaned forward on the couch, my face in my hands. "You're so strange."

"Why?"

"You..." I looked up at him, "you're not fighting anything, not like you tell your followers you are. You are not lying, killing, thieving, leading for any purpose. You simply are. And you exist as you are, in relation to no one."

"Yes."

"You... I guess you don't operate within the limits of similar evils. Like terrorism, which has an agenda."

"It claims to."

"And this group you have created... Its goal is to destroy godly men and women, as you put it. But you don't give a shit about that at all."

Cyrus sat there, looking quite pleased with my budding realization.

"You are not like them at all," I said. It was a tired, belated realization. "You are an evil entirely separate from the borders and understandings of all other evils, because you admit there is no basis for your actions."

"Correct."

"It's not for a god, and it's not because you were abused."

"No."

"It is not because you hate someone who has wronged you or stolen from you or killed someone you love."

"No."

"This is not a reactionary sort of evil. It is not a...human level of darkness. You simply want what you want."

"Yes!"

"And there is nothing driving you on this dark road except yourself."

His eyes flashed. "You have it. We are what we are, Jack. I kill because I want to, not because a man beat me. Lots of children are abused, and they do not murder or seek chaos. It is not nearly a good enough excuse. I murder because I want it, and so do you.

"And that is the point I'm getting at. If you did not have me to understand you as you are, to love the best and worst parts of you, to help you love them too, you would not have anything. You would be lost. Because you are what you are, with me or without me. By betraying me, you do not solve one itty bitty thing. Roland is dead. You are a murderer. The world will not accept you, but I will.

"You have not seen how people treat your kind outside of this house and my protection. If you leave here, you will be caught, and they will drug you, bind you, study you, and torture you. Society will not give a shit about you. They will view you as different, distant from themselves, so they feel better about their lives.

"You will become nothing.

"And the worst part is...if you leave me, there will come a time when you are sitting in your cell, realizing the same thing I realized after my father died—that you want to kill, whether or not I'm alive, and that leaving me did not solve anything. The truth is, I'm always alive and present, in that I'm alive and present in you. That realization will make you very, very alone. It would be useless to leave me."

He placed a hand on my cheek again. "With me, you don't have to suffer, and you don't have to be alone. There is no person so wondrous as you are, and when you realize your error, you will be stronger than anyone could imagine. You will be powerful, and rich, and beautiful, and there will be nothing, absolutely nothing, that you cannot do, no action you cannot commit. A harder, darker coldness will fill you, and it will feel marvelous. It will course through you and lift you up. You will be perfect, without borders, beautifully ungoverned. There will be no yearning anymore, just what is. You are, and will forever be, so lucky by me."

-

"Just say it," Roland said.

I bit the edge of my lip. "It will require your death."

"It doesn't matter."

"But I can resurrect you."

"It doesn't matter."

I frowned, pulled my jacket tighter across my chest. "It matters to me."

Roland sighed. "But I have died so many times now, it would be a blessing to not wake up again. I don't think I really am woken anymore. Do you understand?"

I nodded. I did. Thinking back, I couldn't imagine how Roland had endured what he had.

"So tell me. What's this plan?"

The leaves above us rustled in a gentle breeze. "If you pivot first," I told Roland, "and Cyrus kills you, he will expect me to react to that." I licked my lips and swallowed. "If I pivot second, he might believe it is not out of a true hatred for him but rather out of my love for you. He will, perhaps, pity my teenage rebellion, my idiocy and ignorance, my ability to love, my humanity. He might let me live. He might not want to accept that I have truly betrayed him, especially not if that betrayal arrives immediately after yours."

Roland's eyes narrowed, and he bit his lip.

"The box doesn't say why someone betrays. It only says that one loathes, or despises, or desires to destroy him...or wants to leave him.

"The only thing left to work with, then, is Cyrus's assumptions.

"You...attempt to kill him first. I attempt to kill him second. And we hope he believes the box names me because I have 'overreacted.' Not because I have been building up a subconscious realization for the past week, month, maybe even year, that he is insane and monstrous and maniacal, that I have lost almost all of myself because of him. Not because I can't stand to see hundreds of children who look like me—are like me—march to their deaths and am determined not to let it happen.

"Not because I know, but because I am ignorant. Not because I planned, but because I am emotional. Not because I want to kill him because he is him but because I want to *leave* him for killing you."

Roland stood taller, awakened. "I think," he said, "that just might work."

I breathed a sigh of relief, for I needed Roland for what I was about to do, and I needed his consent. Perhaps more than that, I needed the slightest bit of his confidence. I wasn't entirely certain myself that my plan wouldn't destroy us both and cost the world the lives of thousands.

He had said it, though. It "just might work," and "might" was enough.

-

"I know you miss Roland," Cyrus said. "But you will learn, in time, that I was doing what was best for us. If he threatened my livelihood, whether by desiring to kill me or leave me, he would most certainly threaten the livelihood of you and Alex and everyone here."

Cyrus stood up from the couch and glanced at the clock on the mantle. "Unfortunately, I must cut this conversation short. It is time for me to go. We will continue when I return. Until then," he donned his coat and walked to the edge of the room, "think hard about what I said. Think carefully. Because I want to keep you. I do."

He stepped toward me quickly, grabbed my arm, and dragged me to the edge of the room. I kicked one of the child's blocks, sending it spinning off to the side, ricocheting against a buffet. Cyrus hauled me to the fireplace and told me point blank, "Sit."

Warily, I did as he asked and sat on the edge of the brick. He retrieved a pair of handcuffs from a pocket and slipped one around my wrist. The other end he secured through the thick metal ring protruding from the wall.

He took my gun from me and my knife and everything else I had, and then he leaned close. "You will think for a while about these matters, and I will release you when I return."

In an instant, he was gone.

Jamie's mother came and retrieved him. Then it was just me in the dark living room. I leaned against the fireplace bricks and watched men file out of the house in preparation for the bombing. Soon, all was quiet.

The black stone from the red box waited on the coffee table, taunting me.

The cuff was snug against my wrist. I pressed the metal circle against the brick, tried to spin it. Nothing. It was secure.

The clock on the mantle ticked.

I took a deep breath and spoke calmly to myself. "It's just a hand."

CHAPTER 26—LOVE IS NOT ENOUGH
AGE: 17 YEARS OLD

I loved Cyrus. Even with the new piece Lutin had put inside of me, heating me, I loved him. Love, though, was not enough, and neither was desire—not when children were about to die, when a monster might transcend.

I began to work at the cuff on my wrist.

I slid the metal half an inch past my wrist, and a tendon across the back of my thumb popped. My hand turned white from the pressure. Though I pushed, the cuff would not budge. No matter how small I made my hand by folding my thumb toward my palm, I could not force it further.

Again, I told myself, "It's just a hand."

I grabbed a heavy, clear piece of decorative stone from the fireplace edge and braced myself against the brick hearth. I pressed my hand against the wall, so that my thumb faced outward, curved toward my palm. My pinky and the side of my hand rested against the stone.

Glancing around once to ensure no one who might be left in the house was near, I lifted the large piece of glass and slammed it on my hand as hard as I could.

Pain shot through the tendons and bone like lightning. I clenched my teeth and squeezed my eyes shut. It took everything in me not to cry out. When the pain relented, I quickly swung again so I wouldn't lose momentum, and the piece of glass connected with my hand almost silently. I slammed it down again. The third time, a bone slipped out of place. A tendon tore. I growled a low, guttural scream, gritted my teeth, and forced the sound back down.

My hand bled profusely. I lifted my arm for a moment and let the blood slip down, toward my wrist. I pressed my hand against the wall again, and I raised the glass.

There was a crunching sound during the final blow, like gears grinding against one another, and I placed my mouth against my elbow and bit down while I screamed. A delirium overtook me. I didn't know how long I sat there as the exquisite pain shot throughout me. When I could think again, I slammed the glass against my hand one more time.

My hand broke in two, like a hinge. My thumb met my pinky. I bit down as I slid the cuff through the blood, across my broken hand, off. I collapsed against the wall; my entire body broke out in a sweat. I rested, tears streaming down my face, my teeth locked.

I attempted to stretch my hand, but the pain impaired my vision. All I could hear was one high-pitched note. Tears obscured my sight. Moments passed before I stood, dripping blood on the floor. I managed somehow to make my way across the living room, to the two French doors. I rested a moment, and then I walked to the stairs on my right.

I climbed the stairs slowly, taking my time so I wouldn't pass out and the nausea wouldn't overwhelm me. Each step thrust bile to the back of my throat.

I tried to use my power to heal my hand and ease the delirium, but it didn't work. At the top of the stairs, I quit trying.

When I reached the upper hallway, I bumped into a tray on a table with decanters of liquor. I pulled the crystal top from one of the bottles, lifted it one-handed, and guzzled. I continued to Cyrus's office, swallowing most of the contents as I passed his desk. I set the much lighter decanter on the floor.

Before all the possible books, I stood hopeless, but I reminded myself that I didn't necessarily have to find the right book. If I failed, it might be possible to simply push my power forward, blindly, hoping it would reach the beings behind the wall, bring them life again. If *that* failed, it was possible to go to the basement and bring Lutin up the stairs to Cyrus's office. Maybe he could blast through the bookshelf.

That would take time, though, and I wasn't sure how much time I had. I must move quickly.

I gazed up at the metallic books in the elaborate mechanism before I retrieved the lamp from Cyrus's desk. I bit down as the cord brushed against my broken hand. When the pain subsided, I lifted the light, scrutinizing the books, searching for evidence of dust.

The layer seemed equal. It wasn't thick, just enough to dull the light reflecting off the fake gilded edges. Fear cut through the pain. Cyrus may not have visited the room for years. Perhaps no oily fingerprint would point to the way.

My stomach bubbled. I swallowed, forcing the salty saliva that foreshadowed vomiting back down. I inspected the titles, hoping that Cyrus might have selected the key to opening the contraption via some theme.

Dead Souls by Nikolai Gogol had potential. I held the light above it, searching for thumbprints. My blood dripped on the shelf in front of the book.

To my left was *The Prince* by Machiavelli. It was much larger than it should have been. Perhaps to provide an adequate width to open the mechanism? I placed the pinky of my good hand on the book and was about to slide it out when I noticed that all the books were the same size. My theory was wrong. *The Prince* wasn't larger. It matched the others.

I breathed deeply for a moment to calm my cramping stomach. The liquor curdled before ever flooding my bloodstream, making me nauseous and sick, too sick to think.

Even on my best day, the likelihood of guessing right was low. What had I been thinking? I just had to choose one, any one. It would be wrong, undoubtedly, but it would allow me to move on to a second plan that had a better chance of working. I scanned the titles rapidly. Choose one, just one—any one. *Sons and Lovers. The Art of War. Anna Karenina.*

My breath caught in my throat.

Shakespeare. As I stared at the titles on the shelf, the name popped into mind. *Shakespeare!* It would be too perfect if Cyrus had chosen the answer to his puzzle based on the name of our family pet. That was his style: the truth right there, invisible under everyone's noses.

I found a *The Complete Works of William Shakespeare* in the upper left corner of the bookshelf. I held the lamp up and pressed my fingers along its spine, and the metallic object began to tilt forward.

I paused.

The book on the shelf right beside *The Complete Works...* The tiniest section, the smallest fraction—so small anyone might have easily missed it—of the gold gilt had sloughed away, revealing a speck of silver. I could've easily missed the clue beneath the thin layer of dust. The top of the book was silver because it had been touched many times and then forgotten.

I read the title. *Moby-Dick.* My focus shifted between the book I had chosen and the one beside it. I stood, thinking feverishly.

I made my decision hastily—far too hastily. The agony in my hand motivated me to be hasty—the night would not last forever. The glimpse of silver had spoken to me, and I released Shakespeare and clasped the edge of *Moby-Dick* instead. I pulled.

The entire bookshelf emitted an odd depressurizing sound, and then it receded a few inches into the wall. Still dizzy and nauseous from the pain, I laughed and heaved my shoulder against the shelves. Cathartic chills spread over my body. I thanked fate.

The right side of the bookshelf creaked inward. A slant of light shimmered across Cyrus's office floor. I stepped in and gazed at a crystal chandelier hanging in a long stone hallway. At the end of the hall was a wooden door.

Forcing an inhale, I steadied myself, wiped a bead of sweat from my forehead, and walked forward. My footsteps barely sounded, marking the undisturbed dust on the floor.

The liquor, combined with the pain and the sudden liberating success, made me squat and heave. My hand slid across the thick velvet dust of the floor, and I vomited. Rotten liquor exploded from me, and bile splashed on the stone.

I stood slowly and swiped the dribble from my chin with my sleeve. My vision and head cleared. The ringing in my ears subsided, as well as the nausea and some of the pain. I breathed deeply, rested for just a second, and continued.

When I reached the door, I tested the knob and found it wasn't locked. I cracked it open. Beyond was a room well-lit—this time by two electric chandeliers. The door creaked wide. Four men lay in the center of the gray stone floor.

I had expected skeletons, not supple, perfectly clad men. Their cheeks were full. They appeared not an hour expired. I shivered at the sight and the fresh throb of pain from my hand.

They all had black hair, and their eyes were deeply set. The shadows between their cheekbones and jaws were heavy, and the cracks in their necks and hands—so similar to Lutin's—were not warm red. The cracks were black.

They were frightening, and I stood in the doorway a long, long time before I went to them, dared to disturb them.

I searched within me for that warm, sparkling sensation that had become so familiar and comforting the past week. I shot it down through my limbs toward them. In less than a second, they bolted up, yelling.

The one closest to me was on his feet and grabbed me around my neck. He yanked me up and pinned me to the wall. When my broken hand slapped against the brick, I screamed. I was deaf to him.

"Where are we?" I finally heard. I forced my eyes, which had locked shut, to open. His gaze bore into me like a drill. The others gathered around him, standing very close, each looking angry.

"Cyrus's," I managed between red throbs of pain.

His positively vibrant dark eyes darted around the room. "And who are you?" His grip tightened. A brilliant light now coursed through a deep wound-like streak in his hand.

"Jack."

As he looked me up and down, his fingers loosened slightly. "How long have we been here?"

"I don't know, but Lutin could tell you. He's downstairs."

"Where?" The question came from one of the others. He was tall and thin. His clothes had moth holes in them. All of them did. The liquid fire that swirled around their bodies sparkled brightly through the openings in the cloth.

"In the basement. In a room just past the wine."

"And where's Cyrus?" the one holding me asked. His thick lips were dark pink.

"Gone. He has taken hundreds of children out to bomb schools and churches. That's why I came here—to wake you. To stop him."

He released me, and the easy air entering my throat was sweet. I bent forward and gasped.

Cocking his head, the same man said, "You're the one who brought us back?"

"Yes."

He grimaced. "Let me guess," he said. "You got the power from Lutin, didn't you?"

I hesitated—I hadn't expected him to ask this—and that gave him the answer straightaway.

"How long have you had the power?" he asked.

"I don't know," I said. "A week?"

He analyzed my face and then nodded. He grabbed my arm and lifted my damaged hand. I jerked from him, but he was as sturdy as stone and held me still. He studied the break. An extraordinary blast of pain shot through the hand, far worse than I had experienced before. Before I could cry out, it vanished.

There was no more agony.

The man released me, and I cradled my hand carefully to my chest. I gently moved my tender fingers—no deep ache. I stretched my hand out fully, and every bone, tendon, and ligament moved and stretched as it should. My mouth dropped in ecstasy. What sweet relief.

As I wiped away the blood to reveal undamaged skin, they spoke to each other in a language I didn't understand. It sounded smooth, stressless, easy.

The sensation of curdled milk in my stomach was gone, and I relaxed against the wall. All of me was better, not just my hand.

The apparent leader of the four turned back to me, a fiery look on his face. "You say Cyrus is gone. Where's Roland?"

"Dead," I whispered.

"Where is his body?"

I shook my head. "In the furnace. There is no body." My voice sounded quite sober, but it pained me to say it.

"Lucky to have escaped me," the man said. "Now, assuming you are not lying, how did you slip past Cyrus?" He loomed, and his breath smelled like coal dust. The red labradorite stripes in his flesh flared.

"Roland helped me," I told him. "He planned to kill Cyrus first. His name was submitted as a traitor before mine was. We...hoped Cyrus would think I'd betrayed him for the sake of my love for Roland and then pity me. We were right. Cyrus did pity me."

The man smirked. "How old are you?"

I swallowed. "Seventeen."

He looked me up and down. Then, he walked to the door, and two of the others followed.

"Are you going to kill him?" I asked, unable to stop myself.

"Who?" He paused at the threshold.

"Cyrus."

"Of course. But first we need to remove the protection he has guarding this house, himself, and others."

The last one of them came to stand beside me and nudged me forward. "Show us where Lutin is."

I glanced at each of them and said, "There are still a few people in the house."

"That doesn't matter," the one who had pinned me against the wall replied.

I believed him. "All right."

I led the way through the cold stone passage back to the bookshelf door in Cyrus's office, stepping over my vomit. When the four of them were through, I closed it. I moved toward the outer door, but one of them put his hand against my shoulder to stop me. He gazed at Cyrus's desk, and I looked, too. In the very center was the peeling red velvet box. I couldn't believe I had missed it when I walked in. The pain must have blinded me.

Without a word, the four of them went to it, and the leader of their group picked it up and inspected it. "Perhaps thirty years old at the most. Can you believe it did us in?"

"His quality is increasing," one of them said.

"Whose quality?" I asked, turning back to them.

All four of them regarded me with their holographic black eyes. "The Builder," two of them said at once.

I repeated the name and asked if the Builder was Cyrus. The leader of the group sneered. "No."

I looked at the red box in the man's hands, streaked with tribal hellfire.

"The Builder, then, he builds...boxes?"

"Yes. And picture frames. Vases. Kettles. Cups. Urns."

"Why does he build them?"

He opened his dark lips and paused. "Imagine a loss so great that it turns into a positive, a void so immense that it is full of power. That is what each of these arcas..." he lifted the case, "becomes. The box is important, but not in the way you might think. It is like a magnet. The only important thing is what goes in it. Souls. No soul is enough. The arca is there to create a metonymy."

"A metonymy?" I had heard the word before, but I didn't understand what he meant.

"It provides the endless need for someone like Cyrus to feed it souls, gain more control, in hopes of reaching a larger goal—transcendence. Of course, the amount of control is never enough, and no soul is strong enough to do the trick."

"What trick?"

"Of filling it. Of actually transcending. It is like a bucket with a hole in it. Do you understand? It gives the owner a sense of accomplishing something, of reaching toward a kind of evolution, but the point is to never actually accomplish that evolution, just to go on and on killing."

"Cyrus," I said, "would do that anyway. I grew up with him. I would know."

"That might be true," the man with fire in his veins said. "But, nevertheless, he has kept it all these years. Perhaps it does move him, after all, hm?"

I searched my mind for an answer as to why it might and could come up with none. "That doesn't make sense to me."

"It should. The box makes the monotonous have meaning again. There is no point to murder, but *this* provides the illusion of a point—perhaps the owner will transcend, evolve. With the illusion of a point again comes pleasure. The Builder makes these things to draw out the amount of time with which a killer has to work. Most men who crave evil deeds self-destruct early because they realize there is nothing to gain, or that they are lonely, or they are tired of their success. Maybe they realize they should have been caught. Desire becomes heartless drive. This box," he held it up, "turns heartless drive into something pleasurable again, any drive to any pleasure. It fills in for the half of them that is no longer human so that they do not limp so horribly or fall so dramatically."

I bit my lip. "It gives the tasteless flavor."

"Yes," he said. "And it gives the owner the hope of reaching the fullest flavor possible...which doesn't exist. Cyrus will not transcend. There's no such thing for the owners of arcas."

Although I knew Cyrus had not begun transcending, hearing from this ferric that he wouldn't filled me with relief. Cyrus was not about to gain more power. He never would. Cyrus was merely human and always would be.

"How do you...destroy one of them?" I asked.

"I am going to burn it. When I do, Cyrus's safety net will disappear, and his plans will unravel. His devices, strategies, everything he has used to destroy the world, as you put it, will disintegrate."

He tucked the case beneath his arm and gestured to the door. "Now Lutin, please."

"Right." I paused. "I just want you to know that Cyrus is out there with those children right now, and…"

"He is not going to succeed. Trust us. Now take us to our brother."

I took a deep breath. I didn't necessarily trust them, but I did trust Lutin. Bringing him up to date on everything would help assure me they would stop Cyrus in time.

The best thing would be to lead them quickly to him.

Passing down the hall, I lit a cigarette. I extended my bloody but repaired hand out and noticed it was shaking.

"What is it?" one of them asked.

"Nothing."

The truth, though, was that betraying Cyrus was uncomfortable and painful, despite my resolve.

We took the stairs down to the first floor, and as we rounded the corner, I nearly bumped into Luther, one of Cyrus's top officials. He stared at the five of us. Something inexplicable passed between us before Luther reached for his gun. As I grasped mine, Luther's neck twisted violently, and he dropped to the floor, dead.

"Keep going," the man to my right said.

They followed me through several of the great rooms and halls and met more people along the way. Like Luther, in a matter of seconds they were nothing to worry about anymore.

Then we were at the basement door, and I opened it. We took the stairs quickly. The metal door in the wine room opened on its own—either because of Lutin or his brothers. I twisted to the right and walked to the first door. In a matter of seconds, the second door opened, revealing Lutin in the worn chair.

There was a pause, a brief quiet, like we were in the midst of a soft snowfall, as Lutin looked upon his four brothers and they upon him.

"Twelve damn years you've been sleeping," Lutin said, rising weakly. "About time you thought of someone besides yourselves." He spoke in that other language I didn't understand, and the man beside me responded.

The four of them met him halfway. Two men carried Lutin to the door, and the other two swept their hands down the door jamb.

Black smoke rolled from the top of the doorway, turning over on itself, trying to bolt up as they brought their hands down. The black smoke was unable to climb like it wanted to, as if their hands supported a section of glass that confined it. When their hands dropped toward the floor, there was no more smoke. It had been squelched. Whatever barrier had been there, invisible to me over the years, was suddenly gone.

The two ferrics carried Lutin out, along the hallway, past the metal door, before they set him on his feet in the wine room. He gazed at the red box one of them carried. He shook. The leader of the group grabbed Lutin's shoulder and said something. Lutin dipped his head into his hands. When he looked up again, he seemed more sure of himself.

The brothers spoke briefly. A tiny movement caught my attention. A bottle of wine that had been left on the little island beside a vase of tulips had a crack in it. Cyrus had placed it there because he meant to open it sooner than the others. The crack shined, and then the glass on either side of it flowed to the structural flaw and filled it in. The bottle was whole again.

The tulips, whose petals had withered slightly, were suddenly brightening and flourishing like a *mimosa pudica* ending its play-dead act. The gaps in the mortar between the bricks filled out. The room shifted.

Something brushed against the back of my right hand. I scratched it. The skin looked unusual. The last remnants of my white scar disappeared.

"Holy shit," I whispered. The residual nausea in the pit of my stomach evaporated.

Lutin said something, again in a language I couldn't comprehend, before two of his brothers lifted him and carried him through the corridor. I followed them up the stairs, out of the basement. They set him in a chair by the door. I offered him my cigarette, and, to my surprise, he took a draw.

"Careful," I said. "That stuff'll kill you."

He smiled.

The four brothers lifted a nearby table and set it in front of Lutin. They placed the box on top.

A conversation between the five of them erupted in their strange, deep voices and tongues; they were each bouncing sentences off Lutin.

"What's going on?" I asked.

"I am telling them," Lutin said, "how I came to be stuck here and so weak."

The conversation continued for a few minutes before the tallest brother clapped his hand on Lutin's back. The lightning bolts along Lutin's skin instantly brightened. He closed his eyes and breathed in deeply, and when he opened them, his weariness had vanished.

Lutin rose from the chair like he was a completely different man. Without speaking, he walked to the door that led to the garage and garden. He turned the knob and pulled the door. The garage was open. Lutin's face changed when he looked to his left. The striking creature stared out into the dark night.

Breathing deeply, he placed one foot on the concrete walkway beyond the door, then the other. He took another step, and then two more, and the others followed him outside. After glancing back, I also left the mansion.

The moment was quiet. The air was still quite cool, though the seasons would soon shift from fall to winter. No small animals rustled; no crickets called. There were no fireflies. The night was not that beautiful; the grass was not green, and the moon was not nearly full, but Lutin stood on the ground, his expression conveying that he believed it was the most stunning night in the world. The other four gazed upon the mundane outdoors with similar appreciation. The cracks in their skin fluoresced, mystical furnaces glowed deep within. They glittered in the night, like broken pottery pieces glued back together with gold.

Cyrus's plan with the children was still on my mind, but something in me didn't dare disturb Lutin or his brothers, wouldn't allow me to ask them to hurry, not right then.

"Do you want to hear something frightening, Jack?" Lutin said, his black eyes surveying the tree line and moon and the few stars that poked through the darkness.

I stepped closer to him. "What?"

"I didn't believe you." His breath puffed out like smoke in the cool night air. "You surprised me."

"I still don't believe myself," I said. My right hand trembled. The cigarette's tip blurred.

"Cyrus could have given you everything."

My limbs became heavy. "I don't want him or anything he could give me."

"That's obvious, and also why I like you."

He smiled, walked over, and briefly rested his arm around me. "It's time to end it."

Tension in me released. Yes. It was time.

Lutin hugged me as though he heard my thoughts.

The head of the group returned to Lutin and held up the box. The others circled them and placed their hands on it. Something dripped, slowly at first, and then increased. A thick and dark fluid oozed between the lid and the base of the box, and then the red box shrank until it was just a tiny ball in the man's glowing hand. The box burst into flames like a compressed explosion. Staring into the light was like looking into a galaxy on fire. The tiny galaxy went dark. The remnants of the ooze slid from his hand onto the ground like he was made of glass.

Drip.

Drip.

Drip.

That's how it rang. The bell of liberation.

The four glowing arms returned to the men's sides, and then the tallest one spoke. "Just one more item to deal with." Faster than my eye could see, the same hand that had held the box grabbed my jacket and jerked me forward, dragging me close to the tall one's torso. The familiar scent of coal and dust filled my nostrils. I tripped as he spun me around, holding me tight by the hair on the back of my neck. I now faced Lutin.

"You must take back what's yours," he said.

CHAPTER 27—ENTWINE
AGE: 17 YEARS OLD

I REACHED BACK AND CLASPED the fingers that secured me. They were like soft stone with the texture of skin, but firm, with a cool indestructible core.

Lutin walked toward us. His dark eyes, like holograms in his pale face, were pinned on the ferric who held me. Slowly, Lutin's hands rose and clasped mine. He brought my arms down to my sides. My heart leapt in my chest. Lutin would take back his gift to me.

It only made sense. What he had given me was too good to be true. It would have to be returned. Tears came to me. I didn't want to give him the power back, but there was no way they'd let me keep it.

Lutin winced. He dropped my hands and lifted his own, close to my face. I sensed a slow but sweet release. He pried each of the ferric's fingers from my neck.

"No," he said. One simple word.

What?

The other released me. I stepped away from them, rubbing my hand against the skin that would have bruised if I had not been among creatures that repaired the very air around them.

Lutin clasped the wrist of the taller ferric. The only thing that moved was the grass surrounding their feet, which was becoming thick and turning emerald.

"What do you mean, no?" the one standing between them asked as Lutin released the tall one's arm. "She took a piece of you. It's time to take it back."

"She didn't steal anything." Lutin's gaze flicked back and forth between them. "Nor did she coerce me. I gave it to her willingly."

"Yes, so she could wake us. She did. The job is done, and you must take what rightfully belongs to you."

"Believe it or not, that isn't why I gave it to her."

The tallest, the one who grabbed me, whirled around. Dust puffed from his aged clothes, which by that point looked renewed, the moth-eaten holes filled in.

"I don't believe this. Do you want to be locked away, *again*?" He faced us. "Is that something you enjoy?"

Lutin shrugged. "If that is what they must do, that is what they must do. I have made my decision, and I stand by it." He looked resolute, more potent than the others.

I was quiet, perhaps as shocked as they were as they absorbed Lutin's dissent. Of all the eventualities I'd considered, of all the contingencies I'd planned for the night that Cyrus was to die, this had not been among them.

The decision might not be Lutin's to make. They wanted him to remove his power from me. They could, perhaps, force him.

The tall one's eyes were wide with anger. "Don't think I won't hand you in. Don't believe for a second that what has happened allows you to give a mortal immortal tools."

Lutin pressed the tips of his fingers together. "It was never about that, and what is allowed or required has never concerned me.

"I was in that house for twelve years, Osric, hearing everything that happened in it, knowing each of the inhabitants more and more intimately.

You think after twelve years I would misjudge? You think I would err after all that time?"

"I think you were in a bad place and still are. You're not thinking clearly. You've gone mad."

Lutin tilted his head, weighing the possibility. "Madness can have its useful elements, but I am not mad. Sitting there in the same room, day in, day out, I discovered this child, who was turned toward coldness and cruelty. I watched her in my entrapment. I saw everything. She needed my help, Osric. I provided it, and she provided the same. She saved me. She resurrected you. She keeps the power."

Osric readied to charge at Lutin. "I've never enjoyed the way you violate the rules. This isn't a time for having fun, as much as you might need it."

"If you think I'm joking, you don't understand at all." Licking his dry lips, Lutin turned from them and stepped across the soft grass. "Besides, Alex and Cyrus have been feeding bits of me to the box for over a decade," he said. "That has shortened my patience. It's removed my tolerance for what is an apparent wrong, even if it's 'against the law.' And you know I was very short on that to begin with. This is as it was meant to be."

"If you go back there, the others will imprison you, and I will not stop them. Because this," Osric said, pointing toward me, "is unacceptable. It's an abomination."

Lutin shrugged. "Then I'm an abomination. I won't go back."

Osric's jaw muscles bunched. The lines in his body fluoresced. He walked toward Lutin, a hand straight out toward him. His lips were pulled back, his mouth wide.

Lutin stood his ground, daring Osric.

I waited for a blow. Osric's hand curled into a fist, but then his arm dropped to his side. He backed down.

"There are things we need to do, ferrics we need to alert about what has been going on here. When we do, Cyrus will come," Osric said. "We'll discuss this later." He walked toward the house, his energy boiling. The other three, one at a time, followed.

I released a breath I hadn't realized I was holding.

Lutin stood with me and waited as I retrieved the cigarette I had dropped in the grass. I relit it. I smoked and glanced at him, not knowing what to say in response to what had just happened. At last, I said, "Don't end up in another basement or get hurt. Not on account of me. All this hard work would be for nothing."

He grinned. "You must understand, Jack, that I am moved to complete and make whole all those gaps and cracks around me. Even at the cost of myself. It's as though my very power was custom made to share with you and, though the others can't see it, you were fated to have it. They weren't there when all this occurred. I was. And I do not believe it was accidental.

"The truth does not belong to the majority, and all the power I was born with was not meant only for me. It is now more a part of you than any part of you, and to *remove* it would be the abomination."

His words moved me. Their truth warmed my soul. I agreed with him. If he were to remove the ability he had granted me, I would lose myself entirely.

"Imprisonment, death, punishment, chastisement, an earthly life—I do not care. Besides," he said, "the basements are nicer where I come from." He winked. "In just a bit of time, your power will take root, and I won't be able to take it back anymore. You will mix with it, and it will blend with you. They can't demand I take it then. All of this is just..." he shrugged, "temporary theatrics."

I checked my hand. To my surprise, the cigarette tip was clear and still. I was no longer shaking.

"Jack," Lutin said. He smiled reassuringly and then nodded toward the house. "Osric was right about one thing. Cyrus will be here soon. Let's go."

CHAPTER 28—BURN
AGE: 17 YEARS OLD

CYRUS WASN'T ALONE WHEN HE arrived at the house. Angry, disappointed cursing men quickly filtered into the mansion.

I sat in the living room, the lights off and the double doors pulled almost closed, as they walked past. From the sound of mutterings and yells, things had not gone as planned. Of course, I already knew that. Lutin's brothers had destroyed the box, obliterating every bit of Cyrus's magical protection. They had already called on others like them to go claim the children, rescue them from their deadly mission. Their kind was delivering them in droves to police stations all over the country. Before Cyrus returned, the five immortals had passed through the house, quicker than the fire of a gun, killing everyone left behind.

I saw a flash of silver hair; Cyrus walked past the living room. Soon, he would seek his faithful red toy.

When the front door shut, I rose from the couch and told the five immortals waiting with me where I was going. I glanced once at the glowing orange and red lines, and then I continued on my way.

I slipped between the two doors and ascended the stairs.

Cyrus was speaking to Jeffrey just inside his office, his silver eyebrows drawn down in a furious expression. When he spotted me, his entire demeanor shifted. He looked startled, his eyes wide with concern. Then he took me in fully, his gaze lingering on my right hand, the one he had cuffed to the living room fireplace.

He ran his tongue across his top lip. "Who uncuffed you?"

"Luther," I said. "I had to use the restroom. He let me go. Then I told him I would wait quietly in the living room for you. I have been waiting quietly."

Cyrus stared at me, clearly aware that what I'd just said was a lie. He knew *I knew* it was a lie. Cyrus rushed at me, stopping just inches from my face, every muscle in him full of fury. He yelled, "What do you know about this?"

"About what?" I asked, not reacting to his anger.

He searched my face and eventually found whatever it was he was looking for. He turned quickly and stepped into his office. He threw his jacket onto the chair and glanced at his desk. He swiveled suddenly. "Where is it?"

"What? The box?"

"Yes!" he yelled. "The fucking box, Jack! Where is it?" He looked at me as though I were insane to think he could mean anything else.

I shrugged and pressed my palms together. "I took it down to the living room."

"Why the fuck would you?"

"It was making a strange noise," I said. "I wanted to show it to you as soon as you returned." I beckoned him. "Come on."

For the first time, he appeared a tad uncertain, maybe even frightened of me. I had never seen an expression of doubt on his face, certainly not doubt mixed with fury. He likely wasn't used to such emotions. We stood momentarily frozen in that sudden power shift. Just as he opened his mouth, about to say something—perhaps accuse me of being the catalyst behind all that was happening, and rightfully so—a noise stopped him. It sounded like someone tumbling down the stairs.

We both turned to the doorway before Cyrus rushed past me into the hall. He glanced down the steps, to the bottom of the immense entryway. I came to look, too. Nothing.

"What was that?" he asked.

"I don't know."

He descended the stairs, and I followed. "Exactly what sort of sound did the box make?" Cyrus asked. It amused me that he continued the conversation. The tone of his voice asked something entirely different, perhaps *Is this really happening?*

"Almost like a moan."

He looked at me quizzically.

"What does it mean?"

Cyrus didn't answer.

When we reached the first floor, I told him the box was in the living room, and he glanced that way. He stood for a moment, staring at the double doors and the darkness inside. Instead of entering the living room, he turned right. I followed him, wondering where the hell he was going. We passed the staircase and went down the hall to the very back of the house—the location of the anterooms. Cyrus halted, though, and he looked up at the ceiling.

A strange thumping noise echoed above us and what sounded like a muffled yell. Cyrus clutched his collar, his head cocked to focus his ear on the floor above.

He continued. His footsteps were perfectly silent, and I ensured mine were just as quiet.

At the end of the hall, he approached a door that led to a familiar room. The first time I was there, I was seven, and I'd seen Cyrus, carrying the dark red container, drag Thornton by his hair inside. The second time, I was ten and had cut out a piece of the white curtain to bring to Lutin.

The doorknob squeaked as Cyrus gently turned it; he flung the door wide. He entered the dark space and flicked on the light. A large, beautiful room with blue carpet, blue walls, and soft cream sofas flashed into view. "Fuck," Cyrus said. The white room wasn't white anymore. The gold fleurs-de-lis were back to gold. The cobalt fibers were cobalt again. The empty bird cage was silver.

He spun quickly. I was right behind him, and he almost stumbled over me.

"I know what you've been keeping behind your office bookshelves," I told him, dropping all pretense.

His tongue dashed over his top lip, as it had done many times already. He retreated a step. "How?"

"I figured it out on my own, but Roland confirmed it."

More thumping sounds resounded from the ceiling. My mentor glanced up nervously. When silence once again reigned, his cold, silver eyes slowly dropped to mine. "Jack, where's the box?"

"I told you. In the living room."

He wetted his lips, an increasingly nervous twitch. "Show me."

I pointed back down the hall, toward the south end of the mansion, and headed that way. Several seconds passed before he followed.

We walked silently, retracing our steps. Though my back was exposed, I was unafraid. In little time, we reached the closed double living room doors and paused. He glanced around the large entryway and stairway and listened. Silence: no strange, muffled booms. In fact, there were no sounds at all, despite the fact thirty men had recently come in through the front door.

Something radiated from Cyrus. Not just fear—intensity and knowing.

"I don't believe you," he finally said, immobile. His body seemed to collapse. He was realizing, Yes, this is really happening.

"Very good, Cyrus. Very good."

I crossed my arms and took a deep breath. I sat on a step, wearily, and watched him.

"Did Roland somehow return?" he asked.

I shook my head.

"What about the...ferrics?"

I nodded.

"How?"

"Me."

His eyebrows dropped. He beheld the empty house fearfully, his gaze on the shadows. When he looked back at me, he asked, "What do you mean...*you*?"

I didn't hold back. I explained it all—Lutin had given me the ability to resurrect. Roland and I had plotted against him. And many, many other details. As I continued, the fire in his expression stoked and cool. Desperation and hopelessness passed over his face in waves.

"I know," I said, "that you deeply wanted to believe you were transcending. I know how alluring it must have been, to believe you were evolving beyond all of this, all the pain and misery and chaos and human weakness, to your own level, where nothing could reach you. But I was the one who brought Shakespeare back from the dead. I was the one who carried him up the stairs into your son's bedroom and let him savor a nice, final battle."

I let that soak in. Cyrus's chest heaved, but he said nothing. I continued.

"I also, whether or not you know, resurrected the girls you poisoned a few nights ago.

"Lastly, I'm the one who returned Lutin's brothers, and they destroyed the box. They are passing through your house right now, killing all the members who are left. That's what you've been hearing."

Cyrus's mouth was agape. Confusion pass over him like a cloud. "Wh...why?" he asked, finally. He ran his hands through his hair, grasped the strands tightly. His voice rang confused.

"You've never really known me, have you? The best moments of my life were not when you took me down to the basement to kill Roland. It was when you brought him back. That was what I craved. What I wanted more than anything else.

"When you told me about Lutin, I went downstairs to see him because I desired to meet the one who was able to resurrect. He gave me a piece of his power. He didn't ask for anything. He didn't tell me what to do with it. But he knew me far more than you did, because as soon as he added that ability to me..." I snapped my fingers, "I was an entirely different person.

"All my life you told me to kill—how and when to kill, who to kill. But now I have something no one else has. I have the other half of the circle."

"Why didn't you tell me," he asked, "that he gave you such immense power? We could have—"

"Tell you?" I laughed at the absurdity. "And end up down in the basement next to Lutin? Do you think I'm a fucking idiot? You would never have let me out! You wouldn't have been able to stand me being capable of something you aren't. You would have killed me, or worse."

"That's not true," Cyrus said. He sliced his hand through the air like a knife. "I never would've done that to you."

I frowned. "That's a lie. If it *were* true," I added, "then maybe I am worse than you are, because I'd have no problem locking you in a basement, Cyrus. No problem at all."

Cyrus turned from me quickly and bolted. He grabbed the handle to the front door, twisted it, and pulled the door wide, placing his right hand against the wooden door jamb. He started to run, away from his crumbling empire, away from me, the mentee turned enemy.

In one swift motion, I drove forward from the stairs, my hand already moving behind me, beneath my thin gray sweater. I grasped the warm metal hilt of a knife, retrieved it, and raised it high.

I drove the knife down, through his hand, through skin and muscle and bone, through skin again, straight into the wood of the door jamb itself.

Cyrus screamed.

His body continued to propel forward, forcing his hand to tug against the knife. The blade cut to the right. Blood spurted from the knife edge.

Cyrus's body slammed to a halt, and he shrieked again. He grasped the door jamb with his other hand, steadying himself.

I produced the second knife.

This one was smaller, neatly folded. I flicked it open and tossed it into my right hand. I raised the knife. As soon as Cyrus clasped the door jamb, I brought it down, stabbing through more skin and muscle and bone, straight into the wood. Both his hands were pinned.

Cyrus's shriek was hard and loud and as startling as a gunshot.

"You're not going anywhere," I said, my voice low, almost a growl. I leaned in. The ferociousness he had created in me over the years came fully alive. It launched at its creator. "You're going to stand here and face your creatures. You will look at us!"

The sweat sheen over his face made him look sick and glassy. Large swathes of blood covered his hands, dripping down the door jamb and coating the floor. Cyrus moaned with each breath and collapsed in on his hands.

At last, he looked at me.

"I did everything for you," he said, his voice gurgling, clawing its way out through the whimpers. "And now you're going to kill me?"

I leaned in, ignoring how pitiful he looked.

"No. Not me," I said. "I'd do it. Believe me, I would. But there is someone you owe much more to than me. You imprisoned a man in the basement for over ten years, cutting pieces of his soul away, keeping him weak enough so he couldn't run, strong enough so he couldn't die. That trumps my right to kill you. But your son..." I smiled. "Your son, who chose all those girls who looked just like me, is mine, Cyrus. And his body is going to end up like Roland's. You just won't be there to see it."

Anger mixed with defeat in Cyrus's expression. It wasn't just fury at not getting his way anymore, or fear over losing his empire. It was protective hatred. He loved Alex.

A sound behind me interrupted us, and I turned. A pair of legs took the steps, a brilliant glow of lightning on them. The ethereal man slowly approached, revealing himself as he descended. Lutin.

Cyrus tried to back away, but the knives secured him to the jamb. He gritted his teeth and screamed low in his throat. When he opened his eyes, his gaze was tinged with awe and desperation.

"If I could bring back every dog who was ever abused and allow him his revenge, I would," I said, drawing Cyrus's attention to me. He seemed smaller, a mere child. "If I could return every man who, in just a moment, realizes right from wrong, even as it is too late, I'd do it. All the children killed by monsters like you? I'd bring them back. And families who are naïve to our world—I'd allow them their kind illusions. Every man caught and bound and tortured, I would release from his dark, dreary cage. And every bastard who likes to strip away humanity, I would slaughter.

"You are right, Cyrus. Souls do not have to be either/or, and though you have snipped at mine since the age of seven, a bit still remains. Enough now."

Lutin was beside me then, and my attention shifted to him.

He appeared even healthier than an hour before; the blood dripping from him—others' blood—added color to his pallid skin. His fiery streaks glowed hot. The rusty red gleamed neon.

I backed away, letting Lutin take my place. The pair was close, then, far closer than Cyrus, a man now dethroned, would've ever allowed. From the right, another shining man I had resurrected came forward, and then another from the living room. Another arrived from the side of the stairs. Soon, they were all there, gathered in a circle around Cyrus.

Lutin jerked the knives from Cyrus's hands. My mentor dropped to the ground, shaking, screaming as he lifted them to his chest. He looked at his wounds, his mouth open wide.

"Pick one," Lutin said, "just one of these to eat." A series of daggers arrived from all areas of the house, spinning midair, circling above Cyrus's silver head.

Cyrus grimaced and lifted his broken hands to protect himself. The daggers dropped, clattering one at a time to the floor.

My mentor sat stunned. Hands midair, he gazed in awe at one of his palms. A gray cloud rose above his right hand, from the center of the knife wound. The cloud expanded; beneath it, Cyrus's entire hand turned red, not a speck of cream skin to be seen.

A similar mist gathered before his face, obscuring him. His cheeks, chin, nose, and forehead became crimson. Cyrus screamed.

The red became pale and began to balloon. Every nook and cranny on his face and hands disappeared. He no longer looked like Cyrus—rather a decaying corpse. The threads of his clothes disintegrated, and his skin puffed away. In just a moment, his organs, sinew, and bone were revealed. His eyes popped, and his tongue disappeared; the organic thread had snagged and unraveled. A long, bodiless wail echoed in the entryway. His bones weakened and cracked, ground into dust by some invisible force.

Finally, there was nothing left but dust. Cyrus was gone.

A sound like a tin can hitting glass rang. A circular metal plate with little triangles cut along the rim swiveled through the Cyrus dust.

I bent down to pick up the plate and inspect it.

"Where are you people," I said, "when the violence *starts*? Why do you wait until children have already suffered and murderers are already made?"

One of them knelt with me, and I smelled familiar coal-dust breath. I looked up into Lutin's black eyes.

"There are too many reasons I'm not allowed to share."

I dropped the plate into the dust and stood. "Do you feel better? Now that he's gone?"

"Yes," he said.

"I do…and do not." I was a little stunned, a little lost.

Lutin and his four brothers spoke together in their unfamiliar language. Lutin opened the front door and gestured for me to exit first. I did, and they followed.

As we walked onto the front lawn, I turned back to stare at the house. Distant swirls of light and flame rose from the back.

"Are you going to leave me?" I asked Lutin. Tears welled in my eyes. My stomach hollowed. Everything I had always known was going up in a blaze that I could not—and would not—stop. I had nothing.

"Yes," he said. "I have things to do, and so do the others. But I'll check on you from time to time."

I tried to keep my heart from wilting. "Can I come with you?"

"No."

I wiped my tears. "Why not?"

The flames expanded, shining bright in his dark mirror eyes. "The others would kill you, and you have a life to live. Finally."

A life to live, he said. Right. Where would I possibly go? I didn't understand any world outside of Cyrus. I wasn't sure how I would survive.

Then an image of a smiling older woman with green eyes and red hair came to mind, and I thought perhaps I did not have to be so alone. Close to my heart, in my inner pocket, Margaret Wilhelm's card waited.

Lutin smiled, and it appeared sad, even in the dark. "What do you think angels are, Jack? In relation to demons?"

"They're opposites."

"No," he replied. "That is not true. They are nearly the same. Angels aren't more than the spiders and wolves and snakes that don't bite and slither and slake. Angels and demons aren't opposites. Wings will grow on anything that'll swear off biting.

"We're all wolves, no matter the person, no matter the environment. And all of us, angel and demon alike, start in the same place. Later on, some break their dark patterns. Some don't.

"I'll be here for you when you do."

I slowly nodded, a new hope in my heart. I trusted Lutin. We would indeed meet again if he said we would. That was all I needed to hear. I stood straighter, and my shoulders relaxed.

Something very bright moved in the darkness. It was Lutin's hand. He held it up, the palm straight and welcoming. I stared at it and then slid my hand into his, noticing the warmth that radiated from him. We shook.

And we turned back toward the house.

And watched it burn.

ACKNOWLEDGMENTS

A multitude of people have had a profound influence on the story and journey of *Pivot*, and I must thank them all. They have changed my life in fantastic, irrevocable ways.

The first person I would like to thank is Wayne Alexander, who I met at my first World Horror Convention in Portland, Oregon. He asked me to send him my book the day we met, and then again at the book release party for Josh Malerman's BIRD BOX. I sent him a copy the next day. He read it quickly—he always reads my work quickly, bless him—and then brought another incredible person into the loop.

Ryan Lewis read the book just as quickly, and the three of us talked. I told them my intentions for the trilogy, as best as I had figured them out. The number of revisions they estimated for me on PIVOT alone would have been daunting to anyone else, but I was ready to dig in.

"It's going to be a lot of work," they said.

"I will do the work," I told them.

"It's a marathon, not a race. You have to have stamina," Wayne said.

Boy, was he right.

I was determined, though. For eight months, we talked about the book, they gave me pointers, and I revised. Because of these two individuals, I pushed myself out of my comfort zone every day, stretching myself to my limits. The pricelessness of the lessons I learned from them in the many phone calls and e-mails we exchanged cannot be overexaggerated.

What came next was the hunt for an agent, and fortunately the brilliant Jonathan Lyons took a look at *Pivot* and found something valuable in the manuscript. We talked, he gave me more pointers, and I revised. He recommended I split the book into two novels. At the time, I groaned and protested, but ultimately took his advice, and I am eternally grateful he pushed me to do this. It was the right decision.

About a year or so later, the revised book/s (*Pivot* and *Perish*) landed with California Coldblood Books and the awesome publisher Robert Peterson. Bob offered me a three-book deal for the Jack Harper trilogy and made my entire year (at the least). As for *Pivot*, he gave me more suggestions, I revised, and then the book was copyedited by the wonderful and impressive Sue Ducharme, which was a magical experience in its own right. I give many, many thanks to Sue. She knows what she's doing and helped my book pop.

While the submissions process was occurring with Jonathan, I attended and graduated from USM's Stonecoast MFA program and, fortunately, had multiple workshops with the amazing Nancy Holder. For two semesters, she graciously mentored me. She made my MFA experience and helped me greatly in developing my craft and revising. To her I owe a great debt.

I don't know where I would be without these amazing writing, revising, and publishing powerhouses. A lot of writing is done in a small room on one's own. To bring it into the light of day, especially for a young writer, is difficult, but I always trusted Wayne, Ryan, Jonathan, Bob, Sue, and Nancy. Always.

In addition to the above individuals, I give many, many thanks to my friend Adam Setliff for easing the pressure, always easing the pressure. He is my best friend, the person I can always bounce ideas off of, and I look forward to many more conversations with him.

I would also like to thank Sebron Stoneham, who was like a second father to me and who altered my life for the better in countless ways. "Don't fear," he told me. I have tried my best to live up to his advice. *Pivot* would not be here without him.

Thank you so much to my mother, Helen Barlow, who believes in me and my writing and who has supported me through thick and thin. I don't know what I would do without her. She is so strong, so smart, so capable.

Finally, thank you to my father, Jack Barlow, who passed away in 2017 after seventeen years of illness. I am so happy to have known him, and I am forever grateful simply for his sublime existence. Such a down-to-earth and gentle soul, he was my best friend, beyond strong, patient, and resilient, and he taught me what goodness is. Without him and my mother, *Pivot* would not exist. To both of my parents, I express depthless unconditional love.

ABOUT THE AUTHOR

L.C. BARLOW is a writer and professor. Her work has been published in a variety of magazines and journals and garnered praise, winning multiple awards. Barlow lives in Dallas with her cats Smaug, Dusty, and Fiona.

CPSIA information can be obtained
at www.ICGtesting.com
Printed in the USA
LVHW090819021019
632887LV00004BA/4/P